SINFUL

by

KATE BENEDICT

CHIMERA

Sinful Seduction first published in 2001 by
Chimera Publishing Ltd
PO Box 152
Waterlooville
Hants
PO8 9FS

Printed and bound in Great Britain by
Omnia Books Ltd, Glasgow

SINFUL SEDUCTION

Kate Benedict

For all his wealth and breeding, Lord Edward stank like a fat old pig. He looked like one too, lying there with his mouth open and his puffy red face covered in grey bristles.

Holding her breath, Maggie bent to lay the tray carefully on the bedside table. With a bit of luck she could have the curtains drawn and be out of there before he was properly awake.

But as she stood up his hand shot from beneath the coverlet and grabbed her behind the knee, toppling her onto the bed. She gasped and struggled as he sat up and hauled her alongside him. His sweaty face came down on hers, his breath stinking like an open grave and she gagged as his tongue squirmed its way between her lips like a hot, wet slug.

'Come on,' he panted, lifting his head. 'You know you want it.'

Chapter One

'Get aht of it, you little bitch!' snarled the coach driver. His whip flicked dangerously close to Maggie as she ducked under the horse's hooves and scurried for the safety of the narrow pavement. Once there, she put down the stoneware jug she was carrying and gave him the fingers. Miserable bastard! Thought he owned the whole bloomin' road!

He responded with a mouthful of oaths and his passenger looked to see what the disturbance was. Maggie stared at the bloated, self-indulgent face peering at her and generously included him in her rude gestures. Fat old git! She snorted. Not hard to work out why a posh bloke like him was down here slumming it. He'd be after a bit of rough. One of those poor bitches who made their living selling themselves to all comers for the price of a few gins and a doss-house at the end of the day. She grinned. With a bit of luck they'd give the bleedin' toff a good dose of the pox. That'd wipe the smile off his face!

But the smile was wiped off her own face as the driver lashed out with his whip again and this time connected. 'Ow!' squawked Maggie, hopping up and down and rubbing her leg, where a thin weal was rising beneath the dirt. She looked round for ammunition and spotted a rotting cabbage stalk lying in the muck of the gutter. Picking it up she heaved it at the cabbie's horse, there was a satisfying squelch as it hit its backside, and it reared up and took off as if the devil himself was after it, the driver cursing a blue streak as he hauled on the reins.

Maggie chuckled as the coach disappeared round the corner, its wheels jouncing dangerously on the cobbles. Served him right if he broke his bloody neck! The bastard might not be quite so quick with his whip the next time. Still grinning, she dusted her hands and picked up her jug.

The cracked bell on the church clock chimed eleven and her triumphant smile vanished, to be replaced with a look of apprehension. God strewth! Was that the time already? Ma would be desperate for her gin by now. Her lips set grimly; the last couple of times she'd had to do without she'd started raving on about spiders coming out of the walls.

Clutching the jug to her chest Maggie scurried on as fast as possible without spilling the precious liquid. Dodging the scrawny, grey-faced kids playing in the gutters she made her way through the narrow twisted streets towards the crumbling tenement she called home.

Holding her breath against the stench, she picked her way bare-footed through the noxious puddles in the courtyard. Funny that; once you'd been in awhile you didn't notice the smell, but if you'd been out a bit it hit you like a sledgehammer when you came back. Still, what else could you expect when there was only one outhouse for the whole bloody building?

The cellar door gaped like a rotten mouth and the reek was even worse here. Hardly surprising when their tiny room was sandwiched between the cats-meat man on one side and the bloke who collected dog shit for the tannery on the other.

She negotiated the slimy steps, carefully avoiding a pool of drying vomit; ma would go mad if she dropped the jug now.

The sound of a blow followed by a soft whimper stopped her in her tracks. Oh no – Bert! He should have been off down the docks looking for work by this time. He must've slept in after reeling home from the pub the night before – and now he was taking his spite out on her mother.

Carefully hiding the jug beneath a pile of old sacking she pushed open the door, and a familiar scene met her eyes. Her mother cowered in the corner, holding her hands up as she tried to ward off the blows from Bert's fist. Her left eye was swelling already, a fresh bruise rising to cover the faded one beneath. He was grinning as he raised his arm again.

'Get off her, you bastard!' shrieked Maggie. She flung herself across the room, landing on his back and clinging like a monkey. He didn't even blink. One meaty paw reached back over his shoulder and plucked her off as if she weighed nothing and he threw her against the wall. Her head banged against it and everything went black.

When she came to it was to the sound of grunting. Her mother was spread-eagled on the rag-covered pallet that served for a bed, her skirts flung up around her waist. Bert heaved and panted on top of her, his hairy buttocks clenching as he thrust himself on her. He gave one final thrust, grunted in satisfaction and hauled himself to his feet.

Buttoning his trousers, he glared down at the whimpering woman. 'Useless, drunken bitch,' he snarled. 'You're not even a decent fuck any more.' He gave her cowering body a kick and sauntered out, slamming the door behind him.

'Ma! Ma! Are you all right?' moaned Maggie, crawling across the floor and slipping an arm round her mother's heaving shoulders.

'I... I'm fine, pet,' she quavered, her bruised lips attempting a pathetic smile. 'Tough as old boots, me.' One thin, trembling hand clawed at Maggie's arm. 'Did you get it, love? You know, my gin?' A horrible thought struck her and her hand went to her lips. 'He... he didn't break the jug, did he?'

'No ma, he didn't break the jug,' sighed Maggie. 'I hid it before I came in.'

She gazed at her mother with pity. 'I'll go and get it now. You look as if you could do with a drink.'

Rats scuttled off into the darkness as she bent to retrieve the jug from beneath the sacking. She carried it into the room, dug through the rubbish on the rickety table until she found a chipped enamel mug and poured a couple of inches of gin into it.

'There you go, ma,' she said, putting it into her mother's trembling hands and watching as she gulped it gratefully.

When the mug was empty the woman held it out for more, and half an hour later she was blissfully drunk.

'We didn't alwaysh live like thish,' she slurred, smiling tipsily at Maggie. 'I had a good poshition in a houshe in Eaton Square.'

Maggie sighed; it was always the same. As soon as her mother got a drink inside her she harped back to the good old days. She knew the whole story by heart. How she'd been the assistant cook – and would have become cook herself if she hadn't fallen in love with the footman and left to get married. Still, if telling it again made her mother happy, she would listen to it all as if she was hearing it for the first time.

'He wash a lovely man, your dad,' she muttered, nodding over her drink. 'A lovely man.' A sob caught in her throat. 'He shouldn't have died and left us like that. It washn't fair.' Her head drooped and the empty mug fell from her slack fingers. Maggie eased her down on the pallet and heaped rags over her. She'd sleep now. A temporary escape from the living hell her life had become.

Maggie's mouth set grimly. Her mother never told the rest of the story, but she'd been able to work it out for herself from snippets of gossip she'd overheard in the tenement; even with references, nobody wanted a cook with a kid in tow, did they? Most toffs didn't even like their staff to get married. But God knows, her ma had tried. Taking in sewing at first, then when her eyes had given out, taking in washing instead. Moving from cheap digs to even cheaper ones, the gin gradually becoming not an occasional escape but a necessity.

Her lips tightened even further. And then along came Bert. She'd been old enough to remember that. Nice as ninepence to start off with. Coming round all spruced up and sober as a judge. It was only after the wedding he'd shown his true colours. She could still see her mother's expression of horror when he dragged her back to this hovel.

'We… we can't stay here,' she'd gasped, clutching Maggie protectively to her skirts. 'You said you had a nice little house.'

'Beggars can't be choosers,' he'd sneered. 'It's a roof over your head, ennit? What more can you expect?

There's not many blokes would take on another man's brat.

'And you won't be needing that any more,' he went on, wrenching off her old wedding ring. He'd used the money he got from the pawnbroker to get roaring drunk and came rolling home to celebrate his wedding night by beating up his new bride before taking her savagely against the wall, while Maggie cowered in the corner.

Her lips twisted. His 'steady job' had been as big a lie as his 'nice little house'. He stood at the dock gates – when he wasn't too hung over to roll out of bed, that was – waiting to be taken on for a day at a time. If he did he spent most of the money in the pub on the way home. If he didn't he'd come back and take it out on her mother. And either way they went hungry.

Thinking of food made Maggie's stomach growl. She raked through the debris on the rickety table and came up with the heel of a loaf and a hunk of dry cheese. Splitting it scrupulously in half, so there would be some left for her mother when she woke, she gnawed on it hungrily, and all too soon it was finished.

She glanced longingly at the other half, and then shook her head; it might be tempting, but her mother was rail thin already.

Maggie brightened; never mind, if she went down the market she could pick through the gutter for the stuff the stallholders threw away. It might be half-rotten, but if you cut away the bad bits you'd be all right – and if you were really lucky, you might find a bone with a few scraps of meat still clinging to it.

Pulling the bit of old blanket she used as a shawl round her shoulders, she checked on her mother. There was a gentle snore and she tiptoed out, closed the door quietly behind her – and promptly bumped into a smelly body. Two wiry arms gripped her and she choked with terror.

'Watch it, gel, you very nearly had me over then!' rasped a familiar voice, and she sighed with relief.

'Blimey, Fred, you scared the life out of me!' she gasped, staring at the wizened figure before her.

He grinned, revealing a mouthful of blackened stumps. 'Fancy a trip up west, young 'un?' he asked.

She grinned back. 'Wot for?' she asked cheekily. 'You taking me to the opera then?' She stuck her nose in the air and patted her matted hair. 'Hang on a mo' and I'll just nip back for me tiara.'

'Impudent little madam,' he grumbled. 'Course I ain't; my back ain't what it used to be. Pushin' that bleedin' barrow's murder these days.' He ran his bloodshot eyes over her. 'You're a little 'un, but you're game. You'd do at a pinch.'

'Thanks a lot,' she snorted. 'And what's in it for me?'

His eyes narrowed as he came to his decision. 'Tuppence for the day,' he muttered. 'Take it or leave it.'

'I'll take it,' she grinned, spitting on her hand and holding it out.

Suppressing a smile he took it and shook it solemnly. 'Done,' he agreed. 'Now get your skates on, gel. We haven't got all day.'

The cart was heavy and the cats-meat stunk to high heaven, but the thought of a whole tuppence kept her going. Sweating like a pig she heaved and panted as they made their way through the winding streets, a string of scrawny strays trailing after them, yowling hopefully.

As they reached the better parts of London it was a revelation to Maggie. She stared at the big houses with her mouth open, watching as two well-dressed ladies descended the steps of one and were carefully helped into their carriage.

'You mean there's only one family lives in them places?' she gasped in disbelief. 'Garn! You're having me on!'

Fred shook his head. 'Cross me heart and hope to die,' he grinned. 'Course, there's the servants too. Can't expect nobs to look after themselves, now can you?'

'Strewth!' she exclaimed. 'They must be rolling in it!' She considered this for a moment. 'Stands to reason though, doesn't it? I mean, fancy paying good money to feed bloomin' cats.' She sniffed scornfully. 'They must be off their heads. Cats feed themselves; eat rats and stuff.'

'Not these ones,' he grinned. 'These ain't your common-or-garden moggies. These are aristo-cats.' He chuckled at his own joke. 'Eat better than we do, drink cream, sleep on silk cushions.' He grinned ruefully. 'Wouldn't mind being one, meself.'

He shook himself. 'Anyway, this won't feed the baby. Get a move on, gel.' He slapped a couple of pounds of meat on a sheet of brown paper, wrapped it deftly and thrust it into her hands. 'Number ten,' he said, pointing. 'Down them steps to the kitchen door. And mind your manners,' he warned. 'No cheek; these are good customers. Regular as clockwork every week.'

She grinned; for tuppence she'd be as well bred as bloody Queen Victoria!

But it wasn't as easy as she'd thought. The girl who answered the door, in her neat uniform, was only a couple of years older than her.

'Wot do you want?' she demanded rudely, her eyes

taking in Maggie's ragged clothes. 'Didn't you see the sign? No tramps or hawkers – nor ragamuffins either. Get aht of it.'

Maggie flushed and bit down the angry retort that sprang to her lips. 'Cats-meat, mu'um,' she said, humbly holding out the bloodstained parcel.

'Might have known,' sniggered the girl. 'You look like something the cat dragged in and all.' Grabbing the parcel, she thrust a sixpence into Maggie's hand and slammed the door in her face.

'Snooty cow!' muttered Maggie, as she stamped back up the area steps.

Luckily they weren't all like that. At one house the plump, motherly cook who answered the door took pity on Maggie's cold pinched face and gave her a bit of cold bacon between two slices of bread as well as the money. At another she was given two farthings for herself. She split the bread and meat with old Fred, but the coins she tied into the corner of her shawl for safekeeping, gloating over her newfound riches.

By the time they got home the barrow felt as if it weighed twice as much as when they'd set off, even though it was almost empty now. She was exhausted, her bare feet were sore and swollen from so much walking and her shoulders ached from pushing and hauling the barrow over the cobbles, but her misery disappeared as soon as Fred pressed the two precious coppers into her hand.

'Cheers, Fred,' she grinned.

'You're welcome, gel,' he said. 'You did a good job. Here,' he scraped up some of the leftover meat, wrapped it and handed it over.

'Cor, ta!' she exclaimed. Boiled up into a stew, with a

13

couple of carrots and onion and a few potatoes, it would keep them going for days! She grinned. 'God bless yer, Fred. You're a real gent.'

He blushed with pleasure. 'Go on with you, gel,' he grinned. 'I'm off for a pint. Getcha, before I change me mind.'

Chuckling, she scampered down the cellar steps, the parcel of meat in one hand and her precious tuppence clutched tightly in the other.

Her mother was awake and sitting on their one broken chair. Her elbows were on the table and her head was in her hands. As Maggie came in she looked up with an expression of complete and utter misery.

'I'm sorry, love,' she sighed. 'Your dad's not back yet and there's not a bite to eat in the house.'

Maggie's smile disappeared, to be replaced by a black scowl. 'Don't call him that!' she snapped. 'He's not my dad and he never will be – thank God. He's just the bastard you married.' Her smile returned. 'Anyway, who cares about him? Look at this!' She placed the parcel and coins triumphantly on the table, enjoying her mother's astonished expression.

'Wh-where did that come from?' she quavered. She looked at her daughter. 'You… you haven't done anything you shouldn't have?' Despite the dirt and matted hair, Maggie was still a pretty girl and there were plenty of so-called 'gentlemen' who wouldn't scruple to take advantage of her.

'Don't be daft, ma,' grinned Maggie. 'I worked for it. Pushing old Fred's cart for him. Bloody hard work it was too.' She beamed at her own achievement. 'Tuppence he give me – and one old dear give me two farthings for meself as well.' She rejoiced over her riches.

'We'll put the meat past till I get some veg termorrow, and I'll nip out and get something nice and hot from the pie-shop—' Just then an arm reached over her shoulder and a dirty hand scooped up the coins.

'I'll 'ave that,' said a familiar voice. 'It'll buy me a nice few pints down the Fevvers.'

Maggie whirled round to see her stepfather's gloating face grinning down at her. 'You give that back!' she snarled, kicking him in the shins. 'That's mine! I worked hard for that money—!' His grin disappeared, he lifted his arm and backhanded her, and she stumbled backwards and glared up at him like an enraged kitten.

'It's mine now,' he sneered, 'and I'm off down the pub now – but when I come back I'll deal with you good and proper. I'll teach you to kick me, you little bitch.' He grinned again. 'That'll give you sumfing to look forward to while I'm gone.'

He turned on his heel and stomped out, and Maggie stared at the door and burst into tears. 'It's not fair, ma. I worked me guts out for that money.'

'Never mind, love,' sighed her mother, slipping an arm round her shoulders. 'We've still got the meat. And once he's had a few, he'll 'ave forgotten all about it by the time he gets 'ome.'

A couple of hours later, with a plate of hot stew inside her, Maggie was feeling a bit more optimistic. Ma was right; he'd come rolling home, fall into a sodden sleep and that would be the end of it.

The cellar was hot and sticky from the cooking. Yawning, she pulled off her tattered dress to reveal an equally tattered petticoat and curled up in her pile of rags, and within moments she was sound asleep…

A kick woke her and the next thing she knew she'd been hauled out by the neck of her petticoat and was hanging with her toes barely touching the floor. 'Thought you'd get the better of me, did you miss?' muttered Bert, drunkenly. 'Well, you were wrong, weren'tcha. You're goin' to pay fer it now.'

The material of Maggie's thin petticoat gave way under the strain. There was a ripping sound and she was suddenly on her feet again, trying to clutch the shreds of ragged cotton to her breasts. Bert stared at her for a moment, and then an expression of lustful cunning crossed his face. 'Seems to me there's another kind of lesson I could teach yer while I'm at it,' he chuckled, fumbling at the buttons on his trousers, and Maggie stared at him in horror.

'For God's sake, Bert, no!' wailed her mother, grabbing his arm and hanging on to it like grim death. 'She's your daughter!'

'No she ain't,' he chuckled, shaking her off so that she staggered back and slumped against the wall. 'Now, where was I?' he grinned. 'Oh yes, I remember.' His grubby hands reached for Maggie, and she closed her eyes and shuddered in dreadful anticipation of what was to come... but it didn't. Instead there was a dull thud, and she opened her eyes again just in time to see him crumple slowly to the floor, her mother standing over him with the chamber pot in her hand. 'Oh gawd, ma!' she squawked. 'You 'aven't killed him, 'ave you? If you 'ave, they'll hang you.'

Her mother gave Bert a poke with her foot and he gave a drunken moan. 'No such luck,' she said bitterly. 'I'd be well out of it if they did hang me.'

An equally horrible thought struck Maggie. 'Oh gawd,'

she said again. 'When he wakes up again he's going to kill us!'

'No he ain't,' said her mother contemptuously. 'After the skinful he's had he won't remember a fing. He won't come round till noon.' She smiled at Maggie. 'And by then you'll be long gone.'

'Wh-what do you mean?' stammered Maggie.

Her mother's lips twisted grimly. 'You don't think he's going to leave you alone now he's noticed how beautiful you've grown, do you? That's one thing he won't forget. He'll be after you like a dog after a bitch in heat till he 'as 'is way of you.' She shook her head. 'I made my bed and I 'ave to lie in it – but you ain't going to lie in it too.' Her lips set in determination. 'First thing termorrow I'm getting you out of 'ere.'

'Come on, ma, where are we going?' demanded Maggie, hurrying breathlessly after her mother.

'To see a man about a dog,' came the tart reply. 'Just you wait and see, my girl.'

Maggie groaned with a mixture of frustration, excitement and apprehension. It was just one more mystery in an already bewildering morning. It had started almost before light with a hand on her shoulder, shaking her out of an uneasy sleep.

'Come on,' hissed her mother. 'We've got to get a move on in case His Nibs wakes up.'

Rubbing her eyes, Maggie cast an apprehensive glance across the room, then sighed with relief. Her stepfather was lying sprawled on the pallet, mouth open, still snoring in a befuddled sleep.

She turned back to look at her mother, and her jaw dropped in astonishment. Instead of her usual old dress and sacking apron, she was wearing a respectable black one. Admittedly it had seen better days; the skirt was shiny with wear, there were clumsy darns on each elbow and the whole thing had a distinctly greenish tinge – but compared to her usual ragged garb it was like one of Queen Victoria's blooming ballgowns!

'Cor, where'd you get that, ma?' she asked, wide-eyed.

'Borrowed it offen Missis O'Mally upstairs,' she replied. 'It's her funeral dress.' She grinned with satisfaction, and held up a smaller version and a pair of cracked boots. 'Got these an' all. Belong to her youngest. They'll suit you a treat.' Her smile vanished. 'Now stop all this gabbing. We ain't got time for it. You gotta get washed and make yourself look presentable.'

That was easier said than done. Shivering at the standpipe in the yard, Maggie splashed cold water all over, but it did little to remove the ingrained grime from her hands and feet. The dress was far too small as well. Once it was on she could hardly breath for fear of the seams bursting, and the sleeves finished halfway down her arms, making her wrists look even bonier. She crammed her feet into the boots and winced; they were agony already and she hadn't even started walking in them yet.

'Stick 'em under yer arm then,' muttered her mother crossly. 'Yer can put 'em on when we gets there.'

'Get where?' demanded Maggie, but her mother tapped the side of her nose and winked.

'Ask me no questions and I'll tell yer no lies,' she chuckled, and at the sound there was a sudden drunken muttering from Bert and they both froze in horror. His eyes flickered open and for one terrifying moment it looked as if he was waking up – then he groaned, farted and rolled over again.

They looked at each other in relief. 'Come on girl, shift yer arse,' hissed her mother. 'We might not be so lucky next time.' Rummaging amongst the rags in the corner, she produced the jug of gin, finished off the last few dregs and wiped her mouth. 'Thass better,' she winked again. 'Bit o' Dutch courage never hurt anyone. You know what they says: "A little of what yer fancy does yer good".'

Maggie sighed. One look at her mother put the lie to that saying. Her greying hair was pulled back into an untidy bun, her face was bone-white, apart from the dark bruise around her left eye, and her 'new' dress hung from her emaciated frame. She looked liked an old, worn-out whore masquerading as a respectable housewife.

Her mother rubbed her sweating palms nervously over the skirt. 'Do I look all right?' she asked, suddenly anxious. 'I wants to make a good impression.'

'Yer look loverly, ma,' lied Maggie, loyally. 'A proper bobby-dazzler.'

'Thanks, love,' said her mother. 'Gotta try and look yer best, 'aven't yer?' She smiled. 'Now lets get outer 'ere.'

'Is it much farther?' whined Maggie. 'My feet hurt.' They seemed to have trudged for miles and Maggie was totally confused. They'd left their own familiar streets behind ages ago and were now in a similar area to the ones she'd seen when delivering the cats-meat. The posher the houses became, the shabbier she felt. She shivered; this was no place for the likes of them.

Suddenly her mother turned into a wide tree-lined crescent and stopped before the most imposing house in the row. ''Ere we are,' she announced triumphantly. 'Number twelve, Regent's Terrace.'

Maggie stared in dismay at the imposing steps that led up to the entrance. 'We can't go up there, ma,' she muttered. 'They'd take one look at us and chuck us down them steps.'

'Don't be daft, girl,' chuckled her mother. 'We ain't going in the front door. That's only for the gentry. Come on.' She led Maggie to a tiny side gate and down the steps to the basement. 'Get them boots on, girl,' she snapped, and wincing, Maggie did as she was told. Once that was done her mother smoothed down her skirts, patted her hair, took a deep breath and rapped on the door.

It seemed an eternity before they heard footsteps. The door creaked open and a girl, the spitting image of the one who'd been so rude to Maggie the other day, stared at them in disbelief. Her eyes ran over Maggie's too-tight dress and the bruises on her mother's face and her lip curled in contempt.

'Get aht of it the pair of yer – before I set the dogs on yer,' she ordered. 'We don't allow no beggars here,' and she began to shut the door, but Maggie's mother drew herself up to her full height and glared at the girl.

'None of your cheek, miss,' she said haughtily. 'I wish to speak to the housekeeper, Mrs Hardcastle.' Maggie gawped in astonishment; her accent had undergone a startling transformation, and she stared at her mother with new respect. Blimey, she sounded almost like one of the nobs herself!

The maid must have thought so too. Automatically

bobbing a curtsey, she turned and disappeared.

Five minutes later a plump woman, in an immaculate black dress that made her mother's look like the shoddy article it was, appeared. 'Well?' she demanded, folding her arms on her formidable bosom. 'What do you want? Didn't the maid tell you? We want no beggars here.'

A look of hurt bewilderment crossed her mother's face. 'Don't you recognise me, Moll?' she asked. 'It's me, Kate. We were in service together.'

The woman stared at the ragged apparition. 'Kate? Kate who?' She looked closer and an expression of horrified recognition crossed her face. 'Kate Ellis?' She struggled to hide her dismay at the state of her friend. 'Good heavens! Little Kate Ellis! Well I never! And this is your girl, is it?'

Maggie's mother nodded proudly, and Moll shook herself and forced a smile. 'Where's my manners? You must be frozen stiff standing there. Come into the kitchen and we'll have a nice cup of tea and a chat about old times.'

Inside, Maggie looked round, wide-eyed. Cor, the kitchen was enormous! Their cellar room would have fitted into it four times easy. A massive black range took up half one wall and was covered in bubbling pots. At a long scrubbed deal table two girls with aprons over their brown uniform were sorting eggs and flour. Through a doorway was a scullery where another was peeling a huge mound of vegetables, and the smell of hot food made Maggie's mouth water. Her stomach rumbled loudly and she blushed with embarrassment.

Moll looked at her shrewdly and clapped her hands. 'Emily, make a pot of fresh tea,' she ordered. 'And fetch a couple of slices of that cold game pie from the larder, for me guests.'

Emily hurried to do as she was told – and if she had any thoughts about the pitiful state of Mrs Hardcastle's 'guests', she was wise enough not to express them. Or at least not until she was safely out from under her eagle eye.

Ten minutes later they were comfortably sitting in front of the range, drinking steaming hot tea. Maggie spooned in more sugar, bit into her slice of game pie, wiped the juices from her chin and smiled blissfully. This was the life – a roaring fire and a full belly. She wiggled her toes inside the tight boots with the sheer pleasure of being warm and well fed, and then unexpectedly emitted a belch. She turned scarlet again and looked round furtively to see if it had been noted. It hadn't. Luckily everyone was too preoccupied to notice her lapse of manners. The kitchen maids were bustling about their tasks and ma and Mrs Hardcastle were making polite conversation.

The amenities over, her mother got down to brass tacks. 'I'm looking for a favour, Moll,' she said bluntly.

Mrs Hardcastle looked apprehensive. 'Depends what it is,' she said cagily. 'But if I can help, I will.'

'I need a place for our Maggie,' her mam went on. 'Any chance of you taking her on?'

Maggie squirmed on her chair as Mrs Hardcastle looked her over with the air of someone offered a pig at market and discovering it was the runt of the litter.

'I don't know,' she muttered doubtfully. 'She's a scrawny little thing, ain't she. Don't look very healthy.'

'Don't you believe it!' exclaimed her mother eagerly. 'Strong as a horse that one, for all she's small. Never been sick a day in her life. And she's a grand little worker.'

Mrs Hardcastle plucked thoughtfully at her lower lip. 'Well… I suppose Mrs McAlister could do with another tweenie.' She pointed to one of the girls who was rolling out pastry with a dreamy expression on her face. 'Ellen there's going off to get married.' She snorted. 'Silly young madam! Being some man's slave will soon wipe that smirk off her face. At least in here you get paid for working your arse off.' Mrs Hardcastle's title was strictly honorary, and she had every intention of keeping it that way.

'Where was I?' she asked. 'Ah yes. If I move young Mary up to kitchen maid, then your Maggie can take her place. Nine pound a year all in.' She sat back with the smug smile of one who has manage to do a good turn at absolutely no inconvenience to themselves. 'How's that suit yer, love?'

'God bless yer, Moll,' gasped Maggie's mother, sagging with relief. 'How soon can she start?'

'No time like the present,' beamed Moll, subjecting Maggie to another looking over. 'Course, we'll 'ave to clean her up a bit. Can't 'ave her working here looking like that.' She clapped her hands again. 'Mary! Leave them veg just now and go and get the bath out. Ellen, put some water on to boil.' She fumbled a key off the huge ring at her waist and handed it to Emily. 'Go to the store cupboard and look out a couple of uniforms and aprons from the bottom shelf – one for work and one for best. Oh, and see if you can't find a pair of old boots somewhere till we can buy new. Them ones she's wearing ain't fit for nothing.' She sniffed in disapproval. 'They can go in the fire along with them rags she's wearing.'

23

'Oh no, please, you can't do that!' exclaimed her mother in dismay. 'They ain't mine.' Her cheeks turned a dull red with shame. 'I had to borrow them.'

Mrs Hardcastle's face softened with pity. Poor Kate. To be reduced to this. 'Righto, love,' she said with forced cheerfulness. 'You sit there while we get the young 'un spruced up and we'll wrap her stuff up in a nice bit o' brown paper to take home with yer.' Her shrewd eyes noted Kate's trembling hands. 'And how about a little drop o' something while you're waiting? To celebrate, like?'

Maggie's mother nodded in dumb gratitude.

Half an hour later Maggie found herself sitting in a galvanised iron tub in front of the range. Her initial shock at having to take off all her clothes and submerge herself had melted as the hot water seeped into every pore of her body. Her hair, turpentined, scrubbed and sluiced within an inch of its life was pinned up in a wild tangle on the top of her head. 'We'll take the lice comb to that little lot, once you're out,' Mrs Hardcastle said grimly.

Wrapped in a warm towel, she sat on a high stool as Mrs Hardcastle set to with a vengeance. 'Oww! Stoppit, that hurts!' she protested, pulling away.

'None of your nonsense, miss,' snapped Mrs H, yanking her back. 'It's got to be done. You ain't scratching like a monkey in my kitchen. T'ain't healthy.'

By the time she'd finished, Maggie felt as if her scalp was red raw – but her hair fell in a smooth cascade down her back, gleaming red-gold in the light from the range fire. Mrs H stepped back and admired her handiwork. 'Lovely,' she decided. 'Who'd 'ave thought it?' She smiled at Maggie's mother. 'Wouldn't surprise me one bit if she's a beauty once she's put a little weight on. Just like 'er mum.'

Maggie's mouth fell open in surprise. Mum, a beauty? Well, there was a turn up for the books. Then she sighed; living with Bert would wipe out any woman's looks pretty sharpish. You couldn't exactly be 'a beauty' with your teeth knocked out and your face a mass of bruises. And the gin didn't help either.

'Come on, girl, don't sit there dreaming,' Mrs H said briskly. 'Let's get you dressed. Let your mum 'ave a look at yer before she goes.'

The brown frock hung on her skinny frame like a sack and the boots were cracked and worn and at least two sizes too big, but from the look on ma's face she might have been one of the little princesses herself. 'You look a proper treat, love,' she said, her eyes shining with pride. Tears welled up and she dashed them away with a grubby hand. 'Well, I'd best be off now, pet,' she said, swallowing the lump in her throat. She kissed Maggie's cheek and forced a smile. 'Now you be a good girl and do whatever Mrs Hardcastle and Mrs McAlister tells you and you'll get on fine.'

Maggie flung her arms around her mother's thin body and clung to her tightly. 'You take care, ma,' she whispered. 'I'll visit every month on my afternoon off.'

Her mother pushed her away and shook her head. 'No love, I don't think that's a good idea, do you? I'll try and come here instead, if I can get away from His Nibs.'

She turned to Mrs Hardcastle. 'Thanks again, Moll,' she said fervently. 'You don't know how much this means to me. You'll get your reward in heaven, just see if you don't.'

'I'll see you out, Kate,' said Moll, patting her hand

sympathetically. 'Oh, and before I forget, here's them old clothes back.' She picked up a brown paper parcel, thrust it into Kate's arms and winked. 'And there's a bit of cold meat, some bread and butter and a few eggs in there too, so mind and not drop it.' She rolled her eyes towards the ceiling. 'That lot won't miss a few odds and ends from the pantry.'

Kate opened her mouth to thank her again, but nothing came. Turning on her heel she walked out of the kitchen, before she broke down completely. Moll followed her, and at the door she turned round. 'You lot look after the little 'un while I says goodbye to me friend.'

Suddenly bereft, Maggie stared after, trying not to cry, and at a sound behind her she whirled round to face the other girls, prepared to do battle if necessary to establish herself. She looked at the circle of curious faces.

The one called Emily grinned at her and she relaxed. 'Cheer up, love,' she advised. 'It ain't that bad 'ere.'

'Yers,' chimed in Ellen. 'Mrs McAlister, the cook, is a decent old stick. You do right by her and she'll do right by you. She ain't 'alf strict, but she's fair with it.'

'And the grub's good,' added Mary, patting her belly. 'Soon put a bit of meat on yer bones.'

Mrs H bustled back in and they scattered back to their work, leaving Maggie standing. 'Right,' she said briskly. 'You can start by giving Mary a hand with them vegetables.' She wagged a finger. 'Now mind, I want them peeled fine. We'll 'ave no waste in this house.' Maggie bobbed a curtsey and Mrs H smiled. 'Nice to see your ma's brought you up proper. Now off you go and get on with it.'

An hour later Maggie was finished. Mrs H examined her handiwork and nodded with satisfaction. 'Good girl,' she said. 'Now, while Ellen's putting them on to boil, Mary can take you for a quick look round and show you where you'll be sleeping.'

By the time she had finished her guided tour, Maggie didn't know whether she was coming or going. Her head was spinning as she tried to remember her way round the warren of the servants' quarters. Numbly she followed a chattering Mary up a narrow flight of wooden stairs to the top floor.

''Ere we go,' announced Mary, flinging open the door. 'This is our room.' She looked at Maggie suspiciously. 'Yer don't snore, do yer? The last girl used to snore sumfink dreadful. Could hardly get a wink of sleep for the racket.' Maggie shook her head. 'That's good,' beamed Mary, and waved a hand. 'So what do yer think of it?'

Maggie stared round and nodded again. An iron bedstead with a thin mattress and an equally thin coverlet took up most of the room. A framed embroidery reading God Bless this House hung above it, the only spot of brightness on the bare whitewashed walls. There was a chair on each side of the bed and a rickety chest-of-drawers beneath the window, with a few cheap gee-gaws lying on it. Maggie gasped; compared with a cellar, shared by three people, it was a palace.

'Not bad, is it?' said Mary condescendingly. 'And once yer gets yer pay, we can go down the market on our 'alf day and yer can get a few things of yer own. Make it more homelike.' She grinned. 'Seen enough yet? It's dinnertime and I'm starving!'

Maggie stared at her. It was barely two hours since

she'd had the slice of pie and they were going to eat again? She grinned back. Talk about a cushy life!

By the end of the day she wasn't quite so sure. There had been dishes to wash after the midday meal in the servants' hall, and more vegetables to prepare for dinner at eight. Coal and hot water to carry up three flights of stairs, and the fires to sort while the master and mistress were eating. There were more dishes to wash after that, the porridge to put on to soak overnight, and the table to set in the hall for breakfast. Finally, there was the range to clean out and the fire to bank in readiness for next morning.

Maggie smiled despite her exhaustion; at least she hadn't let ma down. Even the cook, Mrs McAlister back from her afternoon off and confronted with the new arrival, had finally given her grudging approval.

'Better blow out the candle and get some sleep,' advised Mary with a jaw-breaking yawn. 'We'll be up again at five to clean out them hearths and light the fires. Then there's the hot water to fetch... and the... the...' her voice trailed off into sleep.

Lying in a strange bed, wrapped in one of Mrs Hardcastle's voluminous cast-off nightdresses, with a warm body beside her and more food in her belly than she normally saw in a week, Maggie stared wide-eyed into the darkness. So much had happened in the last twenty-four hours, she could hardly believe it. A whole new life, and what a life too! There were so many things to think about, she'd never get to sleep in a month of Sundays!

Five minutes later she was sound asleep and, despite her promise to Mary, snoring like a small contented pig.

Chapter Two

Eighteen! Maggie could scarcely believe it. The time seemed to have passed in the blink of an eye. She stared at her reflection in the cracked mirror. The bright-eyed girl who looked back was a far cry from the scrawny lice-ridden waif who'd had to be scrubbed down in front of the kitchen fire two years ago. And she was a young lady to be reckoned with now – head kitchen maid, if you pleased!

No more peeling mounds of spuds and scouring pots. She was the one who gave the orders now. She smiled ruefully. Or at least, passed on Mrs McAlister's.

Hard work and good food had worked wonders. She eyed herself critically. Perhaps her bottom wasn't quite as voluptuous as fashion demanded, but her bosom and hips curved softly and she could almost span her waist with two hands. Her hair was neatly coiled and pinned just now, but when she let it down at night it fell almost to her waist in a dark, shining cascade.

She winked at her reflection. Mrs H had said she'd grow up to be a beauty. Well, that might be pushing it a bit, but she wasn't half bad. Not if Thomas the footman's reaction was anything to go by. He'd been after her for months now, waylaying her in the corridor, his mouth eagerly seeking hers.

'Come on, Maggie,' he moaned, his hands fumbling at her breasts beneath the heavy serge of her uniform, his excitement obvious by the bulge in his tight breeches. 'Yer know I wants yer.'

For a few moments she'd allowed herself to enjoy the strange new sensations his clumsy gropings produced – before pushing him firmly away. 'I wants don't get!' she said tartly. 'Just you keep your hands to yourself, Thomas Watkins. I ain't that sort of girl.'

And his groan of frustration did nothing to soften her heart. Served the bugger right. It was all very well for blokes; they could take their pleasure and walk away without a second thought. She snorted. They could afford to. They weren't the ones left holding the baby, were they? She shuddered. And marriage – if you could get it – wasn't much better. No money, a brood of snotty kids at your feet – with another on the way every year, as like as not. She should cocoa! She was perfectly happy as she was, thank you very much.

Tucking away a few stray tendrils, she pinned her bonnet in place, smoothed down the folds of her new lilac print dress and smiled. It was her birthday, it was her half-day off – and she had five bob in her pocket to spend exactly as she pleased. The day was infinite with possibilities. She could take a walk along the market and see if she could find a new straw hat to go with her dress. She could sit in the park and watch the soldiers strutting by in their scarlet uniforms. She could even be daring and go to a matinee at the new music hall.

But then these pleasant thoughts were rudely interrupted as the door flew open and Emily burst in, red-faced and breathless. 'Yer gotta come right away, Maggie,' she gasped. 'Mrs H wants yer.'

'But it's my afternoon off,' protested Maggie. 'I'm going out.'

'Not any more yer not,' contradicted Emily. 'Come on, get yer arse moving – don't just stand there gawping like a booby.'

With a sigh of exasperation, Maggie threw her dolly-bag on the bed and followed Emily downstairs, and as she took in the scene in the kitchen her mouth fell open in shock. Mrs H was sitting in front of the range, rocking backwards and forwards, and sobbing in the corner was Millie, her ladyship's personal maid, her bags piled round her in an untidy heap. Maggie gawped at her; this pathetic creature bore no resemblance to the snooty little madam who thought herself a cut above everybody else. There was no sign of her airs and graces now. What the hell was going on?

She soon found out.

'In the club, ain't she,' snapped Mrs H, and at the words there was another wail from the corner. Mrs H ignored it. 'Stupid little cow,' she spat, glaring at the snivelling girl. 'Out on her ear without a reference. And what am I supposed to do now, that's what I want to know? With young master Jeremy back from India next week there'll be all sorts of goings on – not to mention her ladyship going off to the ball tonight and no maid to do for her.'

Her lips set tightly. 'There's nothing for it,' she announced, staring grimly at Maggie. 'You'll have to take over.'

'Me?' squeaked Maggie, in disbelief. 'I've never even been upstairs, 'cept on errands. I ain't no lady's maid.'

'Nothing to it,' said Mrs H dismissively. 'If that half-witted little mare could do it, so can you. You're a smart clean girl. You can sew and iron, can't yer?' Maggie nodded dumbly. 'That's settled then,' said Mrs H in relief. 'Lucky you're the same size as Millie. Get yourself back upstairs and changed into her uniform, then I'll give yer a quick run through while her ladyship's at afternoon tea in the drawing room.'

By the time Maggie returned the pile of bags was gone and Millie had disappeared as if she'd never existed. It was as if the streets she'd come from had opened and swallowed her up again. Maggie shivered; what would happen to her now?

She didn't have time to think about it for long. 'Very nice,' smiled Mrs H. 'Now straighten your cap and apron and come with me.'

Keys jangling she heaved herself to her feet and indicated to Maggie to follow her up the backstairs and through the green baize servants' door into the main house. 'This is her ladyship's room,' she announced, leading Maggie in. Maggie nodded. She'd had brief glimpses of it before, when she'd carried up hot water or buckets of coal, but then she'd had to keep her eyes down and scurry about her tasks as unobtrusively as possible. Now she had time to look round and take it all in at her leisure.

A heavily carved dressing table took up half one wall, its surface cluttered with packets of papier poudre, tiny crystal pin dishes, a silver backed brush and hand mirror and a large leather jewel case. Rich turkey carpets covered the polished floor. A satin spread covered the bed and the pillows were adorned with flounces of the same Honiton lace that her majesty was so fond of. Small occasional tables were covered with ornaments and an enormous vase filled with peacock feathers stood at the window. Over everything hung the cloying smell of attar of roses.

An ornate morning gown lay discarded across the bed, and Mrs H picked it up and shook it out. A torn flounce trailed on the carpet and she tutted. 'That'll have to be sewn back on,' she grumbled. 'You can start with that.' She wagged a finger. 'Remember that; nothing's to be put back in the wardrobe until the buttons and frills have been checked and it's been sponged and pressed.'

Maggie nodded, her head spinning as Mrs H continued to instruct her in her new duties. Fetching and carrying, doing her ladyship's hair, and seeing to her clothes and jewels. Everything, in fact, from dressing her ladyship in the morning to undressing her again when it was time to go to bed. God's strewth, it wouldn't have surprised her in the least if Mrs H had informed her she'd have to pee for her employer as well!

'What are you grinning at?' the woman demanded suspiciously.

'Nothing, Mrs H,' Maggie said meekly. 'Just trying to remember everything.'

'Well see that you do, girl,' came the cross reply. 'I ain't got time to go over it all again. Her ladyship's guests will be leaving soon. You gotta help her out of her afternoon gown, see to her bath then get everything laid out for this ball tonight – and I don't want no complaints either. Just you see you do everything proper.'

Maggie nodded apprehensively and Mrs H softened. 'Don't worry, love, you'll do fine,' she said. 'First time's the worst – but I'll give you a hand to set you off.' She glanced at the fob watch pinned to the front of her black gown. 'Just time for a cuppa before you get started.'

'This is Carter, your ladyship,' Mrs Hardcastle said formally. 'She'll be taking over from Evans.' Maggie bobbed a nervous curtsey as Lady Georgina looked her over.

'I suppose she'll have to do,' sighed her ladyship. 'Though how I'm supposed to manage without Evans I do not know. Her leaving is most inconvenient.'

Maggie bit her lip. Typical. 'Her leaving' indeed. As if the poor girl had any choice. Chucked out with a full belly – and all this pampered bitch could worry about was the 'inconvenience'. Selfish cow!

'Don't just stand there, girl,' she ordered. 'Undress me and loose my stays.' She turned her back to reveal a row of tiny buttons from neck to waist, so Maggie hurried forward and began to undo them. When that was done, and her ladyship helped out of her dress, bustle and petticoats, she turned her attention to the tightly laced stays, and her ladyship gave a groan of pleasure as the rolls of tightly compressed flesh escaped.

'Fetch my wrap,' she snapped, glancing at the ormolu clock. 'I shall have a short nap before this evening's ball. You may bring a tray at six then help me bathe and prepare.' She glared at Mrs Hardcastle. 'I presume she can dress hair?'

'Of course, my lady,' Mrs H said smoothly.

By the time Maggie had sewn the offending flounce back onto her ladyship's morning gown, there was barely time to grab a slice of bread and cheese before it was time to take up her tray. As she ate, her ladyship issued a stream of orders and Maggie found herself fetching gown after gown as madam made her decision. Finally she chose a low-cut maroon silk.

'My jewels, now,' she ordered, and considered the glittering trove as Maggie held the heavy leather box. 'I think I shall wear the garnets,' she decided at last. 'Now where are those idle girls? My bath should have been ready by this time.'

Maggie supervised as the hipbath was brought and filled. Trying to avoid the sight of her ladyship's bulging breasts and thighs, she helped her into it, and afterwards she held a soft warm towel to wrap her in as she stepped out. It was like bathing an enormous, bad-tempered baby! And that was only the beginning.

'Tighter, girl, tighter!' her ladyship panted as Maggie hauled on the laces of her stays. Maggie suppressed a groan; talk about trying to get a quart into a pint pot! By the time she'd done it to her ladyship's satisfaction she could hardly breath – and neither could her employer. Stockings, fresh drawers and the inevitable bustle were followed by a dozen petticoats before Maggie could finally slip the maroon silk over her ladyship's head and begin doing up the tiny buttons.

'Hurry up, girl,' she snapped. 'Look at the time, and my hair's not done yet. His lordship will be here and I'm not even half ready,' and the words were accompanied by a slap that made Maggie's ears ring.

'Yes, m'm,' she muttered, hurrying to obey and receiving another couple of slaps for her pains; once for tugging her ladyship's hair as she brushed it, and then again when her efforts were deemed unsatisfactory.

'Take it down and do it all again,' she was told.

Finally it was finished to madam's satisfaction. Maggie fastened the clasp of the garnet necklace and stepped back with a sigh of relief as her ladyship preened herself in the mirror. 'That will do,' she said grudgingly.

Maggie bit her lip. And thank you too! She might be her ladyship, but she was no lady. Sitting there, her heavy, bad-tempered face flushed from the pressure of her corsets, she looked like nothing more than the fat, overdressed wife of a costermonger!

'What are you gawping at, girl?' the woman demanded. 'Get this place tidied up.' She indicated the discarded clothes strewn around the room.

'Yes m'm,' Maggie said meekly, anxious to avoid yet another blow, and she had barely begun when the door opened and his lordship strutted in.

'Not ready yet, Georgie?' he said genially. 'I've ordered Harris to bring the carriage round in ten minutes.'

'Of course, dear,' cooed her ladyship, fluttering round like an overweight butterfly. 'I only have my wrap to put on.' Her smile disappeared and she clicked her fingers at Maggie. 'Fetch it, girl. I don't want to keep his lordship waiting.'

'Right away, m'm,' Maggie said, bringing the fringed monstrosity and slipping it round the bulging shoulders, and as she did so she was uncomfortably aware of his lordship's piggy eyes on her. Despite the heavy serge uniform, she suddenly felt naked.

'This is a new face,' he commented. 'What happened to Evans?'

Her ladyship turned scarlet. 'Er… I had to let her go,' she muttered, avoiding his eyes. 'She proved to be unsatisfactory.' She waved a dismissive hand. 'This is Carter.'

Maggie bobbed another curtsey, uncomfortably aware of his gaze lingering on her breasts.

'My evening bag, Carter,' ordered her ladyship, turning to give herself one last smug glance in the mirror, and Maggie turned away with relief.

But it didn't last long. As she walked past his lordship to hand it to her, he ran a swift hand over the curve of her buttocks, concluding his explorations with a sharp pinch. Maggie stifled an outraged squeak.

'Is there something wrong, Carter?' her ladyship asked icily.

'N-no m'm,' muttered Maggie, lowering her eyes and restraining the urge to rub her bottom. Bastard! If Thomas the footman had tried that little lark, he'd be nursing a slapped face for his pains.

'In that case, do try to sound less like something from the barnyard,' sighed her ladyship. 'Come Edward, the carriage will be waiting.' As she waddled out, Lord Edward turned at the door and gave Maggie a salacious wink, and she stared after him, seething helplessly. The man was a pig despite his title and fine clothes.

By the time Maggie had supervised the removal of the hipbath, tidied the room, made the bed again and pulled back the sheets for her ladyship's return, she was exhausted.

'My plates are killing me,' she moaned, down in the kitchen.

'Never mind, I saved you a bite to eat, love,' said Mrs H, sympathetically. 'Put yer feet up and get something inside yer.' Gratefully, Maggie slipped off her shoes and accepted the food and the glass of porter that accompanied it. Once it was finished she sighed, fetched the sewing box and set to, replacing several buttons that had failed to take the strain of her ladyship's bosom.

She was nodding over her work when she heard the sound of the front door opening. A quick glance at the kitchen clock showed that it was almost two in the morning. She groaned; she still had her ladyship to see to before she could fall into her own bed. The bell for Lady Georgina's bedroom jangled imperiously and she got stiffly to her feet and hurried to answer it.

'About time too,' snapped her ladyship, putting a plump hand to her forehead. 'I am absolutely exhausted. Undress me – and be quick about it.'

Once again Maggie hurried to obey, but her fingers were slow with tiredness and she earned herself another blow when she fumbled clumsily at the tiny buttons. Finally she slipped the silk nightgown over Lady Georgina's head and held the covers as she slipped beneath them. At last, she could go to her own bed.

But not quite.

'Fetch me a glass of hot milk to help me sleep,' ordered her ladyship. 'And perhaps a few of those little rattafia biscuits.'

Maggie bobbed a curtsey and wearily set off for the kitchen again. Standing over the hob, she willed the milk to boil quicker. Every bone in her body ached with tiredness. She arranged the biscuits daintily on a doily, placed the milk on the tray and carried it across the kitchen, bumping the door open with her hip.

'Will that be all, madam?' she asked, as she put the tray down beside the bed.

'That will do,' muttered her ladyship, reaching greedily for the biscuits. 'You may go now.'

Thankfully Maggie scurried out of the room – and almost bumped into his lordship, his dressing gown gaping to reveal a belly bulging against his nightshirt. 'Oh, I'm sorry, sir,' she gasped, stepping back.

'I'm not,' he wheezed lecherously, and before she could escape he seized and pulled her against him. She shuddered as a gust of alcohol-laden breath brushed her cheek, but worse was to come as his wet, fleshy mouth swooped down on hers, his thick tongue pushing between her lips.

'Bbbmmm… no sir… stop it!' she managed, trying to push him off, but her struggles served only to increase his excitement. Even through her heavy uniform she could feel his thick member pressing urgently into her belly and his free hand was fumbling at her skirts. 'Please, please…' she pleaded as his fat fingers found the soft flesh of her thighs. Was this what had happened to poor Millie Evans?

'That's right, beg for it, you saucy little bitch,' he panted, his face flushed with lust.

'Edward? Is that you?' came a querulous voice, and he let Maggie go as suddenly as he'd grabbed her. She fell against the wall, her breasts heaving.

'Another time,' he promised huskily as he pulled his dressing gown round him, opened the bedroom door, and disappeared inside.

Maggie stared at the door and thanked God for her lucky escape. Another time? Over her dead body! She'd keep well clear of his lordship in future.

Light-headed with relief she fled to the safety of her room. Mary's snoring had never sounded so comforting, and her last thought before she fell into an exhausted sleep was that being a lady's maid was more hazardous than she'd imagined.

Chapter Three

'Strewth! I'm about run off my feet,' panted Mrs Hardcastle, planting herself down with a sigh and fanning herself with a limp hand. 'You'd think it was the queen herself come to visit instead of just young Master Jeremy coming home.' She nodded towards Mrs McAlister, who was rolling out enough pastry to cover a small bed. 'You got them menus wrote out for her ladyship yet, Sarah? If I don't take them up soon, she'll have a blue fit.'

'There on the dresser,' muttered Sarah, pointing with a floury hand, and the words were barely out of her mouth when the bell for the morning room began jangling imperiously.

'Told yer so,' said Mrs H, reluctantly heaving her bulk out of the chair and picking up the handwritten sheets. 'They look fine to me, Sarah,' she said, running a swift eye over them. 'But what's the odds she'll manage to find something to complain about? Ah well, no rest for the wicked, eh?' Straightening her voluminous black skirts, she bustled out.

Maggie put down the petticoat she was mending and looked at Sarah. 'So what's this Master Jeremy like then, Mrs McAlister?' she asked. Sarah stopped her rolling and smiled indulgently.

'A right wee charmer,' she sighed. 'I remember when he was a laddie, he was always in and out the kitchen trying to wheedle me into making him biscuits. "Nobody in the whole wide world makes biscuits like you, Mrs Mac", he'd say.' She beamed proudly. 'And who could resist those big blue eyes of his and that head of blond curls? He was like a wee angel fallen from heaven.' She looked at Maggie enquiringly. 'But have you not seen him yourself? You've been here long enough.'

Maggie nodded. 'Yes,' she agreed. 'But only once, the Christmas after I came.' And that was only a quick glance out of the corner of her eye when the staff was lined up on Christmas morning to receive their gifts; a length of cotton for the female servants and worsted for the men. 'I think he was at boarding school then, and after that he got his commission and was posted to India. I can hardly remember what he looked like.'

'Fancy that,' marveled Mrs McAlister. 'How could anybody forget a bonnie laddie like that?' Maggie suppressed a smile and refrained from pointing out that she'd been more concerned with keeping her belly full and her work done than making sheep's eyes at her employers' son.

'Anyway,' Mrs McAlister went on with satisfaction. 'You'll have plenty of time to see him this time. Three whole months he's back for.' She nodded her head. 'And deserves every minute of it, if you ask me. Living out amongst them heathen savages. His poor mother must have been worried sick.'

Maggie nodded, while wondering if Lady Georgina ever worried about anything apart from her own selfish hide. The last couple of weeks as her ladyship's maid had done nothing more to endear her employer to her. She had worked her fingers to the bone trying to please her and had nothing but complaints and rebukes to show for it. She smiled ruefully. Not to mention the bruises! Her ladyship was quick to show her disapproval with a sharp rap across the knuckles when she was displeased. And she was displeased most of the time. Still, perhaps she was wrong. Perhaps her son's arrival home would transform her. And at least she hadn't bumped into the master again since that first horrible night.

'So when's he coming?' she asked.

'Sometime this afternoon,' announced Mrs McAlister with satisfaction. 'Harris is going down to the station to collect him after luncheon.' She pushed up her sleeves and tackled her pastry with fresh vigour. 'Though if I don't stop blethering and get a move on there's not going to be any luncheon – and I can just imagine what her ladyship would have to say about that!'

At the mention of Lady Georgina, Maggie picked up her needle and began sewing industriously again. If her petticoats weren't mended, no doubt she'd have something to say about that as well.

'He's here!' called Emily, peering excitedly out of the kitchen window. 'He's here! The carriage is back! I can see the wheels!'

Maggie scowled as she set the flat-iron in front of the coals. About time too. If Lady Georgina had tried on one dress, she'd tried on half a dozen – before deciding on the one she'd picked in the first place. The pile of discarded dresses was lying crumpled on the kitchen settle, to be ironed all over again. And she'd had to do her ladyship's hair three times before she'd been satisfied with the result.

She grinned; anyway, God knows why Emily was getting so excited. All she'd see from the window were Master Jeremy's boots. He'd hardly be likely to come visiting the kitchens.

But Maggie was wrong. A couple of hours later the door swung open and a tall fair-haired man stood on the threshold, smiling. Keen blue eyes surveyed the surprised occupants and lit on Mrs McAlister, and in three long strides he'd crossed the room, scooped her up and was swinging her round exuberantly. When he finally deposited her on her feet, grey hair escaping from beneath her white cap, and planted a kiss on her cheek, she was laughing and fluttering like a girl of sixteen.

'Och now, Master Jeremy, will you behave yourself,' she scolded. 'And just you stand still while I take a good look at you.' She beamed up at him, her eyes full of happy tears. 'My, my, you haven't changed one wee bit.'

'Nor have you, Mrs Mac,' he said, with a gallant bow. 'And you're still the best cook in England.' He bent down. 'Do you know what the worst thing about India was?' Mrs Mac shook her head, wide-eyed. 'Not having your famous biscuits!'

'Away you go, laddie,' she chuckled, pride and pleasure written all over her face. She turned and clapped her hands. 'Well, girls, don't stand there staring like boobies. Come and welcome Master Jeremy home again.'

One by one the girls came shyly up to bob their curtseys and have their hands shaken. 'Ellen, Mary, Emily,' he said as they giggled and nudged each other. 'Good heavens, what grown-up young ladies you've all turned into while my back was turned.' Then he caught sight of Maggie. 'And who's this? You're new, aren't you?'

'Not at all, Master Jeremy,' interrupted Mrs McAlister.

'Surely you remember Maggie? She came to us as the tweeny in your last year at school.'

He stared at her for a moment in surprise, taking in the smiling face and the trim figure. 'What?' he blustered, vaguely remembering a distant Christmas morning and a skinny waif with downcast eyes who'd scuttled up to receive her present then fled as if the devil himself were after her. 'That scrawny little creature who looked as if she wouldn't say boo to a goose? I don't believe it!'

'The very same, sir,' said Maggie, smiling up at him. She wasn't the only one who'd changed. Then he'd been a gangling schoolboy with untidy hair and knobbly wrists protruding from the suit he'd obviously grown out of while he was away at Harrow. Now he was a grown man; tanned, broad-shouldered and moustachioed. Piercing blue eyes regarded her with interest and she felt a strange quiver in the pit of her stomach.

'Well, well, well,' he said, holding out his hand. 'Pleased to meet you again then, Maggie.' She took it – and was shocked at her reaction to his touch. Even Thomas' clumsy fumblings had never made her feel like this! Her mouth felt suddenly dry and the quivering became a demanding throb in the hidden place between her thighs. Flushing scarlet, she pulled her hand away and lowered her eyes before he could see the effect he'd had on her.

A quick glance from beneath her lashes showed that he seemed disconcerted too. 'Er, well…' he muttered. 'Time to get back upstairs then.' The bell for the drawing room jangled impatiently and his face cleared. 'Sounds as if mamma's wondering where I've got to,' he said. 'Better not keep her waiting, eh?' He smiled round at them all. 'Keep up the good work, girls.' He grinned at

Mrs McAlister. 'And don't be too hard on them, Mrs Mac.' With a jaunty salute he strode out.

'Isn't 'e luvverly?' sighed Emily, and she winked at the other girls. 'Wouldn't kick 'im out of bed, would yer?' There was a chorus of giggles and Mrs McAlister scowled.

'That's quite enough of that, young woman,' she snapped. 'I'll have none of your smut in my kitchen, if you please. Master Jeremy's not for the likes of you.' She sniffed. 'As if he'd even look twice at a bunch of scullery girls.' She nodded her head in approval. 'Look at Maggie there. She's not carrying on like a moon-struck calf. Just you take a leaf out of her book and behave yourselves like good girls should.'

'Ooooh, miss prim and proper and no mistake,' sniggered Emily, digging her elbow into Maggie's ribs. 'Bet you ain't such a goody-two-shoes as yer looks. You wouldn't say no to Master Jeremy if he asked yer nicely, would yer now?'

Mrs McAlister's face became thunderous. 'Right, that's it, my lady! Since you're feeling so lively, you can just go and give a wee hand peeling those vegetables.'

'But that's not my job,' wailed Emily. 'That's the tweeny's. It'll spoil me hands.'

'It's your job now,' said Mrs McAlister, folding her arms over her formidable bosom. 'And one more word out of you and it'll be your job for the rest of the week and all.' She nodded her head grimly. 'Just you remember what happened to wee Millie Evans. Got herself in trouble and she was oot that door so fast her feet didn't touch the ground. She'll no be laughing now, the same lady.'

Subdued, the girls drifted back to their tasks. Maggie

45

picked up her iron again, her legs still weak from the whirl of strange new feelings Master Jeremy had aroused in her. The harsh material of her uniform seemed to rub against the tips of her breasts with every movement, aggravating the throbbing between her thighs.

'You wouldn't say no to Master Jeremy if he asked yer nicely, would yer?' Emily had said. Maggie shivered at the very thought... and she had the dreadful suspicion that Emily might just be right.

Chapter Four

'Where's that Emily?' demanded Mrs Hardcastle. 'She should have been down here hours ago.' She looked at the table where the breakfast trays were still sitting and her lips set. 'Still lying in her bed, I warrant.'

The door of the kitchen opened and Emily crept in. 'About time too, miss,' snapped Mrs H. 'As if I didn't have enough to worry about with them wanting their breakfasts in bed after last night, instead of in the breakfast room. Now pick up the master's and get yourself up them stairs.' She stopped. 'Good heavens girl, what's wrong with you?'

Emily clutched her swollen jaw and whimpered. 'I've got the toothache sumfing awful, Mrs H,' she moaned. 'Never got a wink of sleep last night for it.'

'Well, you can't go upstairs looking like that,' said Mrs Hardcastle briskly. 'You've got a face like a turnip. Put anybody off their grub, that would.' She pushed the whimpering girl into the chair by the fire. 'Now you sit there while I get my box.'

Five minutes later she was back. 'Open wide,' she ordered, and still whimpering, Emily did as she was told, wincing as Mrs Hardcastle dabbed oil of cloves onto the offending tooth. 'Now,' she muttered, producing a large green bottle and carefully measuring out a small spoonful, 'get this laudanum down yer and get back to yer bed. If this don't work you'll 'ave to 'ave it out.'

Emily opened her mouth to protest, but the laudanum was already having an effect, and instead she yawned prodigiously and smiled at Mrs H. 'Yes m'm,' she murmured, slowly getting to her feet. She staggered then giggled.

'Better see her up to bed, Maggie,' sighed Mrs H. 'Don't want the silly young madam falling asleep on the stairs,' and with Emily leaning heavily against her, Maggie left the kitchen.

By the time she left Emily safely tucked up in bed and returned to her duties, Mrs H had made a fresh pot of tea. 'You'll have to take these up,' she said, indicating the trays. 'The old master's first, then young Master Jeremy's.' She sniffed. 'Her ladyship won't want to be disturbed until near enough midday.'

Maggie stared at her in dismay. 'Me?' she protested. 'But what about my own work?'

'You can do it later,' snapped Mrs H. 'Now don't stand there gawping. Get a move on before them bells start jangling,' and with a sigh of resignation, Maggie picked up the master's tray.

When she entered the bedroom her nose wrinkled in distaste. The windows were closed and the room smelt of stale sweat and lingering farts. For all his wealth and breeding, Lord Edward stank like a fat old pig. He looked like one too, lying there with his mouth open and his puffy red face covered in grey bristles.

Holding her breath, Maggie bent to lay the tray carefully on the bedside table. With a bit of luck she could have the curtains drawn and be out of there before he was properly awake.

But as she stood up his hand shot from beneath the

coverlet and grabbed her behind the knee, toppling her onto the bed. She gasped and struggled as he sat up and hauled her alongside him. His sweaty face came down on hers, his breath stinking like an open grave and she gagged as his tongue squirmed its way between her lips like a hot, wet slug.

'Come on,' he panted, lifting his head. 'You know you want it.' His lips came down on her breasts this time and even through the thick serge she could feel the slobbering wetness against her skin. Holding her down with one hand, he flipped up her heavy skirts and groaned as he found the gap in her pantaloons, his stubby fingers exploring the softness where her thick black stockings ended and the creamy flesh of her thighs began. He pinched her viciously and chuckled as she squealed, and it was that that saved her. Galvanised by the pain she jerked convulsively and broke his hold. Rolling away from him she fell on her knees on the other side of the bed, then leapt to her feet and scurried out the door, his jeering laughter following her.

She was halfway down the servants' stairs before she stopped running. Swallowing down her nausea she scrubbed her mouth, trying to remove the taste of him, then attempted to rearrange her tangled hair. When she had finally regained her breath and restored herself she continued on down, still shuddering at her narrow escape.

'You took your time,' grumbled Mrs Hardcastle. 'What were you doing? Admiring yourself in the mirror, no doubt.' For a moment Maggie contemplated telling her what had really happened, then dismissed the idea. Whose word would she take? That of a common lady's maid or that of Lord Edward Cavanagh, member of the House of Lords and pillar of society? And even if she did believe her story, what could she do? Smack his wrists and tell him not to be a naughty boy?

'Yes m'm,' she muttered, bowing her head to hide the bitterness in her eyes. 'Sorry m'm.'

'Well then,' said Mrs Hardcastle, mollified. 'Take up Master Jeremy's tray. And be quick about it. He's probably awake by this time.'

He wasn't. Putting the tray down quietly, Maggie stepped back and feasted her eyes on him, wondering how an ugly brute like Sir Edward could have fathered such a son. His blond hair was endearingly tousled against the pillow and his lips were slightly parted, making him look boyish and vulnerable, despite the rakish moustache.

Maggie blushed as she realised he slept without a nightshirt. He had tossed off most of the bedclothes during the night, and the remaining sheet was tangled round his waist, revealing his broad tanned chest. Her fingers itched to touch the soft golden hair that made a V in the centre of it, then led tantalisingly downwards. She suppressed a gasp as she realised that the thin cotton outlined every curve of his body – and that she could see his...

'Well, do I pass inspection?' he asked, smiling lazily at her from beneath half-closed lids. If she'd been red before, she was scarlet now! Waves of hot shame washed over her. Even the piano in the drawing room had its legs decently covered to avoid wicked thoughts – and she'd been caught staring at a man's half-naked body like a cheap dockside whore, touting for custom.

'I... I'm sorry, sir,' she stammered. 'I was just about to wake you.' She pointed to the tray. 'I brought your breakfast.'

'Thank you, um…'

'Maggie, sir,' she said, staring demurely at the floor.

'Thank you, Maggie,' he said. 'And I'm sure it'll taste all the better for being served by such a pretty wench.'

The blush, which had been dying away, stained her cheeks again. 'Thank you, sir,' she muttered, bobbing a curtsey. 'I'll be back to bring your hot water and fetch the tray once you've finished.'

'I'll look forward to it,' he grinned, and as he turned his attention to his breakfast she took the opportunity to leave, with as much dignity as she could muster.

'You've been running on thon stairs again,' scolded Mrs McAlister. 'Look at the colour of you. You're as red in the face as a turkey cock. If you're not careful you'll give yourself a fainting fit and end up in bed beside young Emily – and then how will we manage?'

'Don't be daft,' scoffed Maggie. 'I won't faint.' She smiled ruefully. 'There's too much to do. I haven't got the time.'

'Well, at least get something inside you, lassie,' grumbled Mrs McAlister. 'You can't run about like a scalded cat on an empty stomach.' She pointed to the black-leaded range. 'There's porridge in the pan and some tea left in the pot. Get yourself something to eat before you take up the hot water and fetch down the trays.'

'Porridge!' exclaimed Maggie, pulling a face. 'No thanks, I'll make meself a bit of toast.' Pouring herself a cup of tea, she found the toasting fork and stuck the heel of the loaf onto it. Seated in front of the fire, she held the bread in front of the hot coals, staring dreamily at the patterns they made as she went over Master Jeremy's words in her head.

'For God's sake, girl, do you want to set the place afire?' demanded Mrs McAllister, and Maggie came to with a jerk to find her toast in flames. She squeaked with dismay as the fiery remains of her breakfast fell onto the hearth and disintegrated in a shower of sparks.

'Now look what you've done,' said Mrs McAllister. 'Get that swept up and make yourself another slice.' The bells on the wall jangled. 'Too late,' she went on in vexation. 'That'll be them wanting their hot water. Leave it and I'll do it. You'll have to wait for your breakfast now.' She tutted. 'Really Maggie, I don't know what's got into you this morning. You're usually such a sensible girl.'

'Sorry, Mrs M,' apologised Maggie, leaping to her feet. 'But don't you bother; I'll sweep up the mess when I get back.' Gripping a water can in each hand, she nudged the door open with her hip and set off back upstairs.

Outside Lord Edwards door she paused apprehensively. What if he grabbed her again? She might not have such a lucky escape this time. She pushed open the door, peered round it and breathed a sigh of relief. There was no sign of him. He must be in the dressing room, so hitching up her skirt she dashed in, deposited his hot water, picked up the breakfast tray and dashed out again.

Leaving the tray at the top of the servants' staircase, she returned for the second water tin, walked along the upper hall to Master Jeremy's room and tapped on the door. There was no answer and a pang of disappointment ran through her. He must be getting dressed too. Pushing the door open she walked in – then stopped on the threshold, her mouth dropping open.

He was getting dressed all right, but he hadn't

bothered withdrawing to his dressing room to do it. The sunlight coming in through the window illuminated his naked body, highlighting the smooth hard planes of his chest and stomach and the muscular columns of his thighs. He looked like that statue of whatsisname she'd peeked at in one of the books when she'd been dusting the library. With one small – or rather large – difference. She gasped and averted her eyes from the sight of his manhood lying heavily against his thighs, her knees suddenly weak at the wicked images the sight conjured up.

At the sound he whirled round and grabbed the crumpled sheet from the bed to cover himself. 'Good God, girl! Couldn't you knock before you came in?' he demanded.

'I – I did, sir,' she stammered. 'You couldn't have heard me.' She held up the can of hot water as if it were a talisman against the strange feelings the sight of his naked body had provoked. 'I – I only came to bring you this and take away your tray. I didn't mean to disturb you, sir. I'm sorry.'

He looked up from fastening the sheet round his waist, saw the expression on her face and took pity on her. 'Don't look so horrified,' he grinned. 'It's not the end of the world. If having a pretty girl see me in the buff is all I have to worry about, I think I'll survive.'

She bit her lip and looked up at him. 'And you won't tell Mrs Hardcastle about it?' she pleaded. 'She'd give me an awful row.'

'Of course not,' he assured her, then winked and chucked her under the chin. 'It'll be our little secret. I think I'll take that, before you drop it,' he added, taking the water can from her nerveless fingers. 'Don't want you getting into any more trouble.'

Maggie pulled herself together. 'Thank you, sir,' she said, stepping back from him. 'You're very kind.' She edged past him. 'I'll just take your tray and be out of your way.' As she lifted it she discovered her hands were shaking; the breakfast china rattled together, giving her away.

'Good heavens, you're a nervous little filly, aren't you?' he grinned. 'Here, that looks heavy. Give it to me and I'll carry it downstairs for you.'

Maggie stared at him in horror, her nerves forgotten as she imagined what Mrs H would have to say about Master Jeremy doing her work. 'Oh no, sir!' she protested, hanging onto it as if he was going to wrench it from her at any minute. 'You can't do that. It'd be more than my job's worth.' She shook her head. 'I can manage, sir. I'm used to it.'

He stared at the slim, defiant figure and suppressed a smile. She looked as if she was prepared to defend the damned tray with her life if need be. 'Determined as well as pretty,' he said softly, and she flushed again at the admiration in his eyes. 'Well, at least let me hold the door open for you; you can hardly object to that.'

'Thank you, sir, that's very kind of you,' she said formally – then relief made her bold and the words were out of her mouth before she could stop them. 'Better hang on to that sheet though,' she said, dimpling up at him. 'I've had enough frights this morning to last me a lifetime.' She stopped in shock at her own forwardness. God, he could have her sacked on the spot for insolence! She stared at him apprehensively.

'You're quite right,' he agreed solemnly. 'I shall.' Clutching it to his waist, he bowed and opened the door, and as she maneuvered past him he was so close that she could feel the warmth radiating from his body, and the clean male scent of him made her head spin. Sudden heat blossomed in her belly and she could feel the secret place between her thighs moisten in response. He put a hand on her shoulder to steady her and she shivered involuntarily at his touch. Their eyes met and she recognised the answering desire in his – a desire reflected in the burgeoning swell of his manhood beneath the concealing sheet. Her lips parted and she swayed towards him, and if it hadn't been for the tray between them she would have found herself in his arms.

Coming to her senses, Maggie turned and walked away as fast as her burden would allow, the breakfast crockery clattering in her shaking hands. Aware of his eyes still on her, she kept her head high until she was safely round the corner and out of sight. Only then did she allow herself to collapse panting against the wall. She must have been imagining things. He was the master's son. He wouldn't be interested in the likes of her – or if he was it would only be for one thing.

Once her heart had stopped pounding she picked up the other tray and made her way slowly back downstairs.

'I knew it!' said Mrs McAllister triumphantly, taking one look at her face. 'I told you you should have eaten something. You're shaking like a bloomin' leaf.' She took the trays from Maggie's unsteady hands, dumped them on the table and pushed her into a chair. 'Just you sit there, my lass, and get something in your belly before you fall over.' She glanced at the kitchen clock. 'Madam won't be needing you for half an hour, so you just put your feet up. You'll be run off them soon enough.'

Fortified by food, Maggie was more optimistic. The

morning had been a storm in a teacup. She set her lips. She'd put him right out of her head, forget what had happened and avoid both father and son as much as possible. She smiled; she'd be back to her own job once Emily recovered from her toothache, so it shouldn't be too difficult.

But she was wrong.

Chapter Five

'Young Master Jeremy just can't get enough of my home cooking,' beamed Mrs McAllister. 'He's never out of the kitchen. That's the second time he's been down today.'

Maggie avoided her eyes and concentrated on goffering the flounces on Lady Georgina's blouse. She didn't need to be told. Every time he appeared her heart skipped a beat and once, when no one was looking, he'd grinned at her and winked.

She blushed. And if that wasn't bad enough, he had taken to coming into Lady Georgina's bedroom when she was doing her hair – ostensibly to keep his mother company, but in reality to watch Maggie as she worked. Aware of his eyes on her, she made mistake after mistake until Lady Georgina lost her temper.

'For heaven's sake, girl!' she snapped. 'What's wrong with you? You're as clumsy as an ox.'

'Yes, m'm,' she muttered, secretly wishing she could box his ears as easily as she boxed Thomas'. 'Sorry m'm,'

So it was a relief when her half-day next came round and she could get away from the house for an afternoon.

'Wot you gonna do, then?' asked Emily, admiring Maggie in her best frock.

Maggie smiled. 'I'm going to do exactly the same as I was when my last half-day got cancelled,' she said.

'I'm going to 'ave a walk round the market and buy meself a new 'at. Then I'm going ter 'ave a nice stroll in the park, and afterwards I'm going ter treat meself to a visit to the music hall.'

'Lucky bugger,' said Emily glumly. 'I ain't off again for three weeks.' She grinned. 'And just you behave yourself, my girl. No picking up soldiers in the park. You know what her ladyship says about followers.' She rolled her eyes. 'All right for her though; she's already got herself a husband and a title.' She pulled a face. 'Mind you, I wouldn't 'ave 'im. Can you imagine that fat old git putting his hands all over yer? It's enough to turn yer stomach!'

Maggie suppressed a shudder. She didn't need to imagine it, she'd already felt his podgy fingers prying and prodding at her. She dismissed the horrible memory, determined not to let it spoil her day. 'Right, that's me off,' she announced. 'See you later.'

''Ave a good time then,' said Emily. 'Don't do anything I wouldn't.' She giggled. 'And remember – if you can't be good, be careful.'

'I will,' said Maggie.

It was sheer bliss to be a lady of leisure and wander at will without being at the beck and call of Lady Georgina. The market was a riot of colours and smells, with costermongers bellowing their wares and ragamuffins dodging in and out of the crowd. Women with scruffy children hanging onto their skirts tried to find the best bargains to eke out their meagre supply of coppers. Maggie savoured it all. She spent a pleasant half hour at a hat stall, trying on one after the other before finally deciding on a pert straw boater with a pale blue ribbon of watered silk. With the parcel tucked under her arm, she treated herself to a bag of whelks to eat in the park.

Sitting in the shade she watched the world go by. Starched nannies with their high prams and well dressed charges. Toffs out for a stroll. Young couples holding hands. Red-coated soldiers who gave her the eye or winked as they walked past.

The hours flew by until it was time for the matinee at the music hall, so wiping her hands on the grass to remove the smell of fish and vinegar she picked up her parcel and made her way towards the omnibus stop.

Outside the music hall, she hesitated. It was the first time she'd been and she'd have preferred it if Emily had been able to come with her. Some employers had forbidden their servants to go – and what if she was accosted? Or even worse, picked up by a white slaver? She shivered as she remembered the horrible stories she'd heard about innocent girls being slipped Mickey Finns and waking up from their drugged sleep to find themselves trapped in a life of shame.

A couple of girls her own age pushed past, giggling, and she shook herself. If they weren't worried, then neither was she. Marching up to the ticket booth she handed over her sixpence and walked through the ornate doors of the theatre. It was like walking into another world; a world of plush red velvet and gold, of pillars and balconies and sconces and fat gold cherubs that perched on every available surface. She stood stock still with her mouth open, trying to take it all in at once.

'Impressive, isn't it?' said a familiar voice behind her, and she almost jumped out of her skin. She whirled round and found herself staring up at Master Jeremy.

'Wh-what are you doing here?' she demanded.

He raised an eyebrow. 'I paid my sixpence, just like you,' he said. 'After all, a fellow's got to have some entertainment.' He rolled his eyes. 'If I'd had to spend another afternoon making polite conversation over tea with mamma's friends and their simpering daughters, I'd have run mad.'

Maggie suppressed a giggle; since he'd come home Lady Georgina's 'at home' days had been particularly well attended, as mothers touted their marriageable daughters as shamelessly as gypsies at a horse fair. No wonder he'd done a runner!

'Well, my lady,' he grinned, holding out an arm. 'The performance is about to begin. Shall we take a seat?'

For a moment she hesitated, then threw caution to the winds. What harm could it do? They were only going to watch a show – not run off together. 'Thank you, kind sir,' she smiled, accepting the proffered arm.

The next hours flew past as they shared a bag of chestnuts and laughed at the comic turns, watched the jugglers and fire-eaters in awe and enjoyed the music together. When the curtains closed on the last act, Maggie sagged with disappointment.

'I wish it could have gone on forever,' she sighed. 'But I'd better get off home now.'

'We could always go for supper,' suggested Master Jeremy, and she stared at him in astonishment.

'Me? Go to supper with you?' She shook her head. 'It wouldn't be fitting. I'm your mother's maid.'

'So?' he grinned. 'Maids have to eat as well, don't they?'

'I suppose so,' she said reluctantly.

'Well then, that's settled,' he said. 'I know this nice little oyster bar. We can go there,' and before Maggie had time to change her mind he whisked her out of the theatre and into a hansom cab.

'Here we are,' he said after a short ride, rapping for the cabbie to stop. Helping her down he led her inside, and for the second time that day her mouth dropped open in astonishment. The decor was almost as ornate as that of the theatre, and tables set with gleaming crystal and glittering cutlery filled almost two thirds of the room. A long mahogany bar took up the other third. But it was the people who caught her attention. The men were dressed in formal black – but the women! Dressed in vivid satin dresses of every hue, with lace shawls and feathered fans, they laughed and chattered and flaunted their finery like an aviary of exotic birds. In her lilac print dress Maggie felt as out of place as a violet in a bouquet of hothouse flowers.

'I can't stay here,' she protested, shrinking back. 'Look at me; I'm not dressed properly.'

He looked at her seriously. 'Believe me, you'd be twice as pretty as any woman here, even if you were wearing a sack,' he assured her. 'But if it worries you so much, we can soon sort that.' He clicked his fingers and a waiter came rushing up. 'The lady and I would like a private room,' he said.

'Certainly, sir,' said the waiter politely. 'Right away, if you'll just follow me.' He led them through the throng to a door hidden behind a blue velvet curtain with gold swags. Maggie felt a pang of unease as she mounted the richly carpeted staircase. What on earth did she think she was playing at? She should be home by now, not going to supper with the master's son. What if this was a house of assignation and she was being led to a bedroom?

'Here we are,' announced the waiter, throwing open a door, and she sighed with relief. It wasn't some tart's boudoir after all. It was a perfectly ordinary room with a long settee along one wall and a table set for two in the middle. The waiter pulled out a gilded chair for her as if she was the queen herself, and she sat down and smiled at Master Jeremy as he took the one opposite her.

'Cor, this is lovely,' she beamed.

'Just wait till you taste the food,' he smiled back, and nodded to the waiter. 'We'll have oysters and champagne,' he said.

Maggie gasped. 'Champagne? Ain't that expensive?' She'd rather have had a nice cup of tea. The only alcohol she'd ever drunk had been the odd glass of sherry at Christmas in the servant's hall – and it had been horrible. She'd taken one sip and poured it into Mrs McAllister's glass.

'Worth every penny,' said Master Jeremy. 'In fact, let's push the boat out.' He smiled at the waiter. 'Make that two bottles.'

When it came Maggie sipped it gingerly, then smiled. 'It's lovely,' she agreed. 'Like lemonade only fizzy.' She emptied her glass and giggled as he refilled it. 'You'll get me tiddly,' she protested – but drank it all the same.

By the end of the meal she felt she was floating. It didn't seem to matter any more that she was just a maid and he was the master's son. They were just two people – a man and a woman. She watched as he tilted his head back and opened his mouth to swallow another oyster and felt a prickle of heat at the base of her belly. What would it be like to feel those lips touch hers?

'I think I'd better get off home now,' she muttered,

pushing her chair back and standing up. She staggered a little. 'Ooooh, I've come over all dizzy,' she giggled. 'Must be them oysters.'

He leapt to his feet and took her arm to steady her. 'Are you all right?' he asked.

'I'm fine,' she said, then staggered again – and was lost. Her knees weakened as his arms went round her and she felt the hard planes of his body pressed against her. She sighed, her head tipped back, her lips parting in anticipation, and he needed no second invitation. With a moan he pulled her tighter against him, his hungry mouth possessing hers, his tongue eagerly exploring. She could feel his growing hardness pressing against her belly and sighed again.

A hand was fumbling at the small buttons at her neck, undoing them one by one until he could push her dress from her shoulders. It slid down her body and tangled at her feet. He pulled off her chemise and tugged at the laces on her corset. It joined the dress on the floor and she stood before him in only her pantaloons and stockings. He eased her pantaloons down over her hips until only her black stockings remained.

For a moment her senses returned and she attempted to cover her nakedness.

'Don't do that,' he panted, pulling her hands away. 'I want to look at you.' He feasted his eyes on her, gazing at her full breasts, the soft pink nipples hard with a mixture of cold and excitement, and then trailing down to the narrow waist that curved into generous hips. Her stockings were shockingly black against her trembling white thighs and his eyes focused on the V of silky hair that nestled between them. With a groan he began ripping at his own clothes until he was as naked as she, and a bolt of fright ran through her as she saw the full length of his prick, its massive head purple and shiny. He couldn't put that inside her! He would split her open! She backed away until her legs bumped against the settee and there was nowhere else to run.

Then his hands were on her again, soothing her as if she were a skittish horse. His fingers toyed with the swollen buds of her nipples, teasing the delicate flesh, feeling them harden even more. She gasped as he bent his head and his tongue traced the same path as he suckled first one and then the other. Her tightly clenched thighs loosened as the secret place between her thighs began to grow hot and wet.

He moaned again, took her hand and placed it on his cock, rubbing it gently up and down until her fingers closed around it. She marvelled at how it felt; such a strange sensation of powerful, silky hardness. As her hand moved on him he groaned and pushed her back onto the settee and parted her legs to reveal the glistening slit of her sex, and Maggie closed her eyes and braced herself for the onslaught.

But it didn't come. Instead he bent his head, held her open like a ripe fig and explored the soft pink flesh with his mouth. 'The sweetest oyster of all,' he murmured as he lapped at the hard crest of her clitoris, and against her will her hips began to writhe as she pushed herself against the tormenting tongue, then she gasped as he slid first one finger, then two, inside her, moving them in and out, slowly at first, then faster.

'Please,' she begged, not even knowing what she was asking for. 'Please…' He raised himself and knelt between her thighs, grinning down at her rapaciously, his lips and moustache coated with her juices. Taking himself in one hand he spread her sex open and pushed the head of his cock against the swollen lips, watching as it disappeared inside her, inch by slow inch.

For a moment she stiffened as he pressed his way through her maidenhead, then relaxed again as the momentary pain turned to waves of pleasure and she felt the full length of him filling her. He began to move again, gently at first, then harder, withdrawing then pushing forward, deeper than ever. She wound her legs round his thighs and raised her hips to meet each thrust with one of her own, until they were rocking together, faster and faster.

Maggie shrieked with pleasure and release as he gave one last thrust and she felt him shudder, his face twisting as he jerked and spasmed – then he was sagging against her, passion spent.

They lay entwined on the settee, gradually recovering their senses. When he finally lifted himself from her, and began to dress, Maggie sighed again – this time with shame. What would he think of her now? She'd given herself to him like a cheap slut.

She sat up and swung her legs round, wincing at the throbbing pain between her thighs, then blushed with shame as she caught sight of the small patch of blood on the settee. She reached for her handkerchief to wipe it away before he saw it, but she was too slow. She turned scarlet and avoided his eyes as he stopped dressing and looked at her bowed head.

'What is it?' he asked. 'What's wrong?' And then he saw the blood and realised what it meant.

Taking her under the chin he turned her to face him again. 'There's nothing to be ashamed of,' he said softly. 'You gave me the greatest gift a woman could give a man. Thank you.' He smiled. 'And next time it will be easier for you.'

Relief washed through her. He didn't despise her after all, and he wasn't just going to use and cast her away. There was going to be a 'next time'! Her heart was singing as she dressed and even the waiter's knowing looks when he brought the bill – or Mrs Hardcastle's scolding when she finally got home – didn't upset her.

In bed beside Emily's sleeping body Maggie savoured every smile and word and touch all over again. Her last thought before she drifted off to sleep was that she must be mad to get involved with the master's son – but oh, what a glorious madness it was!

The next ten weeks were the happiest in Maggie's life. Even Lady Georgina's constant carping and criticism couldn't dent the bubble of contentment in which she floated through her days, buoyed up by secret touches and glances and kisses stolen in dark passageways.

She and Jeremy grasped every opportunity to make love again and again, sneaking down to the library when the rest of the household was asleep, to indulge their passion in fleeting moments of exquisite pleasure. Twice more on her monthly half-day they met to walk in the park, go to the music hall – and slake their appetites in 'their' little room above the oyster bar – and she returned home, her body aching pleasurably from Jeremy's attentions.

But all too soon his leave was up, and instead of sharing one last night together, Maggie found herself pressed into dancing attendance at his farewell dance. Biting her lip she stood against the wall of the ballroom, watching as he waltzed with the simpering daughters of his mother's friends and, even worse, being forced to listen as the older women speculated on which one he would eventually choose as his bride. It wasn't fair!

Lady Georgina glanced in her direction and clicked her fingers. 'Fetch my Kashmir shawl from the bedroom, girl – and don't dally.' Maggie bobbed a curtsey and hurried off, glad of an excuse to leave.

The shawl was tossed carelessly over Lady Georgina's bed, and Maggie picked it up, enjoying the smooth feel of the rich, silky material. On impulse she flung it over her own shoulders and admired her reflection in the mirror. She could still hear strains of music from the ballroom below, so humming, she closed her eyes and danced a few light steps, twirling round so that the shawl flared out around her in a billow of colour – and came to an abrupt stop as she collided with someone. Her eyes opened in dismay, but she found herself looking up at Master Jeremy.

'Wh-what are you doing here?' she demanded. 'You should be down in the ballroom. What if anyone notices you're missing?'

'Let them,' he snorted. 'Even a gentleman's got to use the necessary sometimes, hasn't he?' He chuckled. 'Not that any of those prim little misses would ever dream of admitting it; for all they know a man could be made of wood from the waist down. Now, you on the other hand…' He pulled her into his arms, kissed her, and she could feel his thick rod pressing against her belly.

For a moment she weakened and allowed him to urge her towards his mother's bed, then she came to her senses and pushed him away. 'I daren't!' she gasped. 'You mother is waiting for her shawl. I must go.' Ripping

67

it from her shoulders she flung it over her arm and fled towards the door, but he caught her arm and pulled her round to face him again.

'The library?' he said urgently. 'Once everyone has gone?'

She stared at him, thinking of all the work that would have to be done before she could get away, and then made up her mind. This would be the last time they'd have together for who knew how long? Perhaps forever if his next posting was a dangerous one. 'All right,' she agreed. 'But I won't be able to get away until all my work's done.'

'I'll wait for you,' he said, and kissed her gently. 'Till the crack of dawn if needs be.'

It almost was. The last guest's carriage drew away at two in the morning and Maggie had to help Lady Georgina from her dress, hang up her clothes ready to be attended to first thing in the morning, help her into her nightgown and brush her hair, then fetch her hot milk and a plate of biscuits before she could finally escape.

Back in the kitchen it was chaos. Pile upon pile of dirty plates and glasses covered every available surface and the tweenie was in tears of exhaustion as she stood at the sink trying to wash them in the lukewarm, scummy water. Mrs McAlister thrust a cloth into Maggie's hands and pressed her into service drying and putting away.

By the time order was restored, Maggie's eyes were gritty with tiredness and her feet ached from being on them non-stop since six the previous morning. When they were finally allowed to stagger gratefully off to their bedroom, Emily hauled off her boots, crawled beneath the sheets fully dressed and was asleep in seconds.

Maggie's first inclination was to follow suit; every bone in her body ached with exhaustion. But instead she slipped out of her clothes and into her best nightgown, and brushed her hair. 'Emily... Emily... are you awake?' she hissed, and the only response was a gentle snore.

Picking up the candle she slowly opened the door, careful that it didn't creak, and slipped out into the passageway and down the wooden stairs. In the main hallway she held her breath and listened. Nothing. Not even the sound of a mouse scuttling behind the panelling. The flickering light of her candle illuminated the features of a family portrait, glaring disapprovingly down on her and she jumped, and then stifled a nervous giggle; it looked far too much like Lady Georgina for her liking!

Tiptoeing along the corridor she pushed open the library door, and her heart sank as she peered around the room. It was empty. The dull remnants of the fire still glowed in the hearth, barely illuminating shelf upon shelf of leather-bound books. A single guttering candle still sat on the little wine table beside a half empty brandy glass – but there was no sign of Jeremy.

A sigh of disappointment escaped her lips – so much for all his protestations of undying love. Their last night together and he hadn't even bothered to wait for her. 'Oh Jeremy,' she whispered. 'How could you...?'

Maggie froze at the sound of movement, and then, as if her words had conjured him up, he leaned forward from the concealing depths of the high-backed chair in front of the fire and smiled at her sleepily. 'Sorry, m'dear,' he yawned. 'Must have dozed off.' Then his eyes widened at the sight of her, barefoot and wearing only her thin nightgown, and the expression of sleepiness vanished to be replaced by one of eagerness. In one panther-like movement he was out of the chair and across the room.

'I don't think we need this,' he said, removing the candlestick from her trembling fingers and placing it on the library table. The halo of light it cast shone though the flimsy material of her nightgown, revealing every curve of her body, and suddenly he was trembling as well.

He kissed her and fumbled with the row of buttons at her neck. Once they were undone he thrust a hand inside, savouring the soft fullness of her breasts, feeling the tips rise and harden against his palm as he cradled each in turn. She gasped as his thumb found them, circling and gently teasing them into even greater hardness, then he was tugging the nightgown over her head, it fell in a discarded heap and she stood naked before him.

For a moment he admired her in silence, then his fingers traced a path down her body, over her breasts and the curve of her stomach to the secret place at the V of her quivering thighs. He parted the soft hair and explored the hidden wetness, and then he moaned and pulled her against him. His other hand slid round her waist, then down over the smooth swell of her buttocks, pulling her even more tightly against him. Whimpering as she felt the length of his pole pressed against her belly, she writhed against him, aching to feel it inside her, but he pushed her gently away and began to fumble with his own clothing. Naked, he pulled her back against him and urged her towards the leather chesterfield in the corner of the room, where they toppled in a tangle of limbs.

For a long moment his hands explored every curve of

her body, revelling in her instant response, then, with a groan, he rolled on his back, his rampant cock jutting in the air. She stroked the long silken length of him, her fingers trembling at his size and stiffness, then with a whimper of pleasure she straddled him and lowered herself, groaning as the massive head pushed its way into her. She sank lower, feeling him slide deep inside, impaling her like a butterfly on a pin.

He reached up, his hands finding her breasts, kneading the soft mounds, rolling the stiff nipples between his fingers. She groaned again, leaning forward so that the quivering globes hung like ripe fruit above his lips. He squeezed them together so that his tongue could dart from one swollen bud to the other and she groaned again.

It was too much, despite her urge to prolong the delicious sensations coursing through her she reared up, threw her head back and began to ride him, raising herself up until only the tip of his cock was inside her, then plunging down again, relishing the feeling as his thick shaft slid in and out between the clutching lips of her pussy.

He shuddered with pleasure, gripping her hips to pull her harder down on him, his own hips bucking as he thrust deeper into her hot wetness. As her climax approached her mouth opened to release a wail of satisfaction – then she suddenly froze.

'Wh-what was that?' she gasped, her hands flying to cover her breasts.

'What?' he demanded, irritated at the sudden interruption of their pleasure.

'I thought I heard someone,' she whispered, her eyes frantically scanning the dimly lit library. But there was nothing – only the flame of the dying candle flickering on the bookshelves.

'Don't be silly, my love,' he laughed softly. 'There's no one else awake. It was only the fire settling.' He tweaked one nipple playfully. 'Now, where were we?'

Maggie quietly laughed too, and then drew in her breath as the movement made his erection quiver inside her. She began to move again, deliberately teasing as she rode him slowly, then her own passion overwhelmed her and she moved faster and faster, his prick slippery with her juices. With a groan he began to come, and she shrieked as the head of his cock swelled and pulsed, spilling his seed inside her. With a final groan she collapsed on top of him, spent, and lay against his chest trying to regain her breath, his hand gently stroking her perspiring flanks.

All too soon it was time to go. If they lay much longer the household would be stirring and their secret would be discovered. Reluctantly she pulled herself away and stood up, feeling the warmth of his seed on her inner thighs. He smiled up at her from heavy-lidded eyes before stretching his long limbs and sitting up too.

Feeling suddenly awkward she retrieved her discarded nightgown and tugged it over her head. 'Better go,' she muttered. 'I could lose my place if I was caught.'

'One last kiss,' he said, pulling her against him. 'I go back to my regiment tomorrow and heaven knows the next time I'll see a pretty girl again.' His mouth came down on hers and again she felt the familiar stirring of lust. Gasping, she pushed him away, grabbed her battered tin candlestick and fled.

There was no need of the candle, for the dim light of dawn was already beginning to filter through the windows as she hurried back to her room. With a sigh of relief she slipped quickly in beside the still-snoring Emily, and despite the thoughts racing through her brain, within moments had drifted into an exhausted sleep.

'Wha-what...?' Maggie spluttered as cold water splashed on her face and trickled down her neck. 'Stop it!'

'Come on, sleepyhead,' grinned Emily, reaching into the ewer for another handful. 'Wake up.' She waved her dripping fingers threateningly. 'Get a bloody move on, gel! If you're not downstairs in five minutes Mrs H'll have the skin off your back.' She snorted. 'Lying there like bleeding Sleeping Beauty. Come on, there's work to be done.' Whistling cheerfully she left, banging the door behind her.

With a groan, Maggie swung her legs out of bed. Every bone in her body ached with tiredness and she felt as if she hadn't slept for a fortnight. Yawning, she hauled herself across to the washstand and gave herself a lick and a promise before dragging on her clothes. Then, still tucking her hair under her cap, she hurried downstairs.

'About time too, miss,' sniffed Mrs McAlister. 'Her ladyship's been ringing her bell this last ten minutes.' She pointed to the tray on the table. 'Take that up this minute before she has a fit of the vapours.' Still yawning, Maggie did as she was told.

For once, Lady Georgina was awake before noon. When Maggie pushed open the bedroom door she was already sitting up in bed, her greying hair in a thin plait over her shoulders. 'About time too,' she snapped, unconsciously echoing Mrs McAlister.

'Sorry, ma'am,' Maggie apologised, setting the laden

73

tray on her ladyship's lap and lifting the metal covers from the breakfast dishes to reveal a heaped plateful of kedgeree.

'Humph,' muttered Lady Georgina, poking at it. She rolled her eyes. 'With Master Jeremy leaving I can barely face a thing,' she complained. 'I have no more appetite than a bird.' Maggie wondered idly what kind of a bird that might be? A bloody big one going by the way she was shovelling it in!

Finished, her ladyship gave a genteel belch. 'Take it away,' she ordered imperiously. 'Then you can come back and help me dress.' She simpered. 'I must look my best to say goodbye to my son.'

Maggie's heart plummeted to her buttoned boots. Until now it hadn't actually sunk in that he was really leaving, that she didn't know when – if ever – she would see him again. He might be sent off to some far-flung part of the empire to fight the hostile natives. Suppressing the lump in her throat, she bobbed a curtsey and lifted the tray, turning away quickly in case Lady Georgina saw the tears in her eyes.

When she returned her mistress was already at her toilette and impatiently waiting for her to do her hair. Maggie's stomach rumbled with a mixture of nerves and hunger as she helped her into a burgundy silk morning gown, so tight her ladyship could hardly breathe. 'Stupid dressmaker,' she panted, fanning her flushed cheeks. 'She has made my dress too small.'

'Yes, ma'am,' Maggie agreed dutifully.

There was a knock at the door and Master Jeremy entered. Maggie blushed and lowered her eyes as she remembered the way they'd pleasured each other shamelessly such a few short hours before. 'Good morning, mamma,' he said, kissing his mother dutifully. 'Good morning, Carter.' She sketched a brief curtsey.

'You may leave now, girl,' ordered Lady Georgina. 'And take my ball gown with you. Two buttons need replacing and one of the flounces needs mending.'

'Yes, my lady,' said Maggie. She picked up the heavy dress, draped it neatly over her arms and went towards the door.

'Here, let me help you,' said Jeremy, gallantly moving to open it for her, and half concealed behind it, he stole one last kiss.

'For heaven's sake, Jeremy,' his mother snapped irritably. 'The girl's only a servant; she can open doors for herself.'

Scarlet with humiliation, Maggie hurried downstairs and took out her feelings by banging the flat iron furiously over her ladyship's mended ball gown and wishing her fat body was still inside it.

The rest of the morning passed in a whirl of activity as the trunks were carried up from the cellar and carefully packed with freshly washed linen and newly pressed uniforms. Mrs McAlister, wiping tears from her plump cheeks with a floury hand, produced one final batch of 'Master Jeremy's biscuits' to be wrapped, along with a game pie and a massive fruit cake, and added to the growing pile of luggage in the hall.

Finally everything was done, and Emily's excited face appeared around the kitchen door. 'He's leaving now,' she squeaked. 'The carriage is here.' She glared at Maggie. 'Come on, the mending'll keep. We're all to line up in the hall to say goodbye.'

Smoothing down her skirts, Maggie hurried up the

kitchen stairs to take her place, her eyes eagerly drinking in the last sight of him as he walked along the line of servants, with a handshake, a word of thanks – and a tip – for each of them. When he reached her she felt a folded sheet of paper pressed into her palm as he shook her hand. Suppressing her excitement, she dutifully bobbed a curtsey as he passed on to the next in line. As soon as he was gone, she'd nip to the privy, tuck it into her bosom and read it the next time she had the chance to be alone.

But this happy thought was suddenly banished by a feeling of unease. Glancing up, she caught Lord Edward staring at her, his wet lips twisted in a knowing leer. He smiled lecherously, his eyes running over her body, then his tongue came out and, slowly and deliberately, he licked his thick purple lips.

Maggie shivered and turned back to Master Jeremy – but he was gone. All she could see was his back as he climbed into the carriage, then a strong hand waving from the window as it drove away. She closed her eyes and shuddered as a feeling of dread washed through her. Lord Edward couldn't know their secret.

Could he?

Chapter Six

'Wot's up with your face?' demanded Emily. 'You've got a phizz as long as a wet week of Sundays.' She regarded Maggie thoughtfully. 'Come to think of it, you've been as miserable as sin for the last fortnight.' She grinned wickedly. 'I know wot's wrong with yer. Yer pining for Master Jeremy, that's wot it is!' She fluttered her eyelashes. 'Oooh, Jeremy,' she cooed in a bad imitation of an upper-class accent, 'come back to me, my love. I'm missing yer somefink rotten.'

'Don't be so stupid,' snapped Maggie. Emily's so-called joke was far too near the bone to be funny.

Emily stared at her in hurt surprise. 'Keep yer hair on girl,' she sniffed. 'I was just kidding – honestly. Some people!'

'Sorry,' apologised Maggie, putting a hand to her brow. 'I didn't mean to bite your head off. I've got a splitting headache, that's all.'

'My fault, ducks,' said Emily, forgiving her instantly. 'I shouldn't 'ave been teasing yer. Tell you what,' she went on, 'I'll bring yer back some whelks from me 'alf day off – cheer yer up a bit. And it's her majesty's afternoon for visiting the other old bats, so you just try and get yer feet up and take things easy.'

'Thanks,' said Maggie ruefully. 'But chance would be a fine thing.'

And she was right. After a fraught hour dressing Lady

Georgina to go visiting, she barely had time to grab a bite to eat before tackling her other tasks. She was sitting sewing a rip in a pair of her ladyship's voluminous pantaloons when the bell for the library jangled, and five minutes later Thomas stuck his head round the kitchen door.

'His nibs wants tea and biscuits,' he announced. 'Sharpish.' He grinned. 'And one of you girls'll have to take it up.' He waved a handful of envelopes. 'He's sending me off to post this little lot.'

'As if we didn't have enough to do already,' snapped Mrs McAlister, wiping her hands on her apron. 'Emily!' she called. 'Emily! Where have you got to now, you lazy wee besom?' She shook her head at her own forgetfulness. 'Och! What a nuisance; it's her afternoon off, isn't it?' Her eyes lit on Maggie. 'Well, you'll have to take it up instead,' she decreed. 'There's nothing else for it.'

'Me?' protested Maggie. 'But I'm busy sewing.'

'Her ladyship's unmentionables can wait,' said Mrs McAlister briskly. 'She'll not be needing them in the next ten minutes, now will she?' She brought out the silver teapot, breathed on it and buffed it with the corner of her apron. Satisfied, she took down the tea caddy, unlocked it and carefully spooned out the leaves. 'There's a good girl,' she said. 'You pour on the water while I lay the tray, and mind and not scald yourself.'

With a sigh Maggie put down her sewing and picked up a potholder instead. Wrapping it round the handle she heaved the heavy kettle from the kitchen range and poured the boiling water into the teapot.

'Thanks, hinny,' smiled Mrs McAlister. She put down the plate of biscuits and regarded the tray, muttering under her breath as she checked off the items. 'Hot water jug. Tea strainer. Cup and saucer, milk, sugar, lemon, biscuits.' She sniffed. 'Better put out a bit o' cake as well, otherwise he'll have you running back down again.' She bustled off and returned bearing a large plateful of plum cake. 'There,' she announced. 'That should keep him quiet for a while.' She picked it up and thrust it into Maggie's hands. 'Off you go now. Don't hang about.'

Maggie's mouth was dry as she tapped on the library door. The last time she'd been in the room had been the night before Jeremy left, and a feeling of unaccountable dread crept through her at the thought of facing the father in the same room where she'd made love with the son. An unintelligible grunt greeted her diffident knock and she took a deep breath and pushed the door open.

He was sitting in the same chair that Jeremy had been that evening – but what a difference between the two men. Where Jeremy had been tall and lean, his father sat, leering at her like some squat disgusting toad. She avoided his eyes. 'Your tea, Lord Edward,' she said, trying to keep as far away from him as possible as she laid the tray on the small table beside his chair. She straightened up, her fingers nervously pleating the folds of her starched apron. 'Will there be anything else, sir?' she asked.

'Yes, there will,' He smirked. 'You can undo your bodice for a start.'

She stared at him, unable to believe her own ears. 'I... I... beg your pardon, my lord,' she gasped. 'Wh-what did you say?'

'You heard me, slut,' he sneered. 'Undo your bodice.

I want to look at your tits.'

Her hand flew protectively to the neck of her dress. 'H-how dare you, sir?' she stammered. 'What kind of girl do you think I am?'

'Oh, I know exactly what kind of girl you are,' he leered. 'You're a cheap little trollop who'll spread her legs for anybody.' He laughed coarsely. 'My son's had you – and now I'm going to have you too.'

She closed her eyes in horror, remembering the noise she thought she'd heard the last time she and Jeremy had made love. 'That was you, that night,' she whispered. 'You were watching us.' Her lip curled. 'You're disgusting.'

'How dare you speak to me like that, you little strumpet?' he sneered. 'You weren't quite so high and mighty when you were riding my son's cock like a bitch in heat.' He licked his lips, his face flushed with lust. 'Yes,' he chuckled, 'and a pretty sight you were too, with those little tits of yours bouncing up and down.' His expression hardened. 'Now do as you're told, or you'll find yourself out on your ear, back walking the streets like the whore you are.'

'I… I'll tell Lady Georgina,' she said weakly, and he flung his head back and roared with laughter. When he'd recovered he looked at her with cold eyes.

'Maids are ten-a-penny,' he smirked. 'Do you really think she'd believe you? Take your word against that of her husband?' He shook his head in mock sympathy. 'I think not, my dear. You'd be branded a liar as well as a slut.'

He leaned back and smiled triumphantly. 'In fact, all I have to do is say I caught you thieving and you'd be out of here so fast it'd make your pretty little head spin.

And not just out on the streets either. In gaol.' He waved an imperious hand. 'Now do as I tell you before I lose my patience.'

'But… but I only did it because Master Jeremy and I love each other,' she protested, making one final appeal to his better nature. 'I was a virgin till then.'

He sniggered again. '"Love each other",' he sneered. 'You must have been reading that cheap rag you servants are so fond of. What is it they call it again? Ah yes, Peg's Paper. Full of stories where the duke falls madly in love with the scullery maid and carries her off to live happily ever after in his castle.' His lips curled into a derogatory smile. 'My son love you? Hah! You were nothing but a convenient lay to save him the cost of a real whore.'

Maggie stared at him in dismay. Was he right? Was that all she'd been? Had Jeremy just been using her? She closed her eyes and shook her head in denial. It couldn't have been like that.

The thoughts whirling round inside her head distracted her, fatally, for despite his bulk Lord Edward lunged from his chair and was upon her. 'If you won't obey me willingly I'll have to make you!' he grunted, his thick fingers tearing at her bodice. She lashed out frantically, her hands curved into claws as she attempted to fight him off. Her fingernails dug into his face and left a trail of bleeding furrows down his cheek. Drawing his breath in pain, he stepped back and touched it gingerly, then looked from his bloodstained fingers back to her.

'You're going to regret that, you little bitch,' he hissed. She raised her hands again, but he was too quick for her. As she flailed at him he caught her wrists, trapping them. Dragging her he strode towards the library table, where a pile of newly delivered books lay, bound in a leather strap. Transferring both her wrists to one hand he undid the strap with the other, used it to bind them together, then hauled her across to a heavy wooden chair.

Breathing heavily he pushed her face down over it, took the trailing end of the strap and wound it round the arm so that she was tethered helplessly. Once that was done he walked across to the door, and she shuddered as she heard the click of the lock.

Shuffling back he stood in front of her and grinned down. 'Not so hoity-toity now, are we missy?' he gloated. 'Now where was I?' Bending over, he slid his hands between her trapped arms and slowly undid her bodice till her breasts tumbled free, like ripe fruit. He fondled the quivering breasts eagerly, relishing their taut firmness – then she squealed in pain as his fingers found their sensitive tips and pinched viciously.

'Like that, don't you?' he panted as they hardened under the rough treatment. Straightening up again he fumbled with the buttons of his flies, and she whimpered as his thick, heavy cock sprang forth. He rubbed his hand up and down the shaft till the head swelled, purple and bulbous. 'You'll like this as well,' he promised. 'But first of all you'll find out it doesn't pay to defy me.'

Walking round behind her he flipped up her heavy skirts and pulled down her pantaloons to reveal the tempting curves of her buttocks. Eyes wide with fear, she craned her neck in a vain attempt to see what he was doing.

And she found out soon enough.

Grinning, he raised his hand and brought it down on her backside, hard, and she squealed again as the soft flesh quivered beneath the blow and a red handprint blossomed against the white flesh. Panting with effort and lust he raised his hand again… and again, until she was whining like a beaten animal. When he finally stopped she closed her eyes in relief.

But it didn't last long. Maggie gasped in horror as she felt his hands pulling her legs apart and his thick fingers invading the soft cleft of her sex. 'No… no…' she whimpered, writhing as he pushed them roughly inside her. 'Please, no…'

'Oh yes,' he sneered. 'You can't fool me. You little strumpets are all the same. You can't get enough of it. Well now you're going to get it! More than you ever dreamed of.' He sniggered like a perverted schoolboy. 'I'm going to shove my prick so far up you, you'll be begging for mercy!'

Sick with horror, Maggie felt his fingers withdraw and the head of his cock press against the lips of her sex. There was a moment of resistance, and then he grunted and thrust himself home, and Maggie moaned as the full length of his member slid inside her.

Grunting like a satisfied boar he began to move, and Maggie protected herself the only way she could – with the power of her imagination. It wasn't Lord Edward's cock inside her, it was Jeremy's. It wasn't Lord Edward's thick fingers kneading her breasts and pinching her nipples, it was Jeremy's. Closing her eyes against reality, she lost herself in memories of their last night together, and felt heat spread through her belly.

It was her turn to groan now as she gave herself up to the delicious sensations beginning to spiral through her. Her quim was wet and slippery now, and with each thrust of the rampant prick her breasts quivered in his groping palms. Then Lord Edward released them, gripped her hips and pushed himself even deeper, but now, instead of trying to pull away, she pushed back against him, writhing as she relished the turgid cock wedged inside her.

He began to move more aggressively and she whined deep in the back of her throat as he reared and plunged, each stroke bringing her nearer to the exquisite moment of release. His fingers dug into her and she screamed as he brought her off with one final thrust, his scalding seed erupting inside her as he came.

He withdrew and Maggie collapsed against the chair, her breasts heaving as she gasped for air, then as she came back to reality shame washed over her like a hot tide. She groaned again, this time with humiliation instead of pleasure. Oh, what had she done? Lord Edward was right; she was nothing but a cheap little whore.

And as if to confirm it he was leering down at her again, his flaccid cock dangling, wet and glistening from his gaping flies. She averted her eyes in sick disgust. Untying her bound wrists he stepped back and watched in contempt as she stumbled to her feet and attempted to make herself decent again.

'I knew you were a trollop,' he said triumphantly. 'And one who enjoys her work into the bargain!' He reached into his pocket, pulled out a guinea and flung it at her feet. 'Here,' he said disdainfully. 'For services rendered, and worth every penny.'

Maggie bent and picked it up, determined to fling it back in his face, but his threatening expression stopped her. 'Don't even think about it,' he said dangerously. 'I've punished you once. Cross me again and next time it'll be worse.' So, suppressing her abhorrence for the man, she tucked the coin into her apron pocket and scurried towards the door.

'Oh, just one more thing before you go, my dear,' he said, his voice stopping her on the threshold.

'Yes, sir?' she said dully.

'Have cook send up another pot of tea,' he ordered. 'This one seems to have gone cold,' and his mocking laughter echoed in her ears as she fled.

'Where on earth have you been till this time? I thought you'd got lost.' Mrs McAlister, looking up from whipping a bowl of cream, caught sight of Maggie's red eyes and white face and almost dropped it. 'In the name of God, lassie, what's wrong with you? You look awful.'

'Just a headache,' said Maggie. 'I had to go to the privy and be sick, that's what took me so long.' She smiled wanly. 'I'll be fine.'

'You'll be nothing of the sort,' said Mrs McAlister firmly. 'Just you get up those stairs for a wee lie down. We can manage without you for an hour or so.' She snorted. 'And if you're not better by the time her ladyship comes back, then I'm sure young Mary can undo her stays just as well as you can, for once.' She put her hands on her hips. 'Now off you go and no arguing.'

Too heartsick to argue, Maggie did as she was told. Wearily she crept upstairs to her attic room and closed the door behind her. Collapsing on the bed she buried her head in the thin pillow and wept for her lost innocence – the golden guinea in her pocket a symbol of her shame. Her last thought before she fell into an exhausted sleep was a disturbing one; what had Sir Edward meant by 'next time'?

Chapter Seven

'I don't know what's wrong with you, lassie,' scolded Mrs McAlister. 'I've told you three times that her ladyship's bell's been ringing and you've not taken a blind bit of notice.' She tutted. 'You've been trailing around in a dwam for I don't know how long. Now get up those stairs before she takes a fit.'

Wearily Maggie did as she was told. Mrs McAlister was right; she'd spent the last three weeks on tenterhooks, jumping every time she was spoken to, terrified that Lord Edward would catch her alone and force himself upon her again.

Even her afternoon off had failed to cheer her. She'd found herself wandering round the same places that she and Jeremy had gone to, miserably remembering how happy they'd been. She shuddered. What would he think of her if he ever found out she'd been enjoyed by his own father? She was soiled goods now, little better than the painted women who plied their trade on Piccadilly. No decent man would have her now.

Not that he'd be likely to find out, she thought bitterly. After that first letter, cracked and creased from constant re-reading, there had been nothing. No doubt he had found someone from his own class at one of the garrison balls. By this time his little fling with his mother's maid was probably nothing more than an amusing tale to tell his fellow officers.

Lady Georgina was still jerking angrily at the bell-rope when Maggie entered her room. 'About time too,' she snapped. 'I have been ringing for you this past ten minutes, you idle baggage. Do you think I have all day to wait till you deign to appear?'

'No, m'm,' muttered Maggie, bobbing a curtsey with downcast eyes. 'Sorry, m'm, it won't happen again.'

Mollified, Lady Georgina nodded. 'Good, now hurry up and dress me, girl. Lord Edward and I are attending luncheon with his cousin, Sir Francis, and I want to look my best.' She looked at her reflection in the glass and simpered. 'Sir Francis admired me too, when I was a girl. Why, if Lord Edward had not asked for my hand first, who knows what might have happened?'

If Maggie thought Sir Francis had had a lucky escape, she wisely refrained from saying so. Instead she went to the mahogany wardrobe and began laying out dresses for her ladyship's consideration, and the bed was piled high with discarded gowns before she finally chose one of bilious yellow satin, with so many flounces and furbelows it looked like a wedding cake.

'Tighter, girl, tighter,' she panted as Maggie tugged on the laces of her corset. 'My waist must be no more than a hand span.'

Chance would be a fine thing, Maggie thought wryly as she hauled even harder. It would take a miracle to whisk away the years of overindulgence. 'Hand span' indeed. It would need a man with bloody big hands to get round that waist!

By the time she'd finished, Maggie was panting as well – and Lady Georgina could barely breathe. So much displaced fat oozed out over the top of her stays that she looked as if she had two bosoms – one at the back and one at the front! Still, Lady Georgina seemed pleased with the effect, so Maggie hurried to fetch her layers of petticoats and tie on her bustle before she changed her mind.

'My dress now, girl,' she ordered imperiously, so Maggie eased the yellow satin carefully over her mistress's head, settled the folds of heavy material over the underpinnings and began to do up the interminable buttons at the back. Even with the stays pulled to their tightest, this was an effort. Finally, much to her relief, she was finished. Only her hair to do and her jewels to fetch and madam would be ready.

Maggie had barely done when Sir Edward strutted in. Lady Georgina lumbered to her feet and gave a graceless twirl. 'Well?' she asked coyly. 'What do you think? Will I pass muster?'

'Delicious, my dear, absolutely delicious,' he said heartily. 'Good enough to eat.' Maggie shivered; his words might have been for Lady Georgina, but his cold eyes were fixed on her and she felt naked again beneath his leering gaze. Luckily her mistress noticed nothing. 'Bring my fan, girl,' she ordered. 'The one with the ivory handle and yellow ostrich feathers.' Relieved to have something to do, Maggie scuttled off to fetch it.

When they had both gone, her ladyship clinging to her husband's arm like a portly galleon being escorted by a dumpy little tug, Maggie collapsed on the bed beside the discarded dresses and blew out her cheeks in a gusty sigh of relief. Thank God for Lady Georgina. She might not be the easiest of mistresses, but at least while she was around she was protected from the master's unwanted attentions.

A man might keep sleep with a different whore every

night and keep as many mistresses as he liked – provided everything was swept discreetly under the carpet. Even Lord Edward would not dare flout convention by fornicating with his wife's maid while she was under the same roof. As long as Lady Georgina was in the house, Maggie was safe.

Feeling more secure than she had in weeks, Maggie set about tidying things away again, humming happily under her breath.

But it wasn't to last.

Three days later, the letter arrived.

'Mr Harris the butler gave me this,' Mrs Hardcastle said to Maggie, waving a narrow envelope as she bustled into the kitchen. 'You'd better take it up with her ladyship's breakfast tray.' She held it up to the light and peered at it. 'It's not Master Jeremy's writing. I wonder who it's from…' She laid it on the tray. 'No doubt we'll find out soon enough.'

'A letter for you, my lady,' said Maggie as she laid the tray on the bed.

Lady Georgina picked it up and slit it open with her butter knife. She scanned it rapidly, then tutted and shook her head. 'Poor Lucy, enceinte again,' she muttered to herself. 'There's nothing else for it, I shall have to go.'

She looked up at Maggie. 'I shall be leaving for the country as soon as possible, Carter. You may start packing as soon as I have dressed.'

'What's "enceinte" when it's at home?' Maggie demanded when she took the tray back to the kitchen.

'In the puddin' club,' Mrs Hardcastle said bluntly. 'It's one of those fancy words them upstairs uses when they're talking about something "not quaite nice". Anyway,' she went on, fixing Maggie with a suspicious stare. 'Why are you asking that? You ain't, are you?'

'Of course not!' Maggie protested. 'Lady Georgina used it and I wondered what it meant, that's all.'

'Ahhh,' said Mrs H, comprehension dawning. 'So that's what the letter was about.' She sniffed. 'It'll be that young sister of hers again. Miss Lucy – or Lady Fortesque as she is now – and a blooming good job she's married, too. This'll be the seventh by my count.' She shook her head. 'Poor girl; all that husband of hers needs to do is look sideways at her and she falls – and she was never very strong to start with.' She sighed. 'He's going to kill her one of these days, you mark my words.'

'Lady Georgina's going to stay with her,' Maggie informed them. 'I've to start packing once she's dressed.'

'More work,' said Mrs H glumly, then she brightened. 'Mind you, once she's gone we can loosen our own corsets a bit, and you'll like it down there, Maggie. It's a beautiful old house. You'll have a bedroom to yourself, and the grub's lovely. Mrs Benson's a grand cook.' She looked at Maggie. 'The fresh air'll put a few roses in your cheeks, too,' she added. 'You've been looking a bit peaky lately.'

'Will I be going, too?' asked Maggie eagerly. The thought of being safely away from Lord Edward was almost too good to be true.

Mrs Hardcastle looked at her in surprise. 'Course you will, love!' she exclaimed. 'Don't you know that by this time? No lady travels anywhere without her personal maid.' She chuckled. 'Can you imagine her majesty trying to put on her own stays? I should cocoa!' She patted Maggie's hand and gave her a wink. 'It'll be like a holiday, and you enjoy yourself while you can, pet. Bit o' new blood? I'll bet them young footmen will be falling all over you.'

Maggie smiled back. She could live without the footmen, but it would be lovely to get away from this place and all her fears, and by the time she got back perhaps Lord Edward would have found someone else to lust after.

Buoyed by the thought she whisked through the rest of the day, oblivious of the sheer hard work involved as she ran backwards and forwards filling trunk after trunk with clothes, underwear and shoes. 'Good grief,' grumbled Mrs H as she carried in yet another pile of freshly washed and ironed petticoats. 'You'd think she was going to bloomin' America instead of to the next county. God help the poor horse that has to cart this lot, that's all I can say.' She laid them on the top of the open case and attempted unsuccessfully to close the lid. 'Come on, love, park your bum on this while I try and shut it.' Giggling, Maggie did as she was told.

The first tendrils of doubt began to intrude as the day wore on and Lady Georgina still hadn't mentioned Maggie going with her. So when Thomas began to carry the trunks down to the carriage she took her courage in both hands. 'Shall I pack my trunk now too, my lady?' she asked anxiously.

Lady Georgina looked at her as if she was mad. 'Of course not, Carter. Whatever gave you the idea that I was taking you?' She snorted. 'There's plenty of work for you here.'

Maggie stared at her aghast. 'B-but, how will your ladyship manage without a maid?' she stammered. 'Who will take care of you?'

'Lady Fortesque will lend me her French maid, Antoinette, of course,' said Lady Georgina. Her lips tightened with resentment at a long-held grudge. 'She should have come with me when I married, but for some strange reason she chose to stay with my sister.' She looked down her nose at Maggie. 'And I have had to put up with years of inferior service as a result.' She glared at her. 'Now don't just stand there gawping at me, girl. I haven't got all day. Fetch my grey kid gloves. The carriage will be leaving soon.'

Numbly, Maggie fetched the gloves, followed Lady Georgina downstairs, settled her in the carriage, and only when it drew away did the dam break. Scurrying down the area steps she fled to the kitchen where she slumped into a chair, laid her head on her arms, and wept as if her heart would break.

'There, there, love,' said Mrs Hardcastle, patting her back while Mrs McAlister looked on wringing her floury hands in distress. 'Don't take on so. It's not the end of the world. You'll get to go next time, I'm sure. That French piece Antoinette's been with them since they were girls. She must be sixty if she's a day. They'll have to put her out to pasture soon.'

'No, you don't understand,' sobbed Maggie. Nobody understood. With Lady Georgina safely out of the way, she was now totally at Lord Edward's mercy.

Chapter Eight

Despite her fears, day followed unremarkable day for the next two weeks and Maggie began to relax. Without Lady Georgina's constant demands, there was a holiday atmosphere in the house. Lord Edward dined frequently at his club, so there were less elaborate meals for Mrs McAlister to prepare, and on Mrs Hardcastle's birthday, Mr Harris the butler unbent enough to 'acquire' several bottles of wine from his lordship's cellar to celebrate the occasion.

'To Moll,' he said, solemnly raising his glass. 'God bless her.'

'And all who sail in her,' sniggered Thomas.

Mr Harris quelled him with an icy glance. 'That will be quite enough of that kind of smutty talk, young man,' he said sternly. 'This is a respectable house, and don't you forget it.'

'Sorry, Mr Harris,' Thomas muttered, lowering his eyes. 'Sorry, Mrs H.'

'As I was saying,' Mr Harris went on, unperturbed. 'Please raise your glasses in a toast to Mrs Hardcastle.'

'To Mrs H,' they chorused. Maggie sipped her wine and pulled a face. It was horrible. How the nobs could drink such nasty, sour stuff for pleasure escaped her. Give her a nice cup of tea or a glass of Mrs McAlister's homemade lemonade anytime. Grimacing, she swallowed it as quickly as she could.

'Here, love, 'ave another,' beamed Mrs McAlister, pouring it before Maggie had time to protest. 'Red wine's good for the blood.'

After the dishes were cleared away there was another surprise. There was a timid tap at the entry door and when Maggie opened it a street urchin stood on the step, clutching a battered fiddle. He shuffled from one dirty bare foot to the other and gave her a gap-toothed grin. ''Ello, miss,' he beamed. 'The toff wot lives here said 'e'd give us a sixpence if I come and played me fiddle.'

Maggie grinned back; Mr Harris would be delighted to hear himself described as a 'toff', and he was certainly pulling out all the stops tonight. First the wine, and now this. Normally a cheeky little bugger like this would be chased off so fast his legs wouldn't touch the ground.

'Right,' she said, 'this way.' She wagged a finger under his nose. 'And mind you don't touch nothing. Keep your sticky fingers to yourself – or else! Anything goes missing and I'll 'ave the constables after you.'

'As if I would, miss,' he said, with a look of injured innocence that Maggie didn't believe for a minute. He followed her through and stopped short, his eyes widening at the sight of the half-eaten food scraped onto an old tin plate beside the sink. His belly rumbled loudly.

'Och, he's hungry, poor wee lamb,' said Mrs McAlister, glancing at Mr Harris for permission. 'Can't he just finish off the scraps before he starts playing?'

'That soft heart of yours'll be the ruin of you, someday,' he grumbled. 'But all right then.' He glared at the urchin. 'Just be smart about it, boy. I'm not paying you good money to eat.'

'Cor, thanks guv,' he gasped. 'You're a real gent.' Mrs McAlister placed the tin plate in front of him, along with a glass of milk and watched with satisfaction as everything was polished off in double quick time. He looked shyly at Mrs McAllister, gave an enormous belch and grinned. 'Lovely grub! Cheers, missis.'

Mr Harris raised an eyebrow. 'Have you quite finished, young man?' he demanded. He tapped his fingers impatiently. 'Because, if so, we're waiting.'

'Right guv, sorry guv,' he said. He scrambled to his feet, grabbed his fiddle and launched forth into a lively tune. Mr Harris gallantly held out his hand to Mrs Hardcastle and Maggie suppressed a giggle as they proceeded to do a stately jig the length of the kitchen and back. Who'd have thought they had it in them?

As the evening wore on and the level of the wine dropped, the fun grew fast and furious. Accompanied by the little fiddler, Mrs McAllister treated them to a heart-breaking Highland lament that would have brought tears to a glass eye. Thomas gave a lively rendition of the latest music hall song, with much winking and grinning at the saucy bits. Mr Harris and Mrs Hardcastle solemnly duetted on Mr Tennyson's Come into the Garden Maud, and even young Mary, blushing, giggling and forgetting half the words, attempted to recite The Wreck of the Hesperus.

'Come on, Maggie, your turn,' said Mrs H, flushed and giggling like a young girl under Mr Harris' attentions. 'You ain't done nothing yet.'

'I couldn't,' protested Maggie. 'I don't know anything.'

'Course you do,' beamed Mrs H. 'Come on, gel, it's me birthday. You don't get off that easy.'

'Oh, all right then,' sighed Maggie. She drained the

last of her wine and got rather unsteadily to her feet. 'D'you know any Irish tunes?' she asked the young fiddler.

'Course I do, miss,' he grinned. He played a few bars and Maggie smiled and tapped her foot to the familiar rhythm. Mrs O'Mally from upstairs, for all her bulk, had been a dab hand at an Irish jig when she had a few gins in her, and it was all coming back now.

'Help us up,' Maggie ordered Thomas. Clutching his sweaty hand for balance, she climbed onto a stool, then onto the kitchen table. Hands on hips she nodded to the boy, and as the music began she let rip, feet stamping, hips swaying, breasts bouncing, her hair escaping from her neat bun and falling about her shoulders as everyone clapped in time. When she finished, flushed and panting, in a whirl of starched petticoats, there was a round of applause.

'Cor, that was better than the pantomime!' chuckled Mrs H, wiping tears of enjoyment from her eyes. 'You'll need another little drink to recover!'

'Cheers, Mrs H,' Maggie said, reaching for the glass. She gulped it down and swayed. 'Oooh, I'll need to have a sit down now. All that dancing's made me dizzy.'

All too soon the last glass was emptied, the last song sung and the clock on the kitchen mantelpiece chimed midnight. 'Right,' said Mr Harris, clapping his hands. 'Time for bed.' Groans of disappointment met his announcement, but he was adamant. 'No arguing; there's work to be done tomorrow.'

He fished in his waistcoat pocket, produced the promised sixpence and handed it over. 'There you are, young man. You deserve it.'

The urchin examined it, bit it, then tucked it away

somewhere amongst his rags. 'Thanks guv,' he grinned, touching a finger to his forehead. 'And if you ever wants me services again, you knows where to find me. I'll be in me usual place, foot of Mile End Road.'

Maggie disappeared for a few moments then returned to lead him out. As they reached the door she reached under her apron and produced a greasy package, wrapped up in string and brown paper. 'Here you go,' she whispered. 'A bit of grub to take home with you.'

His eyes widened. 'Thanks, miss,' he muttered. 'You're a diamond, a proper diamond.' The parcel vanished into the same mysterious place as the sixpence, and he looked up at her and grinned. 'You know what they says, miss: one good turn deserves another, so you ever need any help, you send the word. Eddie's me name.' His scrawny chest swelled with pride. 'Me mum called me after the young prince. You just ask for Eddie the fiddler and I'll come running.'

'Thank you, Eddie,' Maggie said solemnly. 'That's very kind of you. I'll remember that.' She watched him strut off, fiddle tucked under his arm, and suppressed a giggle. Anything less like a prince was hard to imagine, and the chances of her ever needing to call on a guttersnipe for help were few and far between! She smiled indulgently. Still, his little heart was in the right place, God bless 'im!' She was still smiling as she returned to the kitchen to begin helping tidy everything away.

'Never mind them dishes, Mary,' yawned Mrs McAlister. 'They'll still be there in the morning. Just you get yourself off to bed before you falls over.'

Once Mary had gone, Mrs Hardcastle fluttered her eyelashes at Mr Harris. 'Can I tempt you to a nightcap, Mr Harris? Just a little one before bed?'

Mr Harris smiled. 'That would be most acceptable, Mrs Hardcastle,' he agreed, and she fumbled with the keys at her waist, unlocked a cupboard and produced a half-full bottle of brandy.

'There we go,' she beamed, pouring it into glasses and handing them round.

'What, am I to have one too?' asked Maggie in surprise, as one was thrust into her hand.

'Course you are,' said Mrs H, so Maggie sipped it and gasped as it burnt its way down her throat and the heat spread through her belly.

'You'll have me drunk,' she protested.

'Nonsense,' said Mrs H briskly. 'You're a big girl now, and a little tot of brandy's good for you.'

'That's right,' agreed Thomas, winking at her over the rim of his glass. 'Medicinal, that is. Get it down yer.'

As the brandy hit the wine she'd already drunk, Maggie's head spun. 'Oh dear,' she giggled. 'I think I'd better get to me bed now too.' She got to her feet, staggered and giggled again. 'Ooops! Think I'm a bit squiffy. Night all. See you in the morning.' Walking with exaggerated care, she headed towards the kitchen door, bumping off the jamb as she went through.

She had reached the landing where the green baize door led from the servants' quarters to the main house, when a pair of hands grabbed her round the waist and spun her round. She recoiled as Thomas' stale breath, smelling of wine and brandy gusted into her face.

'Come on,' he panted, pulling her against him. 'Give us a kiss. You know I fancy yer,' and before she had a chance to protest, his wet mouth came down on hers and his free hand tugged at her skirt. He pushed her against the wall and panted with excitement as he managed to wriggle his fingers beneath the heavy material to the silken flesh underneath.

'Gerroff, you bastard!' she squawked, made even more furious by the fact that his probing fingers, combined with the effect of the alcohol, had triggered an unwanted response. But her struggles merely served to inflame him further as she squirmed against him, her firm breasts pushing against his chest. He grunted with satisfaction as he found the soft lips of her sex and he thrust first one finger, then two inside her, relishing the hot wetness that met his touch. Even through his breeches she could feel the massive swell of his cock.

'You want it as much as I do,' he groaned, pushing his hips against her. Heat spread through her belly and she felt herself begin to weaken. Then there was a creak, a flicker of light, and they both froze.

'What was that?' gasped Thomas, pulling away and trying to bring his breathing under control. 'I heard something.'

'It was the baize door,' she hissed, staring at him with frightened eyes. 'The only one in the house is Lord Edward. It must have been him! What if he saw?'

Thomas forced a nervous laugh. 'Course it wasn't Lord Edward,' he blustered, wilting rapidly. 'He's asleep. It must have been a draft.' He turned to look and Maggie took her chance; picking up her skirts she ran for the stairs, and before he could recover and come after her she was safely in her own room with the door locked behind her.

Giggling tipsily over her narrow escape, Maggie flung off her clothes and snuggled down beside Emily's warm body, and her last triumphant thought before she fell asleep was that Thomas would never have her. Never!

There were a few heavy heads in the kitchen the following morning. Emily dropped a plate and promptly burst into tears when Mrs McAlister scolded her crossly and told her that it would be taken out of her wages. Mrs Hardcastle pleaded a migraine and didn't appear at all until ten. Thomas, white-faced and red-eyed, retreated to the butler's pantry, ostensibly to clean the silver but in reality to doze. As for Maggie, she found a pile of Lady Georgina's stockings that needed mending and kept her own aching head bent over it, vowing never to drink anything stronger than tea in future.

She was feeling better by the time luncheon was laid on the table in the servants' hall, and was just reaching for a second helping of potatoes when Mr Harris spoke.

'Lord Edward wishes to see you in the drawing room, young lady.' He took his fob watch from his waistcoat pocket and consulted it. 'In precisely one hour.' He put it back and looked at Thomas. 'And you too, young man.'

Maggie's hand froze in mid-air and appetite deserted her. 'B-but... why?' she stammered.

'Lord Edward did not see fit to enlighten me as to the matter concerned,' he said stiffly, obviously aggrieved by this flouting of protocol. Matters of discipline were normally dealt with either by himself or Mrs Hardcastle, depending on the sex of the offender. For the master to involve himself personally was virtually unheard of. He glared at them both. 'But I trust there is no reason for his lordship to reprimand either of you?'

They exchanged frightened glances and shook their heads.

'Good,' he went on. 'Then once you have finished

eating, you may go and tidy yourselves up.' His stern gaze raked them from top to bottom. 'You can change into clean breeches and polish those buttons for a start, young man. And as for you, miss, comb your hair and put on a clean apron and cap.'

Maggie gulped, her stomach churning. Pushing her plate away she got to her feet. 'May I go now?' she asked; Mr Harris gave a curt nod and she hurried out.

In her bedroom she splashed cold water on her face and looked at her reflection in the mirror. Frightened eyes stared back from a white face as she remembered the incident the previous night. Had that been Lord Edward at the baize door? She shivered. He seemed to have a talent for creeping round spying, and even the most debauched employer expected his servants to be above reproach. If he had seen, she and Thomas could both be sacked on the spot – even though it hadn't been her fault. It wasn't fair!

With trembling hands she tied on a fresh starched apron, combed her hair back until her scalp ached and added her lace cap. From her room she could faintly hear the grandfather clock in the hall below, chiming the half hour.

Another thirty minutes to go. She sat on the bed to wait, her hands twisting nervously in her lap.

The next fifteen minutes seemed to take years to pass, but when the clock chimed again she reluctantly got to her feet and made her way slowly down the stairs to the drawing room door; better not keep his lordship waiting. Thomas was there already, fidgeting from foot to foot and running his finger round his tight collar.

'What does the old bastard want to see us for?' he hissed. 'We ain't done nothing.'

101

'I don't know, do I?' she muttered bitterly. 'But we're going to find out soon enough.' As if on cue, the clock rang out the hour. Thomas cleared his throat and tapped gently on the door.

There was a grunt from inside. Thomas pushed the door open and ventured inside, with Maggie close behind. Lord Edward was sprawled in his armchair with a glass of brandy in his hand, and they stopped in front of him. Thomas bowed stiffly and Maggie bobbed a curtsey.

'You wished to see us, my lord?' said Thomas, his voice cracking with nerves.

Lord Edward took a sip of his brandy and smiled genially at him, ignoring Maggie. 'You've been with us quite some time now, haven't you, my boy?'

'Erm... yes, my lord,' said a bewildered Thomas. 'Since I was twelve. Eight years now.'

'And you like it here?' he went on.

'Of course, my lord,' Thomas said. 'This is an excellent situation, sir. I—'

'Good, good,' interrupted Lord Edward. 'I like an ambitious young man. So you'd like to stay with us then? Perhaps take over Harris' position – in the fullness of time?'

Thomas' eyes glittered greedily. 'Of course, my lord, that would be wonderful. Why, I'd do anything for that. Anything at all!'

'I thought you'd say that,' purred Lord Edward. 'Very well, you can start by locking the door.' Puzzled, but anxious to impress, Thomas hurried to do as he was told, and as Maggie watched the first tendrils of cold fear began to twine through her body.

'Anything else, my lord?' Thomas asked eagerly.

'Why yes, my boy,' the loathsome man chuckled. 'You

can finish what you started last night.'

For a moment Thomas stared at his master in confusion, then in horror, and then Maggie saw delighted comprehension crawl across his sly face. 'You mean I can…?'

'You can do whatever you like with her,' Lord Edward confirmed. 'She won't tell anyone. She wouldn't dare.' His lip curled in contempt. 'Not if she wants to keep her job.'

Maggie looked from one flushed face to the other, hoping to see a glimmer of mercy. But there was none. And going by the swelling at his crotch, Thomas found the idea of rogering her while his master watched enormously exciting. She began to back away. 'Leave me alone,' she whimpered, shaking her head in denial as he advanced on her.

'Cock-teasing little bitch,' he sneered as he fumbled at the front of his breeches, and her wide-eyed stare fixed in fascinated terror on the swollen member that sprang forth as if it had a mind of its own. 'Thought you were too good for me, didn't you?' he spat. 'Well, I'll teach you to turn me down.'

Maggie turned desperately to run to the door but he was too quick for her. One arm snaked round her waist and pulled her back while the other skilfully undid her buttons. Grinning, he wrenched her dress from her shoulders and down over her hips, pulling her pantaloons with it. Naked except for her black stockings she cowered away, frantically trying to cover her breasts with her hands.

'Oh no you don't!' he snarled. Grabbing one of her wrists he jerked her back towards him, hauled her towards a chair and flung her over his knee.

'This is for the time you kneed me in the balls,' he grated, raising his hand and bringing it down on her unprotected buttocks. The sound of flesh on flesh echoed around the room like a pistol shot and the mark of his palm rose, shockingly scarlet against the tender white flesh. Maggie squealed with pain and humiliation.

'Bravo, my boy,' chuckled Lord Edward, and thus encouraged, Thomas raised his arm and brought his hand down again… and again and again. Maggie whimpered and squirmed in a vain attempt to escape her tormentor, legs kicking and breasts trembling with each fresh blow.

Lord Edward shifted uncomfortably in his chair, his own excitement mounting, as he feasted his eyes on the sight of the naked girl writhing helplessly. His prick rose, straining against the heavy material of his trousers, and groaning he undid the buttons and began to stroke his shaft as he watched.

Maggie's buttocks were aflame with pain now and each convulsive wriggle made her more aware of Thomas' rigid cock jabbing into her belly, and to her horror she realised that the heat of her beaten bottom was spreading to the base of her belly, transformed by some dark magic into insidious tendrils of pleasure. She felt herself moisten and moaned again, this time in despair at being betrayed by her own body.

Finished with his punishment, Thomas turned to satisfying his pleasure. He pulled Maggie's unresisting body up, spun her round until she was facing away from him, then pulled her back onto his lap. She wailed with a mixture of pain and pleasure as his rigid young cock parted the soft lips of her vulva and, forced by the natural weight of her body, speared its way inside her.

Utterly impaled she writhed helplessly, one of Thomas'

hands holding her firmly round the waist as he began to thrust, the other roving freely, pinching and kneading the engorged crests of her nipples, and lingering on the swollen bud of her clitoris.

Lord Edward stared, mesmerised, a thread of saliva drooling from his lips as he played with his own prick. Maggie's legs, spread for balance, pulled apart the lips of her cunny, and he watched in fascination as Thomas' cock, glistening with her juices, slid in and out of the succulent wetness, her pert young breasts jiggling every time the footman grunted and thrust. Lord Edward grinned salaciously; this was far better than anything in the books he kept carefully under lock and key in his study.

Maggie was moaning now, her head flung back as she gave herself up to the sensations coursing through her, oblivious of everything but the thick cock that was pleasuring her. She ground herself against it, savouring every last inch, feeling it swell even further as he reached the point of no return. As the young footman exploded inside her she shrieked her release, shuddered, and then sagged back against his chest.

When Maggie drifted back to shameful reality she realised her ordeal was not yet over. Lord Edward had got to his feet and was lumbering towards her, his prick bobbing with every step. 'My turn now,' he croaked, pulling her from Thomas' lap. She fell weakly on her knees before him, whimpering as he pushed the shiny purple head towards her lips.

'No, please, no…' she protested, turning her head from side to side to avoid touching the disgusting thing. But it was useless. Gripping the back of her head he pulled her inexorably towards it. She gagged as it pushed against her lips, forcing them open. He moaned as it slid into the warm wetness, and it was Thomas' turn to watch in fascination as his master's thick cock, slick with Maggie's saliva, pumped in and out of her warm wet mouth, stretching her glistening pink lips.

But at least it was mercifully brief. Excited beyond endurance by what he had seen, it took only moments for the bloated pig to climax. Maggie felt the head swell to bursting point, then gagged again as he grunted, jerked his hips and his sour seed spurted against the roof of her mouth. As he released her she collapsed in a heap, the taste of her shame bitter on her tongue.

'Cover yourself up, you cheap little slut,' ordered Lord Edward, turning towards a grinning Thomas. 'And you too, boy.' Thomas' grin disappeared as he hastened to obey, hastily tugging on his clothes.

Once they were clothed again Lord Edward glared at them. 'One word out of either of you about this and you'll both be out on the street,' he threatened viciously. 'Understand?' They nodded. 'Good,' he said, lifting his glass of brandy again. 'Now get out of here and get back to your duties. Do you think I'm paying you good money to stand around doing nothing?'

As they hurried back about their business, Maggie couldn't bear to look at Thomas' smirking face. He would despise her now too – the same way she despised herself.

The grandfather clock in the hall chimed and Maggie listened in disbelief, closing her eyes to hold back the tears. Only half an hour had passed yet she had taken one more fateful step downwards – and who knew what other horrors were yet to come?

Chapter Nine

In the days that followed Maggie went through her work as if she were an automaton. Like the clockwork model of a brass band that sat on the shelf in the library, jerking into imitation life as soon as someone turned the key, she went about her tasks.

But if she was calm on the surface, underneath she was racked with helpless fear. Her heart leapt into her mouth every time Lord Edward's bell rang, and even if he only wanted tea or a brandy or a letter posted, her trepidation was only temporarily assuaged. It might be all right this time, but next time... With an effort she broke off that train of thought before it drove her mad, busying herself with needless work to fend off further terrifying speculations.

If it had not been so awful, it might have been amusing. Who would have guessed that she would long for the return of her demanding mistress almost as much as she longed for the return of her lover?

'Post been?' she asked hopefully every morning. 'Any more news about Lady Georgina's sister?' The letters might have been addressed to Lord Edward, but their contents were know in the servants' hall almost as soon as he'd read them.

'Aren't you a kind-hearted lass,' smiled Mrs McAlister. 'Thinking about that poor lady in her time of trouble.' She shook her head sadly. 'Nothing since last week – still in her bed, the wee lamb. The doctor says she musn't put foot to floor for fear of loosing the wee one.'

'What a shame,' said Maggie, forcing herself to smile sympathetically, but inside the bitterness welled up again. Who cared if Lady Muck lost the brat? Pampered bitch! Poor women couldn't take to their beds and be waited on hand and foot, could they? They lost children every day to poverty and disease and no one shed a tear.

Even if the child were born safely, what then? One more 'superior' to dance attendance on. Nurses and nannies and servants pandering to their every whim so that they grew up thinking they could do what they liked with those 'beneath' them. Even just thinking of another of Lord Edward's kind coming into the world made her sick.

'Don't you worry, pet,' said Mrs McAlister, mistaking Maggie's scowl for an expression of concern. She patted her hand. 'I'm sure she'll be fine.'

'I'm sure she will be,' agreed Maggie. That sort always were.

The bell of the breakfast room jangled, making her jump so much that her spoon rattled against her plate. Her mouth went dry as all her fears rushed back.

'Emily, go and find out what the master wants!' bawled Mrs M. 'And take the tray with you; you can start to clear the table while you're at it.'

Maggie sagged against her chair with relief as Emily scurried off to do as she was told, and her lips twisted in self-mockery. Lord Edward would hardly be likely to want his oats at this time in the morning. She was jumping at shadows.

With that thought Maggie began to feel a bit better. It

had been almost a week and there had been no further calls to 'serve' Lord Edward. Perhaps now he had slaked his base appetites he would leave her alone? Another happy idea struck her; he was old – sixty if he was a day – and unhealthy with it. A lifetime of overindulgence in good food and strong spirits had made him fat and flabby. Men like that often lost their powers. She smiled; perhaps he'd shot his last bolt? It was a comforting thought.

But it didn't last.

'Penny for your thoughts,' Thomas smirked from the other side of the table. 'Bet I know what they're about, too.'

Maggie smiled sweetly back at him, then drew back her foot and kicked him under the table as hard as she could. She grinned with satisfaction as his self-satisfied smirk was replaced with an expression of shock and he let out a squawk of pain.

'What's wrong, love?' asked Mrs McAlister in surprise.

'Poor Thomas,' said Maggie with mock sympathy. 'I think he bit his tongue.'

He glared at her and her smile vanished. If Lord Edward hadn't recovered from his sexual perversions, Thomas certainly had. He was even randier than he had been before. He was never done brushing up against her or surreptitiously attempting to fondle her breasts or fumble beneath her skirts when no one was looking. So far she'd been lucky, but it had taken all her skill to avoid his attentions.

'Think you're so bleedin' smart, don't you,' he hissed, as soon as Mrs M rose to clear the table and was safely out of earshot. 'Well you're not. I've 'ad you once, you little cow, and by God I'll 'ave you again. Just you see if I don't.' Mrs McAlister returned and he had to content himself with one last glare before he subsided into a resentful silence.

Maggie bit her lip; perhaps she had goaded him too far? But then she brightened again; so what? She'd avoided him before, she could do it again.

Oh, but she was so wrong.

It was her own fault. When several more days passed without a summons from Lord Edward she relaxed her constant vigil. As she headed for the linen cupboard with an armful of freshly washed sheets, the only thought in her head was what to wear and where to go on her next afternoon off. Humming, she bumped open the door with her hip, walked in and began to lay them away on the shelves.

Then the sound of the door closing made her spin round. Thomas was leaning against it, grinning at her wolfishly.

'Wh-what do you want?' she stammered – though the bulge in his breeches made his intentions all too clear. 'Get out of my way,' she snapped, but with less conviction than she'd hoped for. 'I've got work to do. You ain't the master, you can't make me do anything I don't want to.'

Instead of obeying, he licked his lips and slowly rubbed his swelling cock through the thin material. 'Garn! All that hoity-toity talk doesn't fool me,' he said hoarsely. 'Pretending you're little miss priss when you can't get enough of it.' He smirked and thrust his hips at her obscenely. 'And I'm just the boy to give it to you. So get your drawers down, gel. It's your lucky day. I'm going to fuck you into the middle of next week.'

Shaking her head, Maggie backed away until she was pressed against the shelves. She looked round wildly, but he was between her and the door. There was no way out. She bared her teeth at him like a cornered rat. 'You keep away from me, Thomas Higgins,' she warned. 'Lay one finger on me and you'll regret it.'

'I'll lay more than a finger on you,' he sneered, tugging at his breeches until his cock sprang free, its swollen head purple and shiny, a bead of clear liquid welling from its blind eye. 'I'm going to shove this so far up you, you'll choke.'

Her hands fumbled along the shelves frantically seeking for something to use against him, but nothing but the soft folds of linen met her seeking fingers, until... they closed gratefully round a pair of heavy scissors left behind forgotten from some long-ago sewing session. She whipped them from behind her back and lunged at him. He stopped short, the colour draining from his face as the wicked blades snipped closed barely an inch from the end of his prick. 'Come near me and it'll be the last time you'll want any woman,' she hissed, snapping the shears open and closed again.

His cock wilted rapidly and he hastily tucked it back in his breeches out of harms way. She made another lunge and grinned as he shrieked girlishly and fumbled for the door handle.

He paused on the threshold, his eyes full of hate and thwarted lust. 'That's the last time you play me for a fool,' he snarled. 'I'll get you for this, just you wait and see.' The door banged shut and she was alone.

Shaking with reaction, Maggie began to giggle hysterically. Neither Thomas – nor his John Thomas, for that matter – would be bothering her again in a hurry, if she was any judge. The mental picture of his menacing weapon shrivelling to the size of a whelk set her off into a fresh peel of amusement. She'd have needed a pin to winkle it out again!

Wiping the tears of laughter from her eyes she tidied the shelves and tucked the scissors away beneath the sheets – just to be on the safe side. She just hoped she'd be able to keep her face straight when she next saw Thomas in the servants' hall. She was still smiling as she entered the kitchen.

'For heaven's sake, lassie!' exclaimed Mrs McAlister, looking up, hot and flustered from stirring a pot on the range. 'You were only putting the sheets away! Where have you been till this time? Mrs Hardcastle's been up to high doh shouting for you.'

'Sorry,' Maggie apologised meekly, and began to clear the table to help make up for her remissness. 'I had to tidy the shelves and it took longer than I thought. Did she say what she wanted?'

'Oh, it's not her that wants you,' said Mrs McAlister. 'It's the master.'

The pot Maggie was carrying slipped from her fingers and rolled with a clatter beneath the table.

'Now look what you've done,' tutted Mrs McAlister. 'If that had been one of the soup tureens you'd have had it taken out of your wages for months.' She stared at Maggie's white face in surprise. 'Och, don't take on so – it's no' the end of the world. It's just an old pot.' She stooped and picked it up, panting with the effort. 'See? It's no' even dented.'

Maggie's lips were stiff with the effort to stop them trembling. 'What... what does the master want?' she managed.

'I don't know, I'm sure,' Mrs McAlister said. 'He's not going to tell the likes of me, is he?' She smiled to take the sting out of her words. 'Maybe he's trying to take a hand in the running of the house since the mistress isn't here?' she suggested vaguely. 'Though heaven knows why, when there's Mrs H and Mr Harris to keep things ticking over. But it's not really proper now, is it?'

She shrugged helplessly. 'Still, look at Lord Wilcott, f'rinstance. Insists on tending his own horse even though he's got a whole staff of stable lads to do it for him. Who knows what gets into their heads sometimes?'

Maggie shuddered. She knew exactly what had got into his head. The sound of a throat being cleared made her look up. Thomas was lounging against the door, leering at her. The expression on his face made her feel sick. He sauntered in, stuck a finger in a bowl of cream and licked it slowly off, never taking his eyes from hers.

''Spect he wants to see me as well,' he said smugly.

'You?' snapped Mrs McAlister. 'You flatter yourself! Why should he want to see you?' She slapped his hand and moved the bowl smartly out of his reach. 'And I'll thank you to keep your dirty fingers to yourself, young man. Other people have to eat that.'

The look of disappointment on his face would have been comical under other circumstances, but Maggie didn't feel like laughing. Even though the master had excluded Thomas from whatever perverted performance he had in mind today, the thought of his podgy fingers exploring her secret places and his gross body forcing itself on hers were enough to wipe any trace of amusement from her mind. But dully, she resigned herself to the inevitable.

'Ah, there you are, Maggie,' said Mrs Hardcastle,

bustling in. 'I've been hunting high and low for you. Did Mrs McAlister tell you Lord Edward wishes to speak to you again?' She smiled her reassurance. 'Now you're not to worry. You aren't in trouble. With the mistress away he seems to be taking an interest in the younger staff. Isn't that kind of him?'

Maggie's lips twisted. Little did Mrs H know that she was in more trouble than she'd ever imagined possible. As for 'taking an interest' – he was doing that all right, the randy old bastard!

Mrs Hardcastle stared at her, surprised that she wasn't flattered and delighted by her employer's concern for her welfare. 'Well,' she demanded, raising her eyebrows. 'What are you standing there for, girl? Off you go. Don't keep his lordship waiting.'

'Yes m'm,' muttered Maggie, and with leaden feet she turned and walked towards the door.

'Slut!' Thomas hissed malevolently under his breath as she passed. 'I hope the fat old whoremonger gives you the pox!'

Maggie barely heard him; the nightmare to come filled her head, shutting out everything else. She walked up the stairs and along the hall to the library as if she was in a trance.

He was waiting for her. Her gorge rose as she looked at him, sitting in his armchair like some dreadful bloated toad, lying in wait for an unsuspecting fly.

'You wished to see me, sir,' she muttered from between frozen lips.

'Close the door,' he ordered, and like an automaton she did so. 'Good, good,' he purred. 'Now take off your clothes.'

There was no point in resisting. If she did he would

merely take a wicked pleasure in forcing her, possibly chastising her for being impudent. Her only hope was to get the whole thing over with as quickly as possible, so, feeling numb, she began to undo the buttons on her dress, her fingers stiff and clumsy with foreboding.

'Get a move on, you little bitch,' he snarled. 'I'm waiting.'

The last button came free and the heavy dress slipped from her shoulders and down over her hips. She fumbled with the laces on her camisole and it joined the dress on the floor. Finally she stepped out of her pantaloons and stood before him in nothing but her black stockings and her high-buttoned boots.

He drew in a rasping breath as his eyes roamed over her, taking in her firm breasts, her narrow waist and the smooth curve of her hips, lingering lasciviously on the soft pink nipples, hardening in the cold air, then crawling down to the soft downy V between her slender thighs. She shuddered as his eyes glazed with lust and his thick tongue flopped out to lick his slack purple lips.

'Turn around,' he said hoarsely. Stiffly she did so, and he licked his lips again as the luscious globes of her buttocks quivered tightly as she moved. 'Now bend over,' he ordered, and puppet-like she obeyed, and his breath came quicker and more hoarse in his throat.

He smiled wolfishly. 'Sit down there,' he told her, pointing to the chair opposite his own, and fixing her gaze on a point over his shoulder so that she did not have to endure the expression of gloating lust on his face, Maggie did so. He licked his lips again. 'And spread your legs.' A wave of humiliation washed over her as she parted her thighs to display the secret places of her body to him. She felt like a piece of meat on a butcher's slab.

'Now play with your titties,' he croaked, his hand stroking the bulge in his trousers. 'And finger yourself.'

Reluctantly, Maggie raised one hand and began to caress the tight pink buds of her nipples, and he watched greedily as they rose to meet her touch. Closing her eyes to shut out the picture of his fat red face, she concentrated on the sensations in her body, imagining it was Jeremy's lips and fingers that caused them. Her breath caught in her throat and her other hand strayed lower, parting the downy lips of her vulva to reveal the hidden place beneath, pink and glistening, as sweetly inviting as a succulent fruit. Lord Edward grunted in animal satisfaction, but lost in her own world, she did not even hear him.

Maggie sighed as she delicately teased her swelling clitoris, then slipped first one finger, then two inside her hot, wet cleft. She began to move them, slowly at first, then faster as her need mounted, her hips squirming.

It was all too much for Lord Edward. In two steps he was looming over her, fumbling at the buttons on his trousers... and it was then that the door swung open and Lady Georgina walked in.

'I'm home, dear, I'm...' Her mouth dropped open at the sight of her husband standing over a naked girl. For a few seconds she was stunned into silence, then her face turned as red as a turkey cock.

'What is going on here?' she shrieked as Maggie leapt to her feet and scrabbled for her discarded clothing in a vain attempt to cover her nakedness. 'What is this slut doing in my house?' She finally recognised Maggie. 'You!' she hissed venomously. 'I might have known!'

'Um, thank goodness you're home, my dear,' blustered

116

Lord Edward. 'I walked into the library to find this... this... creature disporting herself in this appalling manner.' He waved a disgusted hand in Maggie's direction as she stared up at him in horror. 'Then when I told her to make herself decent, she attempted to seduce me into joining her filthy games.'

'It wasn't like that!' Maggie protested desperately. 'He forced me to do it!'

Lady Georgina's mouth twisted as if she'd bitten into something vile. 'You lying young trollop!' she snarled. 'As if Lord Edward would look twice at a common little guttersnipe like you! How dare you even suggest such a thing?'

She looked round wildly and her eye fell on a sturdy wooden ruler lying on the library table. Seizing it, she advanced on Maggie, arm flailing. Whimpering, Maggie tried to avoid the rain of blows, but it was useless. Grinning salaciously, Lord Edward seized and held her as his outraged wife beat her unmercifully, raising red weals on her lily-white skin, taking the opportunity to rub his tented trousers between the poor girl's writhing buttocks.

'Quite right, my dear; chastise her! "Spare the rod and spoil the child", the Good Book says,' he intoned piously as Maggie squealed in pain and squirmed helplessly against him. By God, he hadn't had this much fun in a long time. It almost made up for being interrupted before he'd had a chance to fuck the little bitch!

Finally Lady Georgina panted to a halt and Lord Edward flung the sobbing girl to the floor.

'Now get out of my house and never darken my door again,' snarled Lady Georgina. 'Get back to the gutter where you belong.'

Still sobbing, Maggie slipped into her dress, gathered her underclothes and fled along the corridor, barely noticing Thomas grinning in the shadows until he stepped out in front of her, barring her way. 'Not so smart now, are you?' he sneered.

She stared at him in horror. You… you brought Lady Georgina to the library,' she gasped as the penny dropped. 'Even though you knew what he'd be doing to me?'

'Course I did.' He smirked in malicious triumph. 'Told you I'd get even.'

'But how could you?' she wailed. 'I've been flung out without a reference. I'll never get another position now, anywhere.'

'Course you will.' He laughed coarsely. 'On your back with your legs open!' He pushed her against the wall and grinned down at her. 'And when you're walking the streets with the other whores, you'll be glad of my custom.' He squeezed her breasts viciously. 'In fact, you'll do whatever I want.' Laughing, he sauntered off, leaving her life in ruins.

Maggie stared after him in horror. Oh God, he was right!

Chapter Ten

Her few pitiful belongings didn't take long to pack. The last six years of her life fitted neatly into a Gladstone bag, with room to spare. Defiantly she put on her best lilac frock and stood in front of the cracked mirror for the last time as she adjusted her straw hat with the matching ribbon.

It was only then that she broke down. She had bought that hat the day she and Jeremy met. The day that had been so happy and yet had brought her to this. She would never see him again now. How would he find her – even if he wanted to – when even she had no idea what was to become of her? Careless of her finery, she flung herself on the bed and sobbed hopelessly.

Eventually the storm of weeping passed. She sat up and wiped the tears from her face. Damn them! She wouldn't give them the satisfaction of seeing her reduced to this. She'd show them! She'd walk out of this house with her head held high and a contemptuous smile on her face if it bloody killed her!

Getting up she splashed her face with cold water from the ewer, smoothed the creases from her dress and examined her reflection once more. Apart from a slight puffiness round the eyes, she'd pass muster. Straightening her shoulders, she seized the handle of her bag and, without a backward glance, marched out of the room she'd shared with Emily for the last few years.

All conversation stopped as she walked into the kitchen, and the look of pity and horror in the eyes of her former friends and workmates almost unmanned her again. She could see in their faces that they already knew her shame. She swallowed the lump that rose in her throat. Were they going to despise and ignore her? Watch her leave without even a last kind word?

It was the sight of Thomas' sly face that stiffened her backbone. If he thought he'd reduced her to a snivelling wreck, he was wrong.

'I expect you've heard the news,' she said, grateful that her voice sounded so normal, and it was enough to break the awkward hush.

Mrs McAllister rushed forward and enfolded her in a warm cinnamon-scented embrace. 'My poor wee lamb,' she sobbed, emotion making her accent stronger than ever. 'What'll ye dae noo?'

'Not to worry,' said Maggie, patting the broad, heaving back. 'I'll find something.' She pushed her away gently. 'I'm not afraid of hard work.'

Mrs McAlister dabbed her eyes. 'Well, you'll not leave here empty-handed,' she said defiantly. 'I've packed ye a wee basket. That'll keep ye going a couple of days.' Maggie smiled. There was probably enough in the 'wee basket' to feed a family of four for a fortnight.

Emily stepped forward. 'Good luck, Maggie. We'll miss you,' she whispered, giving her a quick hug while little Mary bobbed her agreement in the background. Even Mr Harris managed a stiff nod before he left to go about the business of attending to the master.

Finally Maggie turned apprehensively to face Mrs Hardcastle, her heart sinking again at the grim expression on her face. She'd been the one to give Maggie her chance. Did she regret it now? Did she feel that Maggie's shame reflected on her own bad judgement?

'I'm sorry to see you go, lass, but there's nothing I can do about it,' she said, and the relief made Maggie's head swim and chin quiver as she fought back the tears of sadness. 'You're not the first and you'll not be the last,' she went on, and then her lips twisted. 'Not while his lordship still has an eye for a pretty face and a neat ankle.' She snorted. 'I'd have to be blind not to know what goes on. Hypocritical old bastard!'

She collected herself again. 'Still, that doesn't help you, does it?' Fishing in the pocket of her black apron she produced two envelopes. 'There's your due wages, and another month's in lieu of notice,' she said, handing over the first one, then she held out the second. 'And this is a letter from me to say you've been a good, honest girl.' She shook her head. 'Not that it's much good without a proper reference from her ladyship, but it'll have to do. Maybe it'll help get you a post as a maid-of-all work with the likes of someone in trade who doesn't know any better.'

'Thank you,' said Maggie. It was better than nothing and more than she had any right to expect. She slipped them both into her reticule.

'Now you'll have a last cup of tea before you go,' said Mrs Hardcastle. 'Thomas, you can go and look for a hackney cab.'

It was a sad little group that sat round the table in the servant's hall for the last time. Mary and Emily punctuated sips of tea with sniffles and Maggie was hard put not to join in. She looked round at their faces. They'd been her family for the last six years and she'd probably never see them again. She forced herself to be cheerful.

'I'll write once I get settled in a new position,' she said. 'Let you know how I'm getting on – then when you've got my new address you can write back.' She smiled at Emily. 'Maybe if we have the same days off we can meet up – catch up on all the gossip.'

'Luvverly,' sniffed Emily. 'That's what we'll do. You just see if we don't.' Both of them knew it was unlikely.

It was almost a relief when Thomas stuck his grinning head round the kitchen door.

'Carriage for her ladyship,' he called mockingly, and Maggie reluctantly got to her feet. There was a last flurry of goodbyes and promises to keep in touch, and then she was walking up the back steps for the last time. Her single bag and Mrs McAlister's 'wee basket' beside her in the evil-smelling cab, she leaned out of the window as it drew away and waved until the house and the little group on the steps were nothing but a memory.

Slumped in despair, she watched from the cab window as the fine houses gave way to lesser ones, then to middle class villas and finally to the crowded tenements of the poor. When they reached the entry to the warren of slums and back streets that contained Maggie's former home, the hackney drew to a halt, the horse snorting and stamping.

'Right, out you get,' ordered the cabbie, rapping on the door. 'But... but the housekeeper said you'd been paid to take me home,' Maggie protested.

'Not likely,' he snorted. 'I ain't taking me 'orse and cab in there. We'd never get out alive! You're on yer own now, gel. And God 'elp yer!'

Fumbling for her bag and basket, Maggie climbed out

and stood watching as the cabbie disappeared round the corner as if the devil himself was after him. The last link with her new life was gone. There was no choice but to return to the old one.

Taking a deep breath, she gripped the handle of her Gladstone bag more tightly and began to trudge through the narrow lanes. She gagged as the smell hit her. The stench of poverty and desperation hung like a miasma in the air, settling on her skin and into the folds of her clothes. She had barely gone half a dozen steps before the hem of her skirt was dark with mud – or worse.

She had forgotten how bad it was. The scrawny, grey-faced children. The swaggering louts leering and catcalling from crumbling doorways. The women either exhausted and downtrodden or drunk and flaunting themselves. It was like a scene from the anteroom to hell. One little girl, her hair a tangle of matted curls, was sitting on a doorstep stroking something small and furry. At first Maggie thought it was a kitten, then she shuddered as she realised it was a dead rat.

Her appearance brought unwanted attention. The women eyed her clothes enviously and a group of children followed her like stray cats, demanding money or food or both.

'Gerr out of it!' she snarled, turning on them, the veneer of painfully acquired politeness falling away as if it had never existed. She had no room for pity; it was survival of the fittest here. The food Mrs McAllister had given her would save her spending her meagre hoard of coins while she looked for work. They scattered, jeering, and she marched on, ignoring them.

All too soon Maggie reached her former home, even filthier than when she'd left it. She swallowed her disgust as she picked her way through the pools of ordure that filled the courtyard, holding her skirts high to avoid the scummy surface. The only thing that kept her going was the thought of seeing her mother again. Although she had sent a postal order faithfully every month, there had been no contact apart from a loving letter of thanks in return – and even those had tailed away to nothing recently.

Holding her breath, she fumbled her way down the cellar steps and stopped on the threshold of the room, her mouth twisting in distaste. Nothing had altered; the same bundles of rags; the same old rickety table. Even the pile of dirty straw in the corner looked as if it hadn't been changed since she left. But the room was empty. Where was her mother?

She laid the basket on the table and looked around for somewhere clean to put her bag. There was nowhere. Wincing she tucked it away in the least dirty corner and hung her cape on a nail on the wall. What now?

Just then the door swung open and she turned with a smile on her face. 'Ma!' she exclaimed, but the smile was wiped away at the sight of the shambling hulk who stood there, swaying. Her stepfather.

'Oo the 'ell are you?' he demanded, peering at her suspiciously from narrowed eyes. In one step he crossed the floor, gripped her by the neck and shook her like a terrier shakes a rat. 'And wot the fuck do yer think yer doing in my 'ouse, yer thievin' little bitch?'

Choking, she broke free and stepped backwards. 'Keep yer 'ands to yerself,' she rasped, rubbing her throat. 'I ain't stealing nuffink. It's me!'

He peered at her again. 'Maggie? That's never you, is it?'

'Course it's me,' she insisted. 'Who did yer think it was, the Queen o' bleedin' Sheba?'

He grinned, revealing a mouthful of blackened teeth. 'Little Maggie,' he crooned with drunken sentimentality. 'Come 'ome at last.' His bloodshot eyes crawled over her and his mood swung dangerously. 'And all growed up as well. Turned into a proper good-looking little gel, too,' he slavered, the grin became a leer and he licked his lips. 'Aintcha got a kiss for yer old dad then, my dear?'

'Not on you life!' she snapped. 'Anyway, where's me ma? Down the market?'

'Down the cemetery,' he grinned.

'What's she doing there?' Maggie demanded in bewilderment. Then his words sank in and she groped for the rickety chair and sat down. 'She... she's not...' Her voice trailed away as realisation dawned, and tears of loss welled up in her eyes.

'As a doornail,' he chuckled. 'Gin-soaked old cow! Been gone this last four months. Took the consumption and just faded away. Nuffink but skin and bone by the time she went.'

Maggie stared at his hateful, grinning face and anger replaced grief. 'You cold-hearted bastard!' she hissed. 'My own ma dead and gone and you didn't even have the decency to let me know.'

He raised an eyebrow. 'Wot? And 'ave you stop sendin' them postal orders every month? Not on your nellie! Come in very handy that money did.' He chuckled again. 'Bought me a fair few pints, that's fer sure.'

'You're nothing but scum,' she said wearily. 'You'd sell your own granny for the price of a drink. Well, you've had it now. There'll be no more money coming in. They chucked me out.' The loss of her mother coming so soon on the loss of her position suddenly hit her and she crumpled. Oblivious to everything but her grief, she laid her head on the filthy table and sobbed as if her heart would break.

It was Bert's voice that finally roused her from her storm of weeping. ''Ere, get this down yer, gel,' he muttered, putting a cracked cup in front of her. She looked at the colourless liquid suspiciously. 'Just a drop o' gin,' he went on with an ingratiating smile. 'For the shock.'

Holding it in both shaking hands, Maggie sipped the fiery liquid, feeling the warmth trickle back into her belly. 'That's a girl,' he grinned. 'No need for you and me to fall out, is there? We got to stick together.' He patted her shoulder. 'Now get the rest of it knocked back and you'll soon feel the better for it.'

Grimacing at the taste, she did as she was told. Perhaps she had misjudged him? Her head swam as a wave of giddiness washed over her and she swayed in the chair. With difficulty she raised her head, and attempted to focus on his leering face. 'Bass'ard…' she slurred through slack lips. 'Tha' wasn' jus' gin. Wha… what wass it?'

'Yer ma's laudanum,' he gloated. 'There was still some left in the bottle.' He leaned down and his foul breath hit her as he sneered into her face. 'Not so clever now, are yer, yer little bitch?' He snorted. 'Yer come in 'ere with yer hoity-toity airs thinkin' yer better than everybody else. Well, yer ain't!'

Maggie drew back her head and spat straight into his grinning face, and the grin disappeared as he recoiled, her spittle running down his chin. He wiped it away with the back of a grimy hand.

'You're goin' to regret that, me lady,' he grated, reached for her, dragged her to her feet and backhanded her across the face, but lost in her drugged haze she didn't even feel it. She tried to lift her arms and break free of his grasp, but her limbs were made of lead, each movement taking years to make. Only his iron grip prevented her collapsing on the floor.

It was as if it was all happening to someone else and she was only an unwilling onlooker. She floated above it all and watched as the unshaven brute stripped the clothes from his human puppet. Watched as he ran his dirty hands over the naked body, mouthing and slobbering at the soft breasts. Watched as he parted the slack thighs and thrust his thick fingers inside.

Even when he scooped up the unresisting body and flung it roughly onto the pile of filthy rags in the corner, she felt nothing more than a vague dreamy sympathy for the poor girl. She watched as he knelt between the pale slender legs, unbuttoning himself. Watched as he shoved his gnarled swollen cock roughly into the puppet and his hairy buttocks began to jerk and heave. The stream of vile obscenities that ran from his drooling lips as he thrust and strained was nothing more than a soothing murmur in her ears. When he finally grunted in release and withdrew his dripping prick, her eyes closed and she drifted off into darkness.

When she came to she was lying on the filthy pallet, naked, and every bone in her body ached. She groaned as she attempted to sit up, her hands going to her throbbing head. What had happened? She felt the disgusting stickiness between her thighs and her groan became a sob as it all rushed back to her. Her stepfather had taken her like a boar in rut!

Maggie shuddered in disgust then glanced fearfully around, expecting him to leap from a corner and force himself on her again. But thankfully the room was empty, so she staggered to her feet and looked frantically for her clothing. Wherever he was, she had to get away before he came back.

Her expression became bewildered as her gaze searched the room. Her clothes! Where were her clothes? She bent and raked through the pile of dirty rags, then pushed her hands through the straw beneath. Nothing!

Panic threatened to overwhelm her and she forced herself to be calm. She had other clothes. She could wear those instead. In fact, that would be even better, she reassured herself. In her ordinary dress she wouldn't attract so much attention when she fled. So wrapping herself in the best of the rags from the bed, she tiptoed across the room to where she had hidden her Gladstone bag and reticule – then stopped in dismay.

There was nothing there! Her bag had gone! Her reticule, containing Mrs Hardcastle's precious letter of reference had gone! Her purse with two month's wages was gone! Maggie sank down, sobbing in despair.

She was trapped, naked and alone in this filthy room and her stepfather had disappeared, taking everything she possessed in the world with him.

Chapter Eleven

Shivering with cold and fear, Maggie crept into the darkest corner and cowered there, casting frightened glances towards the door. Seconds stretched into minutes and minutes into hours, but still there was no sign of her stepfather. Eventually she was driven by hunger to venture out and rake through the basket Mrs McAlister had given her – and which thankfully remained – for something to eat.

Clutching a wedge of game pie she retreated to her corner and crouched there, devouring it hungrily. The taste of the good food reminded her again of everything she had lost and she salted it with a few bitter tears. Finally, worn out by her emotions, she curled up on the filthy pile of straw and rags like a beaten dog and drifted into a restless doze.

The sound of the door creaking open made her start upright in confusion. For the first few seconds she was blissfully unaware of her surroundings, imagining herself back in the bedroom she shared with Emily, then it all sank in again. Hands and feet scrabbling in the dirty straw, she pushed herself away from him until her back was against the wall and stared up at him fearfully.

'On yer feet,' he growled. 'We ain't got all night for you to lounge around like a bleedin' lady.'

For once he seemed to be sober; there was no smell of drink coming from him, just the usual stench of his sweaty, unwashed body. Gaining confidence, Maggie pushed herself to her feet and stood holding her rags to conceal her naked body.

'What you done with all me stuff, you thieving bastard?' she demanded, glaring at him defiantly.

'Sold it,' he said indifferently, and jingled the contents of his pockets. 'And a pretty penny it brought too. Enough to keep me in drink and whores for weeks.'

'You had no right,' she protested. 'Get it back or I'll have the coppers on you.'

He began to laugh. 'Coppers?' he sneered. 'Where you going to find a copper in this place? It'd be more than a peeler's life was worth to come down these alleys.' His grin vanished. 'Anyway, you won't be needin' your stuff no more. Not where you're going.'

The colour drained from her face. Was he going to murder her? Strangle her and fling her body in the river? She gulped; he could do it easily. Nobody knew she was here. Nobody would even miss her. She'd just disappear, swallowed up by London, like so many other girls before her. Her mouth went dry. She'd seen a body hauled out of the water down by the docks once. Bloated and putrefying, its features had been eaten away until it didn't even look human any more – just a slab of dead, rotting meat. Was that going to be her fate too?

'What do you mean?' she quavered, not sure that she wanted to know the answer.

'Got you a new job, ain't I,' he grinned. For the first time she noticed he was carrying an old sack in one hand. 'Here, get this on,' he ordered, flinging it at her.

The relief she'd felt at his words disappeared as she opened it and pulled out the contents. 'I ain't wearin' this,' she gasped, holding up the dress. It was made of red satin, creased and dirty from years of use and the hem was in tatters. Rings of stale sweat stained the armpits and it was cut obscenely low. 'It's filthy,' she complained, throwing it to the floor. 'Gawd knows what I'd catch off it. I wouldn't touch it with a bargepole.'

'Gerrit on!' he growled, picking it up and shaking it under her nose. 'Or I'll drag you through the bleedin' streets stark naked! And a pretty little thing like you wouldn't last five minutes once some of the blokes clocked you in your birthday suit.'

The sound of the whistles and catcalls from the shadowy doorways echoed in Maggie's memory. He was right; they'd fall on her like a pack of wild dogs. Shivering, she grabbed the dress again and slipped into it, trying to hide her nakedness as he watched closely.

'Very nice,' he grinned, as she tugged it over her shoulders. 'Very nice indeed.'

The dress was too small for her and the bodice was so low it barely concealed her breasts, pushing them together and up until they threatened to spill over it. Smiling lustily, he shuffled closer and cupped the soft globes, pinching her nipples viciously till they stood out against the shiny material. Whimpering in pain, she closed her eyes to shut out his loathsome face and braced herself for another attack. But it didn't come.

'Better not,' he muttered regretfully to himself. 'Don't want to bring the price down.'

Maggie opened her eyes and stared at him in bewilderment. 'What... what do you mean?' she asked cautiously for the second time in as many minutes.

'You'll soon find out,' he chuckled, then delved into the sack again, produced a pair of shabby red high-heeled shoes and flung them at her. 'Here, get these on,' he ordered. 'Time's gettin' on.' He sniggered. 'Don't want to keep your new employers waitin'.'

Maggie pushed her feet into the shoes, wincing as the cracked leather pinched her toes, and they were barely on her feet when he grasped her by the wrist and pulled her towards the door. Teetering awkwardly on the unaccustomed heels, she had no option but to follow him or be dragged along like a sack of coal.

What followed was a ghastly parody of the last time she had left this hellhole, stumbling along behind her mother in a borrowed dress and ill-fitting shoes. Then she had been on her way to a new life – one of hard work, but also of safety and comfort.

Now she was being dragged weeping behind her stepfather – and God only knew what lay ahead!

Chapter Twelve

Maggie was exhausted by the time Bert suddenly stopped on the opposite side of the road from a large house. She staggered against him. They seemed to have walked for hours and she had a stitch in her side from trying to keep up.

'This is it,' Bert said with satisfaction, and relief for Maggie at the unexpected respite was tinged with fear at what lay behind the heavy mahogany doors. It was not exactly the 'best' area of London, but it was still good – and the house was well maintained. Red velvet curtains masked the tall windows, but warm light escaped from the chinks and she could hear music and laughter. But she shivered as an icy finger touched her spine, for despite the reassuring façade, there was something about the house that made her skin crawl – and was it her imagination or did the female laughter have a note of desperation to it?

As she watched a carriage rolled up outside and two men alighted from it, walked up the steps and knocked on the front door. There was a pause, then it was opened and Maggie's eyes widened as an immensely tall black manservant, dressed in green and gold livery, appeared. He smiled and welcomed them with a bow. As the light spilled over the men's faces, it illuminated their predatory grins and she shivered again.

Her uncomfortable thoughts were interrupted as Bert

jerked her by the arm. 'Don't just stand there gawpin',' he ordered, hauling her behind him. 'Pick yer feet up; old Ma Wilkes don't like to be kept waiting.'

Reluctantly she followed him across the road and down the kitchen entry, trying not to slip on the uneven steps. He released her wrist long enough to bang on the door and she took the opportunity to try and tidy herself up, and was still attempting to pull her tight bodice higher when the door swung open.

'Wot you want?' demanded the slovenly maid who answered, her jaws still champing on a mouthful of food. She looked them up and down with contempt, and spat a lump of gristle on the ground at Bert's feet.

He pulled himself up to his full height and scowled at her. 'None of your damned business,' he snarled. 'I talks to the organ grinder, not the bleedin' monkey.' He smirked. 'I got an appointment wiv Mrs Wilkes. She's expectin' me.'

'Please yerself,' shrugged the maid. 'It's no skin off my arse.' She pulled the door open for them and Bert swaggered past her, clicking his fingers at Maggie to follow.

A wave of homesickness washed over Maggie as she walked into the kitchen. At first glance it was the twin of Mrs McAlister's domain; the same black range, with its constantly boiling kettle and a shabby wooden armchair at each side of the fire. The same cluttered shelves. The same long, deal worktable.

But there the resemblance ended. It was obvious that the range hadn't seen black lead and a polishing cloth in a month of Sundays. The shelves were cluttered all right, but not with sacks of flour and sugar. Instead they were filled with rank upon rank of rot-gut spirits. As for the deal table, it was covered with spills and ring-marks from the dirty glasses and empty bottles that had been dumped there and forgotten. Maggie smiled ruefully. If Mrs H saw this lot, she'd have a fit.

But her smile disappeared as quickly as it had come. If the condition of the kitchen was a shock, its occupants were even more so. The grubby maid, her duties done, ignored them and sauntered off to finish her interrupted supper.

At a hastily cleared corner of the table a fat woman in a filthy apron was decanting cheap wine into expensive bottles. As Maggie stared, she wiped her snotty nose with the back of her hand, and then wiped her hand on her apron. Maggie shivered with disgust.

But Bert had no such scruples. He watched the woman greedily and then cleared his throat, and when she looked up from her task, he winked at her. 'Aintcha goin' to offer your guests a bit o' hospitality then, sweetheart?' he suggested with an ingratiating smile. The woman simpered back, filled a tankard and held it out to him, and he grabbed it before she could change her mind. 'Cheers, love,' he grinned, knocking half of it back and belching.

'I'll have a glass too, Gladys,' came a husky voice. 'And make sure it's a clean one.'

Maggie and Bert both turned to look at the unseen speaker, and Maggie's jaw dropped. She'd been too busy looking round the rest of the kitchen to notice the woman sitting in the chair by the fire with her feet propped up on the edge of the range. But now that she had, she couldn't take her eyes off her.

She was wearing a red satin dress too, but that was the only similarity. If Maggie had thought her own was indecent, it was nothing compared to this. It was so low-cut that the shoulder had slipped and one plump breast was totally exposed. The front panel was slit almost to the waist and had fallen away to reveal a pair of shapely legs in black silk stockings and garters, but even more shocking was the fact that one slender hand held a cheroot. As Maggie watched in amazement, the woman took a long draw and blew out a thick cloud of blue smoke.

Bert couldn't take his eyes off her either. They were fixed in lustful fascination on the soft white flesh of her bosom, until with a cynical smile the woman tugged up the neck of her dress. 'Shut your mouth, love,' she advised. 'The flies'll get in.' Bemused, he did as he was told.

'There you go, Miss Millicent,' said Gladys, waddling across and handing her some wine. The woman accepted it with a gracious nod, and taking another puff on her cheroot, she ran her eyes sympathetically over Maggie and raised her glass in an ironic toast. 'To the newest lamb to the slaughter,' she said. 'Here's to a short life and a happy one.' She flung her head back, swallowed the wine and got to her feet. 'No rest for the wicked,' she chuckled. 'Better get back to work.'

Maggie watched as she left. Despite the outlandish clothes and behaviour there was something familiar about her, but for the life of her Maggie couldn't figure out what.

Her disappearance broke the spell and Bert suddenly remembered what he'd come for. 'Where's old Ma Wilkes?' he demanded. 'I ain't got all night to hang around 'ere.'

'Keep your hair on,' muttered Gladys. 'And it's Mrs

Wilkes to the likes of you. She hears you calling her old Ma Wilkes and she'll 'ave yer guts for garters.' She waddled over to the door and pulled it open. 'Eddie!' she bawled. 'Get yer arse in 'ere!' She shook her head. 'Blasted boot boy's never 'ere when you want him. Gawd knows what he gets up to.'

The pattering of feet heralded Eddie's arrival, and Maggie smiled despite herself. If her eyes didn't deceive her, it was the little urchin who'd played his fiddle at Mrs H's birthday party. My, how he'd come up in the world. Instead of rags, he was wearing a neat black uniform and he actually had some meat on his bones.

'Sorry, Gladys,' he panted. 'I was 'umping coal up them stairs. Wotcher want?'

'Tell Mrs Wilkes she has…' she ran her eyes disparagingly over Bert and Maggie '…visitors.'

'Yes m'm. Right away, m'm.' The lad looked at the 'visitors' and his grin disappeared as he recognised Maggie. 'Wot you doin' here, miss?' he gasped. 'This ain't no place for a lady like you—' but a swift clip round the ear from Gladys brought the conversation to a premature close.

'None of your bleedin' business what she's doin' here,' she snapped. 'Just you get about your own and tell Mrs Wilkes she's here.' She raised her hand again. 'Before I gives yer another one.'

Clutching his ear Eddie fled, but his words had filtered through Maggie's fog of fear and it finally dawned on her exactly what kind of place Bert had brought her to. It was a house of ill repute, and her stomach churned with consternation and distaste. Waiting on Lady Georgina had been bad enough, but at least she'd been respectable – even if her husband hadn't. Did Bert really expect her to be a maid here? Dance attendance on a houseful of loose women?

Her horrified thoughts were interrupted by Eddie's return. 'I'm to take 'em up to Mrs Wilkes' office,' he announced. 'She'll see 'em now.'

'Get on with it then,' sniffed Gladys, nodding brusquely at Bert and Maggie. 'Just follow Eddie. He'll take you up.' Bert jerked his head and Maggie reluctantly did as she was told.

As they walked through the green baize door that separated the servants' quarters from the main house, she stopped and gawped around her. Even her former employers hadn't lived like this! The carpet was so thick that the heels of her shoes sank into the pile and the hand painted wallpaper, illuminated by the flaring gas mantles, was a riot of exotic birds and plants.

But it was the oil paintings that caught her breath. She'd never seen anything like them in her life. Instead of portraits they were depictions of scenes of sexual depravity. Naked women writhed in ecstasy with one man, two men – she shuddered – even with animals! It was disgusting!

Maggie was unaware that she'd stopped walking until Bert's heavy hand thumped her between the shoulders. 'Gerra move on,' he snarled. 'You heard wot that Gladys said; old Ma Wilkes don't like to be kept waiting.'

Eddie stopped in front of a heavy mahogany door and tapped gingerly. A muffled voice called, 'Come in', he pushed it open, stepped back to allow them to enter, then closed it discreetly behind them. Swallowing nervously, Maggie walked forward, with Bert on her heels. She didn't know what she'd been expecting; some fat vulgar slut with her face plastered with powder and rouge? Whatever it was, Mrs Wilkes did not fit her mental picture. Small, neat and dressed in sober black, her grey hair drawn tightly back beneath the kind of lace cap favoured by the queen, she sat primly behind a heavy oak desk, with her hands folded in her lap. She could have been a respectable housekeeper on some country estate rather than the madam of a notorious brothel.

But it was her eyes that gave her away. Maggie remembered a picture she'd seen in a book once, of a snake mesmerising a helpless rabbit, and the eyes that regarded her now were as cold and dead as that snake's. The thin lips parted in an icy smile. 'Well?' she asked, her voice as well bred as her appearance. 'And what can I do for you?'

Bert shuffled his feet and smiled back ingratiatingly. 'I brung me daughter,' he blustered, waving a hand in Maggie's direction.

'So I see,' said Mrs Wilkes, leaning back and running her eyes over Maggie. 'And what, pray, am I supposed to do with her?'

'Well, I thought she could work 'ere,' he muttered.

Mrs Wilkes raised an eyebrow. 'Did you indeed?' she smiled. 'And what makes you think I would want her?'

'She's a pretty gel,' he said, beads of sweat beginning to break out on his forehead. 'And nice fresh meat too,' he went on eagerly. 'She'd be worth a packet. A virgin. Never been touched.' Maggie whirled round and stared at him in horror. He hadn't brought her here to work as a maid at all!

A burst of harsh laughter made her turn back to the woman behind the desk. Her shoulders were shaking with amusement. 'A virgin!' she cackled, her veneer of culture disappearing. 'That's a good 'un! You must think I've still got straw stuck behind me ears! She's no more a virgin than I am!' Maggie turned scarlet with humiliation, as Mrs Wilkes wiped away her tears of laughter and regarded her with the intent gaze of a farmer contemplating buying a new cow. 'Still,' she mused, 'the punters ain't going to know that, are they?' She waved her hand imperiously at Bert. 'Strip her off then, till I get a proper look.'

Hands crossed protectively over her chest, Maggie back away in horror. 'Get away from me, you bastard,' she warned as Bert moved towards her, but it was no use. He reached out, grabbed the bodice of her dress and in one violent motion ripped the rotten material to the hem, and the dress fluttered to the floor leaving her standing naked before them.

Refusing to be cowed, Maggie lifted her chin and stared defiantly at Mrs Wilkes. Mrs Wilkes stared back, taking in the proud thrust of the heaving breasts, their soft pink nipples hardening in the cold. She ran her eyes calculatingly over the narrow waist, the smooth swell of the girl's hips, the tantalising V of soft hair at the juncture of the slender legs, and the white unblemished skin. Finally she began to smile.

'Not bad,' she agreed. 'Not bad at all.' She looked at Bert. 'I'll give you five guineas for her.'

'You can't buy and sell me!' gasped Maggie. 'I'm not an animal!'

'Oh yes I can,' smirked Bert. 'You're me daughter, ain't yer? Until yer twenty-one, yer still my property. I can do what I bleedin' well like with yer. It's the law.' He turned back to Mrs Wilkes and scowled. 'Make it twenty and we've got a deal.'

140

'Seven,' the woman countered. 'And that's my last offer.' She shrugged. 'Girls are ten-a-penny. Take it or leave it.'

Bert shook his head. 'She's worth more than that,' he said. 'Make it ten.'

'Done,' Mrs Wilkes agreed, smiling inwardly. The stupid fool; the girl would make ten times that in her first night alone.

Maggie watched in dismay as the woman opened the desk drawer and counted out ten gleaming gold sovereigns. 'There you go,' she said with contempt, pushing the pile towards Bert. 'Now get out of here and never come back. If I see you round here again, one of my boys'll give you a beating you'll never forget.'

Burt grabbed the coins and shoved them into his pocket. 'Thanks, missus,' he grinned, tugging his forelock mockingly. 'It's been a pleasure doing business with yer.'

Maggie watched in dismay as he turned on his heel and swaggered out. She bent, pulled her torn dress about her and turned back to Mrs Wilkes. 'I'm not staying here either,' she said. 'And you can't make me.'

'Oh, but I think you'll find I can,' purred Mrs Wilkes, picking up the bell that stood on her desk and ringing it. A few moments later the door opened and the huge black manservant walked in. Maggie stared at him in horror.

'Take this young lady to her room,' the woman smiled, he nodded silently, and ignoring Maggie's kicks and screams he scooped her up as if she weighed no more than a feather and carried her, still shrieking, along the carpeted corridors and up two flights of stairs to a tiny, uncarpeted room. Depositing her on the narrow bed, he left as silently as he had come, locking the door behind him. Sobbing with fear and rage Maggie flung herself against it, beating her fists against the thick wood. She had to get away! She simply had to!

Chapter Thirteen

She might as well have been a captive bird beating its wings against the bars of its cage for all the effect she had. The door remained stubbornly shut. Finally she gave up and retreated sobbing to the narrow bed. She tugged the tattered remains of her scarlet satin dress about her and sat there, knees pulled up to her chin, her frightened eyes riveted on the entrance to her prison.

It seemed like hours before she heard the sound of movement in the corridor outside. The key turned in the lock and she leapt to her feet, looking round wildly for a weapon to defend herself against whatever monster should enter. The only thing she could find was the flowered chamber pot beneath the bed. The idea of facing the devil armed only with a pot might have been amusing if she hadn't been so scared.

The door creaked slowly open and she raised it above her head, prepared to crown whoever came through it – then stopped just in time.

'Going to brain me, were yer?' grinned the girl she'd seen earlier in the kitchen, the one Gladys had called Miss Millicent. She held out the tray she was holding; there was a steaming mug of tea, a pile of bread and butter and a plateful of hot sausages that gave off a tantalising aroma. 'I come to bring yer a bit o' grub and you try and bash me 'ead in. Fine thanks for doing yer a good turn, that is.'

Maggie's gaze moved from the proffered tray to the open door, and the girl's eyes narrowed. 'Oh no yer don't,' she said, kicking it shut. Balancing the tray on her hip, she pulled the key from her cleavage, turned it in the lock and slipped it back again. 'Old Ma Wilkes would have the skin off me back if I let yer out.'

Sulkily, Maggie sat back down on the bed and studiously ignored the food, but the gesture was spoilt somewhat by the audible rumbling coming from her empty stomach.

'Please yourself,' shrugged Miss Millicent, plonking herself down beside her and putting the tray between them. 'All the more for me.' Maggie watched, her own mouth watering, as she picked up a sausage and bit into it with relish. Grease coated her lips and fingers, and Maggie's belly growled again. She gave in.

'Atta girl,' grinned Miss Millicent as Maggie wolfed down the food. 'Life's hard enough without starvin' yerself into the bargain.' She wiped her hands together, produced a delicate lace hankie from somewhere and began to mop the grease from her scarlet lips.

It was the handkerchief and the bowed head that did it, and Maggie's mouth fell open as the penny finally dropped. Miss Millicent – of course! How could she have been so stupid?

'Millie?' she gasped. 'Millie Evans?'

Miss Millicent raised her head and looked at Maggie, puzzled. 'That's me,' she confirmed. 'But how did you know?'

'I used to work for Lord Edward and Lady Georgina, too,' Maggie explained. 'I'm Maggie. Remember? I was an upper housemaid. I became Lady Georgina's maid after you…' Her voice trailed off as she remembered the circumstances. 'After you… er… left.'

'After I was chucked out, you mean,' Millie corrected bitterly. She ran her eyes over the swell of Maggie's breasts beneath the torn dress. 'Well, well, well. You were a skinny little thing when I left. Who'd of thought it?'

Maggie waved a delicate hand in the direction of Millie's flat stomach. 'What happened to…?'

'Lord Edward's bastard?' Millie said harshly, raising an eyebrow, and then her face softened. 'I shouldn't call the little bleeder that. He's a smashing kid.' She smiled. 'Takes after his ma.' Her face darkened again. 'Thank God.'

'So where is he now?' asked Maggie. 'With your folks?'

'Them?' Millie snorted scathingly. 'That'll be right. Delighted to have their precious daughter back with a bun in the oven – I don't think.' Her lips twisted in a sneer. 'Disowned me, didn't they, for "bringing shame on the family". "Get out and never darken me doorstep again", me dad said.' She shook her head. 'I pay this woman to look after him.'

'A baby farmer?' gasped Maggie. She'd heard about them; dirty basement rooms packed with babies, fed on laudanum to keep them quiet. Most of them were lucky to see out their first year, but who cared? There were always plenty more to take their place.

'Course not,' scoffed Millie. 'I ain't that daft.' She smiled. 'Me folks might have chucked me out, but me Auntie Nan was a real trump. She stood by me.' The smile became wicked. 'Mind you, it ain't surprising. She was barely up the aisle before her first nipper popped out.' She chuckled. 'Practically had the wedding and the christening on the same day!

'Anyway,' she went on. 'Her old man's a coach driver. Got a tied cottage on one of them big country estates. She took me in, looked after me till the kid come, then sorted out this woman to take care of the nipper.' She sighed. 'She'd have kept him herself if she hadn't had five of her own already.' She forced a smile. 'Still, the woman as has him can't have none of her own. Treats him like he was her own.'

She shrugged. 'As for me, with no job and no references, I ended up here.' Pushing the empty tray onto the floor she kicked off her shoes, lay back on the bed and lit up one of her cheroots. 'It ain't so bad,' she advised, blowing out a cloud of smoke. 'Roof over yer head, decent grub.' She gave an ugly laugh. 'And it certainly beats sleeping in a doss house and hawking your mutton on a street corner.'

'How can you bear it?' demanded Maggie. 'All those men poking and prodding you with their filthy hands and their, their...' her voice trailed away and she shuddered.

'Cocks?' sniggered Millie. 'Just close yer eyes and think of England, gel. It don't last long. Anyway. Old Ma Wilkes might be a money-grabbing whoremonger, but at least she's fair. You get a cut of every piece-of-mutton yer flog.' She gave a smug smile. 'Some of the girls spend theirs on clothes and drink, but not me. I'm putting mine past to open a little milliners.' She laughed coarsely. 'That'll be a laugh, won't it? Selling hats to snooty ladies after selling me cunt to their fine husbands.'

She crossed her ankles and her skirt fell open again to reveal her slender legs in their black silk stockings, and Maggie gasped as she saw the dark bruises on the white flesh of her thighs where the stockings ended. 'Course, the gentlemen who come here like it rough,' she admitted, flipping her skirt back over her legs. 'But I just thinks of me little hat shop and it's all worthwhile.' She smiled confidently. 'I'll be out of here in another couple of years.'

Maggie shuddered again. Of course she would – but it might be in a wooden box if she ended up with the pox or one of the 'gentlemen' got too rough. At the thought she began to panic again. 'I can't stay here,' she whimpered, grabbing the other girl's arm. 'Please, Millie, you've got the key. You could let me out. Please.'

Millie shook her off with a scowl and got to her feet. 'And risk me own neck?' she said. 'No chance. The old bitch would skin me alive. I'll tell you sumfink for nothing. I'd rather come up against the worst bloke in London than cross Ma Wilkes.' She shook her head. 'And if you've got any sense, you won't try to cross her either.'

She looked down at the trembling girl and her expression softened. 'You'll survive, love. We all do. We ain't got no choice.' Picking up the tray, she unlocked the door and closed it behind her. As the key turned again, the candle beside the bed flickered out and Maggie was left alone in the darkness with her despairing thoughts. Exhaustion overtook her and she dozed fitfully, starting half-awake at the smallest sound then falling back into a pit of nightmares in which she fled endlessly down a door-lined corridor with something dreadful at her heels. As she ran the thick red carpet sucked wetly at her feet, as if it were soaked in blood, impeding her flight as the horror behind her drew inexorably closer. From behind the shuttered doors came wails and shrieks from the other lost souls trapped in this house of hell.

Gasping and sweating she sat up, suddenly aware that one of the sounds she'd heard was real. It came again and she realised it wasn't the despairing scream of a doomed soul; it was the squeak of a floorboard outside the room. A faint line of light shining through the cracks outlined the shape of the door and she could hear heavy breathing. Her first thought was that Millie had changed her mind and come to release her, her second – and infinitely less comforting one – that the creature from her nightmare had somehow escaped the bounds of her dream and was crouched outside, waiting and listening as it prepared to pounce on its hapless prey.

The door swung slowly open for the second time that night and she realised it was neither. On the threshold stood old Ma Wilkes, candle in hand, panting and wheezing as she tried to catch her breath.

'Bleedin' stairs,' she gasped, patting her chest. 'Ain't good for me at my time of life.' Taking a final shuddering breath, she regained control and stepped into the room. Holding the candle high she gazed down at Maggie's heaving breasts and soft smooth flesh, glowing in the candlelight. Her thin lips parted in a satisfied smile. Yes, she'd got a real bargain with this one. The gentlemen would be queuing up to sample her wares.

'What do y-you want?' stammered Maggie, shrinking away.

'Why, nothing my dear,' she said soothingly. 'I merely came to welcome you to our little house.'

Maggie stared at the dreadful old harridan defiantly. 'Well, yer should have saved yer breath to cool yer porridge then, shouldn't yer,' she said as bravely as she could. 'Cos I ain't staying.'

'Oh, I think you are, my dear,' Mrs Wilkes said calmly. 'I paid good money for you, and I intend to get it back – and more. A lot, lot more.'

'Forget it,' Maggie said defiantly. 'I'll be out of here first thing in the morning.'

Mrs Wilkes raised an eyebrow. 'And exactly where do you think you'd go, my dear? Hmm? Back to your happy home and your loving father?'

'Stepfather,' muttered Maggie. She closed her eyes, remembered Bert's foul, sweaty body forcing itself on hers and shuddered. There was no way she'd ever go anywhere near that bastard again.

'I thought not,' smiled Mrs Wilkes. 'So where does that leave you? Go back into service?' She shook her head. 'No sensible woman is going to employ a girl without references.' She ran her eyes over Maggie. 'Particularly such a pretty one; not with a husband or sons in the house. That would just be asking for trouble.' She looked at Maggie with false sympathy. 'So what are your choices?' She shrugged. 'I suppose you could always go to the poorhouse.'

Maggie stared at her, wide-eyed in shock, the very word striking fear into her heart. The poorhouse was the last resort of the completely desperate – almost as bad as prison. In fact, they were prisons. Huge, soulless institutions that split up families and worked their inmates into the grave in return for their 'keep'.

In the poorhouse she'd be segregated in the women's section, and as one of 'the able-bodied' poor she'd spend her days picking oakum, or slaving her guts out in the hellhole of the laundry in exchange for a bed in a filthy dormitory and a couple of plates of gruel a day. She shuddered; she'd be gaunt and toothless in three months and dead in a couple of years.

'I see that doesn't appeal,' smiled Mrs Wilkes. 'Perhaps you'd prefer one of the sweatshops? Do you sew? I hear that if you work eighteen hours a day stitching shirts you can make a living.' She laughed. 'Well almost – I believe most of the young ladies have to do a little light whoring on the side to survive.'

Her smile became vicious. 'Which brings me to your last option. Do you really want to spend the rest of your life standing on a pavement in Piccadilly offering yourself to all comers? Having some pimp walk off with the results of your efforts or cut that pretty face if you don't make enough? Or how about when he dumps you when your looks have gone? Perhaps the thought of ending your days a pox-ridden dock-whore appeals to you?'

She leaned over and patted Maggie's hand. 'Come, my dear, be sensible. It's not so bad here. A few years and you can retire while you're still young. Look at Millie, she's going to set up her own little hat shop – and all she has to do is open her legs. Now what do you say?'

'I'll stay here,' said Maggie. 'But I won't whore. I'll do anything else you want; clean, wash, lay fires, wait on table, make beds…' she tried to keep the desperation out of her voice. 'But I won't whore.'

Mrs Wilkes' lips thinned. 'I've got Gladys for that sort of thing,' she smiled coldly. 'What do I need you for?' She leaned closer. 'You'll whore all right, my girl. In fact, you'll do any damned thing I tell you to.'

Suddenly at the end of her tether and without thinking, Maggie drew her head back and spat full in the old bitch's sneering face. 'Go to hell!' she snarled. 'I'd rather go to the damned poorhouse! I'm not staying in this place – and you can't make me!'

Apparently unruffled, Mrs Wilkes calmly wiped the spittle from her face and smiled down at Maggie. 'Oh, yes I can,' she said softly, and Maggie recoiled from the hidden menace in her voice. 'And as for whoring – I think tomorrow will change your mind. In fact, this time tomorrow night you'll be begging to spread your legs.' She began to laugh as she turned to go. 'Goodnight, my dear. Sleep well, and sweet dreams.'

Maggie stared after her, the woman's mocking laughter still echoing in her ears. She swallowed anxiously, her mouth dry as she pondered the hag's words. 'Tomorrow will change your mind'. Why? What was going to happen tomorrow?

Chapter Fourteen

When Maggie woke there was a figure looming over her. Still somewhat dazed with sleep her first terrified thought was that her stepfather had returned, and with a muffled cry of fear she lashed out at it.

'Wassup with you?' demanded an aggrieved voice. 'Silly little mare! Yer almost had me over.' Blinking, Maggie discovered that the threatening figure was nothing more frightening than old Gladys, clutching a tray. Her belly rumbled at the smell of food, the bread and sausage from the night before nothing more than a distant memory.

'Sorry,' she mumbled, sitting up and wiping the sleep from her eyes.

'I should think so, too,' sniffed Gladys, unwilling to give up her position of moral superiority. 'Traipsing up all them stairs with yer breakfast and that's all the thanks I get. And me with me bad leg and all,' she added self-pityingly.

'Thank you,' said Maggie. 'It was very kind of you to think of me, and I hope it hasn't made your leg worse. Is it very sore?'

Mollified by Maggie's concern, Gladys permitted herself a smile. 'Agony,' she announced with relish. 'Been a martyr to it for years.' She shook her head with the expression of long-suffering, bravely borne. 'Nothing they can do about it, though,' she sighed, 'so I just gotta live with it.'

'You're very brave,' said Maggie, with a sympathetic smile.

'I don't complain,' Gladys lied smugly. 'What's the point? You just gotta get on with it, don't yer? Here,' she added, plonking the tray down on Maggie's knees. 'Get that down yer, gel.'

Maggie lifted the covers to reveal a plateful of eggs, bacon and the ubiquitous sausages, all swimming in stale grease.

'Good honest English grub, that is,' said Gladys. 'Some of the gentlemen that stays over likes that foreign muck.' She wrinkled her nose in distaste. 'You know, rice and fish and boiled eggs all mixed together like a dog's dinner. Rubbish! Give me a good fry-up every time.'

She watched with approval as Maggie bolted it down ravenously. There was a steaming mug of tea on the tray and Maggie picked it up and sniffed it surreptitiously. Who knew what might have been added to it? She'd heard about white slavers who drugged girls into submission. Then she smiled ruefully at her fears; it was a bit late to start worrying now. She was locked up in a brothel already. Why should they bother?

Anyway, the tea smelt of nothing worse than slightly sour milk, so she drank it thirstily, wincing slightly at the taste. Gladys must have put half a dozen spoonfuls of sugar into it, at least.

'That was delicious,' she lied, pushing the tray away. 'Thank you.'

'That's a good girl,' beamed Gladys, picking it up. She leered at Maggie and gave her a knowing wink. 'Gotta keep yer strength up for today, doncha?' she chuckled.

Maggie stared at her in horror. For a few brief, blessèd

moments she'd forgotten all about Mrs Wilkes' words the previous night, but now they came back to her in a rush. The greasy food suddenly felt like a lead weight in her belly and she could feel her gorge rise. Only the thought of Gladys' reaction if she suddenly spewed her 'good, honest English grub' all over the clean counterpane helped her control the sickness rising in her throat.

'What do you mean?' she asked.

Gladys winked again. 'You'll soon find out,' she grinned, but the sight of Maggie's white face clearly made her regret her cruel teasing. 'Don't worry, gel. Relax and enjoy it,' she advised. 'You'll get over it soon enough. Look at me. Never done me any harm, did it?' Limping exaggeratedly, she shuffled out of the room in her down-at-heel carpet slippers, locking the door carefully behind her.

Maggie stared after her with consternation as it suddenly dawned on her that Gladys wasn't just an ordinary servant. At some point in the past she must have been employed in a different capacity in this house and, impossible as it might seem now, she must have been young and pretty once too. Maggie tried to imagine the fat old woman as one of the scantily clad 'young ladies' – and failed miserably.

She shuddered. Would that be her in twenty years' time? A drunken clapped-out old trull, kept on out of charity – if she was lucky – to dance attendance on the girls who had taken her place? A never-ending cycle of demand and supply?

Maggie's lips set. She'd rather sleep in the street and pick food from the gutter than stay here. There had to be some way out. There had to be!

Swinging her legs out of bed she padded round, naked, investigating the room. In daylight it was equally uncompromising. Apart from the chamber pot she'd almost clouted Millie with, a tiny sliver of soap and a basin and ewer filled with cold water, there was nothing she could use as a weapon. The window was so small there was no way she could wriggle through – and even if there were, it was barred. Through the dusty panes she could see an endless vista of chimneys and rooftops and, in the distance, the winding silver ribbon of the Thames. The whole of London laid spread out before her – just out of reach.

Maddened by frustration she paced backwards and forwards, and then sighed. This was getting her nowhere. Her only chance was to make a break for freedom the next time the door was opened. In the meantime, she might as well get washed and dressed. She smiled ruefully; even if she were successful she'd hardly get far running through the streets naked, now would she?

Pouring the water into the basin, she washed herself as best she could. The cold brought a rosy glow to her skin and she shivered, her nipples rising and hardening as the icy water trickled down her breasts and dripped from their tips. Despite the discomfort, she scrubbed herself scrupulously. Lathering her hands she soaped the warm secret place between her thighs as if she could remove all trace of her stepfather.

She shivered again, this time with pleasure, as her fingers parted the soft lips of her sex and grazed the tight pink bud of her clitoris. She stroked it gently, feeling herself moisten as a delicious sensation of heat built in the base of her belly – then she stopped herself. Was she mad? This was no time to be pleasuring herself.

Someone could walk in at any time. She scooped up a double handful of cold water and splashed her face to bring herself back to her sense.

Drying herself on the threadbare towel, she picked up the torn remains of her dress and slipped it on over her damp body, then groaned in dismay; it was worse than being naked. Even if she held it at the neck, she couldn't cover her breasts. Their pert nipples peeped provocatively from the tatters of red satin, inviting attention.

Then an idea struck her. It was a matter of moments to slip the dress off and put it on again – back to front. She smiled as her confidence returned. Not only was she decently covered, but also the tight material compressed her breasts till she was as flat chested as a boy. Now, provided she kept her back turned to the wall, she looked as prim and proper as any governess. Perhaps Mrs Wilkes would reconsider her bargain after all?

But as the day wore on Maggie's newfound self-confidence wore off. Hour after hour dragged past and no one came near. She strained her ears for the sound of footsteps on the stairs, but there was complete and utter silence. It was like being shut up in a tomb.

With nothing to do but stare out of the window at the rooftops or at the four blank walls of the room, her mind ran riot, imagining the possible horrors that lay in store for her. She paced restlessly, unable to sit or lie for more than two minutes at a time before fear goaded her to her feet again, and it struck her that this was how a prisoner in the condemned cell must feel, as he waited to be dragged to the gallows. It was not a comforting thought.

So it was almost a relief when she finally heard a

heavy tread on the attic stairs. At least the dreadful waiting was finally over. And nothing could possibly be as bad as her fevered imaginings – could it? She stood, defiantly facing the door, waiting for Mrs Wilkes to make her appearance.

And she didn't have to wait long. The sound of her asthmatic wheezing outside was followed by that of the key turning in the lock. The door swung open and Maggie gasped.

Mrs Wilkes was not alone.

Behind her stood the menacing figure of the huge black manservant who had carried her, kicking and screaming, to her prison. In the clear light of day he was even more frightening. He must have been well over six feet tall and the material of his clothes strained to contain the muscles beneath. His hands were so large they looked as if they could encompass her waist without even trying.

Close behind him stood a man she had never seen in her life before, and given the choice, would never have wanted to. He was low browed and brutish, with a nose that had been broken and badly set more than once. A scar that looked like a souvenir from some pub brawl twisted his lips into a permanent scowl. Dark greasy hair fell across his forehead and the narrow eyes beneath regarded her with avid anticipation.

Her heart sank as all hopes of making a run for freedom died. She might as well try and run through a brick wall. Trying to ignore the two men, she got to her feet, straightened her shoulders and stared at Mrs Wilkes, her calm demeanour masking her wildly beating heart.

'What do you want now?' she asked coolly. 'I told you last night I was leaving.'

'I think not, my dear,' said Mrs Wilkes. 'As to what I

157

want, that's quite simple. I want an answer to the little business proposition I put to you last night.' She smiled. 'I do hope you've had time to reconsider your hasty words.'

Maggie laughed harshly. '"Business proposition"? That's the first time I've heard it called that!' She spat on the floor at the woman's feet. 'I'd rather go to hell than turn strumpet to fill your pockets!'

Mrs Wilkes shook her head in regret. 'I'm sorry to hear you say that, my dear,' she said. 'Had you been willing, our little arrangement could have been settled quite amicably to our mutual benefit.' Her face hardened. 'Now I'm afraid you leave me no option.'

'What do you mean?' Maggie quavered.

Mrs Wilkes tutted in exasperation. 'Come, come, my dear, you're a sensible girl. Think about it. If a horse won't go, it must be driven. With a touch of the whip, if necessary.' An insincere smile flickered across her lips. 'Now, are you quite sure you won't reconsider your decision?'

'Never!' Maggie cried passionately.

'Very well, my dear, on your own head be it,' said Mrs Wilkes in resignation. 'You can't say you weren't warned.'

Maggie stared into the woman's cold grey eyes and her stomach lurched. Somewhere in their depths, like an ancient pike at the bottom of a muddy pool, lurked a glint of evil pleasure. She was enjoying all this. Far from being disappointed at Maggie's defiance, she was delighted! If Maggie had agreed to her proposition, she would have been deprived of her wicked game.

As if in response to Maggie's thought, Mrs Wilkes' smiled widened. She took her hands from beneath her black silk apron and Maggie gasped. In one of them the woman held what looked like a short shuttledore bat, padded with soft black leather. She clicked the fingers of the other and the black servant stepped forward. 'Hold her down,' she ordered.

Shaking her head, Maggie edged away until her back touched the wall. It was a waste of time. In two strides he crossed the tiny room. She lashed out frantically, but he caught her wrists in one huge hand, flung her facedown across the bed and flipped her skirts up over her head. Kicking and squealing she struggled to rise, but he held her down as easily as if she'd been a naughty child.

Mrs Wilkes looked down at the flailing legs and the soft white curves of the girl's bottom and nodded in satisfaction. Her clients would pay dearly for the privilege of savaging that tender flesh – but first the silly chit must be made to realise the futility of resistance. She rolled up the sleeves of her gown and raised her arm.

Maggie tensed her buttocks as she heard the sound of the bat whistling through the air – then gave a muffled gasp as it connected with her bottom. The tender flesh went white beneath the force of the blow, then turned pink as the blood rushed back. She writhed as she attempted to escape the pain, biting her lip to remain silent. She wouldn't give the despicable woman the satisfaction of hearing her scream. She wouldn't! Mrs Wilkes raised her arm again.

At the second blow all Maggie's fine resolutions deserted her. The globes of her bottom quivered and jumped as the bat smacked down. Coming so close on flesh already throbbing like an aching tooth, the pain was indescribable. She shrieked aloud in agony.

Beneath the third and fourth blows she lost track of time and place. Nothing existed but the pain that filled her world. Her backside was no longer pink; it was a fiery red – and felt as if it had been scalded, the muscles tensed beneath the skin. Finally it was over and she huddled in a whimpering heap upon the bed.

'Well,' panted Mrs Wilkes, 'have you changed your mind yet?'

Maggie pulled herself upright with difficulty and glared at her from tear-filled eyes. 'Never,' she whispered again, her voice hoarse from shrieking. Despite the pain, her lip curled in a triumphant smile. 'If that's all you can do, you're wasting your time.'

Mrs Wilkes smiled in amusement. 'All?' she said. 'Why, my dear, I haven't even begun.' She clicked her fingers again. 'I do believe Miss Carter needs a little more instruction. Tie her to the bed.'

Eagerly the two men obeyed. Hauling Maggie to her feet they ripped the remaining tatters of her dress from her quivering body. As one held her, the other tore a strip from the skirt and twisted it into a makeshift rope. As Maggie struggled they forced her back down onto the bed, bound one wrist, looped the material through the iron bedstead and bound the other. She tried to break free, but she might as well have been manacled in iron for all the good it did. Naked and exposed, she lay there looking up at them in horror.

Smiling, Mrs Wilkes seated herself on the chair beside the bed and nodded to the black manservant. 'Jebediah, if you would be so good as to introduce Miss Carter to her new duties, please?' He grinned back, revealing startlingly white teeth against his black skin.

Horrified comprehension dawned on Maggie as he began to undress. The wicked old woman was going to sit there and watch while this monster ravished her! 'No! Please, no!' she begged, gazing wide-eyed at the sadistic old witch.

'There's still time to stop, my dear,' smiled Mrs Wilkes. 'Have you changed your mind?' Maggie gritted her teeth and shook her head. 'In that case Jebediah, carry on, if you please.'

He was naked now and Maggie looked in fearful fascination at him, unable to drag her eyes away from his body. He was terrifyingly beautiful, like a huge statue, carved from the wood of some dark, exotic tree. Her eyes took in the broad, gleaming chest, tapering down to the narrow waist. As her glance fell lower she gasped in trepidation; even without being aroused, he was huge. His cock lay against the bulge of his balls like a sleeping snake.

As she watched with dread it began to twitch and swell, rising massively from the patch of dark curly hair, until it jutted from the base of his belly like a thick black club. She whimpered as he loomed over her, his prick bobbing as he moved.

He climbed onto the tiny bed and knelt beside her, his hands reaching for her breasts. He fondled the soft mounds – then she gasped as he pinched her nipples until they rose between his exploring fingers. He grunted with satisfaction, then leaned over and took first one, then the other between his lips, flicking his tongue across their tender tips and grazing then with his teeth. As he bent over her she could feel the thick rod of his cock pressing against her belly.

Maggie closed her eyes and whispered a soft

protestation. The scorching pain radiating from her beaten bottom still pulsed through her, but now it was being joined by a different kind of heat. She felt herself moisten and moaned in complaint, struggling to break free – but her helpless writhings served only to inflame him more.

He swung himself up and straddled her shoulders, his swollen cock only inches from her flushed and spellbound face. She tossed her head from side to side, trying to escape, but he seized her hair and held her in place as he pushed the bulbous tip against her soft wet lips. They slowly parted and he groaned as he slid into the warm moistness of her mouth. She gagged, hardly able to breathe as he moved his hips and sank even deeper, his thick shaft almost choking her.

Just when Maggie thought she would suffocate, the weight shifted from her breasts and he withdrew. She drew in a ragged breath, gasping with relief – all too soon! Instead, he dug his fingers into the tender flesh of her thighs, pulling them roughly apart to reveal the pink, glistening cleft between. She whimpered again as he thrust first one, then two fingers inside her, slipping them in and out faster and faster. She sighed, but this time with reluctant pleasure.

When he withdrew them they were wet and gleaming. Grinning down at her he oiled his cock with her juices, then knelt between her legs and hauled them up onto his shoulders. Unable to drag her eyes away, Maggie watched as he parted the lips of her vulva and rubbed the turgid purplish-black head of his prick slowly against the swollen opening, each movement a torment.

Just when she thought she could bear no more, he pushed forward and she shrieked as there was a moment of resistance before the full length of his massive organ slid slowly inside her. Gripping her hips he began to move, and she gazed down between her breasts in fascinated lust as it pumped, black and glistening, in and out of her wet cunt – each thrust taking her nearer her own moment of exquisite release, and when he finally exploded inside her she threw back her head and screamed her pleasure like a cat in heat.

A cruel chuckle brought her back to reality. 'The blacker the berry, the sweeter the juice, eh, my dear?'

Maggie shrivelled inside with shame. She had forgotten the old woman sitting there watching. She had forgotten everything but the huge black cock pleasuring her. Tears of humiliation leaked out from between her closed lids. How could she have behaved like that?

'Now,' Mrs Wilkes went on briskly. 'I'm sure we can forget all about this little incident and get on with things. I take it we are agreed?'

Biting back more tears, Maggie shook her head.

'My, what a stubborn girl you are,' Mrs Wilkes said regretfully. 'I see that we shall have to continue the lesson until we are. Perhaps Arthur can school you better.' She nodded to the other man, who gave her a lecherous wink.

Maggie's eyes widened in shock as she realised that her ordeal was not yet over. As she watched helplessly, he stripped to reveal a barrel chest, thick thighs and an incipient paunch, beneath which poked a rigid prick, as stubby and thickset as the rest of him.

'Arthur used to be a bare-knuckle fighter, you know,' Mrs Wilkes said conversationally, and then gave a ladylike titter. 'And I'm afraid his tastes are still a trifle vulgar.'

Maggie stared at the other woman. What on earth did she mean? She was soon to find out.

Grinning wolfishly, he leaned over and groped her breasts, squeezing and mauling her already tender nipples so roughly that she groaned. His hands then went lower and for a few minutes he entertained himself plundering her swollen vulva, still wet and sticky from Jebediah's seed. Maggie was just resigning herself to being ravished again when he suddenly flipped her over onto her belly as easily as a stranded fish. The movement made the cloth that held her wrists tighten further, trapping her even more. She twisted her neck to crane fearfully over her shoulder. What was he going to do?

In answer he wrenched the pillow from beneath her head, folded it in half and thrust it beneath her stomach so that her bottom lifted beautifully into the musky air. But instead of plunging into her vulnerable wet sex, he gripped the rosy cheeks and pulled them apart to reveal the puckered pink O of her anus.

'Nooooo!' she wailed, stiffening in horror as it dawned on her what he was about to do. Then her wail became a shriek as he shoved his fingers roughly inside her again, coating them with her own juices, before forcing one into her arse. She squirmed as it slid slowly inside her, and the movement rubbed her breasts against the rough cotton of the sheets, exacerbating the tenderness of her swollen nipples. She groaned again, pain and pleasure mingling in exquisite torment as the probing finger awoke a host of new sensations in her weary body.

Satisfied, he withdrew it and rubbed his cock till it stood out like a rod of iron, its throbbing purple head glistening wetly. A bead of moisture leaked, showing his readiness. She whimpered again as he pushed against her and she felt her anus opening beneath the insistent pressure, then she sobbed as it gave and the whole length of his thick, stiff prick slid into her bottom.

It was as if a red-hot poker was impaling her. She writhed helplessly, her squirming serving only to excite him further. She mumbled incoherently as he began to pump his hips, grinding her breasts against the sheets, his balls slapping against her wet labia with every shunt. One hand slid beneath her to toy with her clitoris as he rutted against her, his humid groin grinding against her spanked buttocks, and she whined as a delicious heat filled her belly.

Forgetting herself once again, Maggie instinctively began to push back, meeting each thrust with one of her own as he heaved in and out of her, forcing him even deeper. He gave one final, convulsive lunge and she felt his cock jerk and spasm as his boiling seed erupted, and she moaned helplessly as a second orgasm shook her sweating body, then slumped weeping as he pulled away...

Maggie buried her head in shame. Her treacherous body had betrayed her, and the horrible old woman had triumphed again.

And she knew it too.

'I take it you have come to your senses,' she said smugly. 'Or do we have to repeat this lesson until you do?' She smiled. 'I'm sure Arthur and Jebediah would be delighted to continue your instruction – and there are avenues we haven't even begun to explore yet.'

Maggie shuddered. Lifting her tearstained face she stared at the gloating woman. 'You win,' she said dully.

'Excellent, my dear,' she smiled. 'I knew you'd see things my way eventually. What a pity we had to go through all this nonsense first.' She waved a hand at the two men. 'Off you go, boys. I shan't be needing you again – for the moment, anyway.'

'Now,' she went on briskly, leaning over to undo Maggie's bonds. 'We'll just untie these silly knots and you can get yourself tidy again. I'll send someone with fresh clothes and something to eat. We don't want you fading away now, do we? Our gentlemen like a nice shapely figure.' She bustled out, leaving Maggie staring after her. On the threshold she paused and smiled again. 'I'm sure you'll make an excellent strumpet, my dear.' She flung her parting barb, 'You seem to take a real pleasure in your work.'

The door banged shut behind her and Maggie sat up rubbing her wrists where the bonds had chafed her skin. As the full horror of her future overwhelmed her she bowed her head and began to sob once more. If she ever saw Jeremy again, he would want nothing to do with her.

Not now she was a whore.

Chapter Fifteen

Maggie lay for what seemed like hours, staring blankly at the ceiling as the light slowly dimmed and day turned into evening. Sick at heart she did not even feel the lack of food or drink, and when the key turned in the lock again she barely had the strength to rouse herself. What could they do to her that had not already been done?

'Come on, lazybones,' said Millie, putting down the bundle of clothes she was carrying and looking down at her friend, hands on hips. 'You can't lie there, like a lady. Mrs Wilkes wants you downstairs.'

A wave of apprehension washed Maggie's lethargy away. 'She... she doesn't want me to start...' she could barely bring herself to say it '...work... already?' she asked fearfully.

Millie shook her head. 'Keep your hair on,' she grinned. 'This ain't a tuppenny knocking shop. This is a high-class house. Take a look at yourself; you ain't fit to be seen in polite company just yet.'

Maggie examined her body for the first time since... it... had happened. She was a mess, and her wrists were still marked where she'd been bound and where rough hands had seized her.

'Can't have you attending the gentlemen looking like you'd been pulled through a hedge backwards,' Millie went on. 'They likes their young ladies lily-white and as pure as the driven snow.' Her lips twisted in a bitter smile. 'Any marks on yer, they likes to put there themselves.'

She sat down beside Maggie and patted her hand sympathetically. 'Bad, was it?' Maggie nodded and bit her lip. She'd managed to bear up so far, but Millie's unexpected kindness brought the tears to her eyes. 'Never mind, love, it's over now,' Millie went on. 'You're like me. One of life's survivors.' Her eyes took on a faraway look. 'Not like some. I remember one girl,' she said softly. 'Pretty little thing. Vicar's daughter, or summat. Couldn't take it.' She shivered. 'Came up here afterwards and found her dangling, dead as a doornail. Tore the sheets into strips, tied them together and topped herself, poor gel.'

She shook the memory away. 'Cheerful bloody cow, ain't I?' she said, with forced brightness. 'But you and me ain't like that. We'll get through it and have the last laugh, just you see if we don't.' She picked up the clothes and dumped them on the bed. 'Now, shake a leg and get this lot on. Once you're dressed we'll go down and you can meet the other girls.'

Maggie swung her legs stiffly over the side of the bed, every bone in her body aching. Reluctantly she picked up the clothes, but they were not what she expected. Instead of the gaudy silks and satins Millie wore, there was a pair of plain cotton pantaloons, a threadbare chemise, and a voluminous brown dress at least two sizes too big. She held it up, looked at Millie and raised a quizzical eyebrow. 'The gentlemen ain't going to see you, so it don't matter what you look like,' Millie explained, and then chuckled. 'You could stick the coal-scuttle on your head for all old Ma Wilkes'd care – so long as it don't cost her anything.' She nudged

Maggie with an impatient elbow. 'Come on, girl, get a bleedin' move on. If you don't hurry up the girls 'll have started working.'

Obediently Maggie put on the shabby underwear, slipped the brown dress down over her shoulders, and was promptly drowned by it. There was a brief moment of stunned disbelief as the girls looked at one another, then they both burst into hysterical giggles.

'Christ, you look a proper fright!' crowed Millie, wiping tears of mirth from her eyes. 'Talk about bleedin' Aunt Sally! That ain't a dress, it's a bloomin' marquee! Last time I seen something like that was the living skeleton at the Whitsunday fair.'

Maggie minced round the room with her nose in the air, holding up the skirts to stop herself tripping over them.

'Stoppit! I'm gonna wet me drawers!' wheezed Millie. 'Or I would if I was wearing any!' She grabbed Maggie's hand and dragged her towards the door. 'Come on downstairs; the girls have gotta see this.'

Stumbling and giggling, Maggie followed her down the bare wooden staircase and into the main house. The gaslights were still off and without their mellow glow to soften it, it looked harsh and garish. It no longer seemed opulent – merely vulgar and overdone, as if someone had decorated it with money but no taste. Even the erotic oil paintings looked as if they'd been churned out by some threadbare, back street hack – which they probably had.

Maggie had no time to take in even half of it before they arrived in front of a door at the far end of the house. Millie flung it open and pushed her through into a large room. Maggie stopped on the threshold, stared round in bewilderment, and then blushed furiously.

There were girls of all shapes and sizes in various stages of undress – an abundance of ripe, casually displayed flesh. She watched in amazement as one girl rouged her cheeks while another rouged her nipples until they stood out scarlet against the white globes of her breasts.

She turned her eyes hastily away, only to have them fall on another girl, who was sitting, legs parted wide as a friend crouched in front of her, carefully shaving her pudenda. Once done, she patted it dry, and then planted a smacking kiss on the rosy nether lips, her tongue darting between them to flick at the soft pinkness within. Maggie gasped, but no one – apart from her – turned a hair.

'Ta-raaa!' bellowed Millie, and the babble of voices suddenly stopped as all eyes turned towards them. Maggie blushed again, this time with a mixture of shyness and self-consciousness, but she forced herself to advance royally into the room, concluding her performance with a deep curtsey, almost disappearing into the puddle of material in the process.

And the chorus of laughter was worth it. Within seconds she was surrounded by the girls, her head spinning as Millie tried to introduce her to them all at once. Their names and histories went in one ear and out the other just as fast. Rosie, Ethel, Grace, Florence…

It all became a blur.

Was Rosie the governess who'd been seduced by her young charge's father? Florence the one who'd been sold into the house at the age of twelve by her gin-sodden mother? Grace the one who'd marched up to the door and asked to be employed when she decided she'd rather be paid than continue to be abused by her father and brothers in return for nothing but a drunken beating? She didn't know.

But what she did know was that these weren't monsters of lust and depravity. They were ordinary girls like her, forced into surviving the only way they knew how – by selling the only thing they had left. Their body. How dare society condemn them? And what real difference was there between them and the respectable housewife who spread her legs for an overbearing husband in exchange for the food on her table and the roof over her head?

Maggie's wave of indignation lasted until the door opened and Mrs Wilkes stalked in.

'What's going on here?' the woman demanded coldly. 'Aren't you girls ready yet? The gentlemen will be arriving soon.' With frightened glances the girls scurried back to finish their preparations for the evening's entertainment. Dresses were hurriedly tugged down over smooth, powdered shoulders; stockings and garters adjusted; lips hastily rouged. All in total silence in case a word should bring Mrs Wilkes' wrath down on them. Finally they filed out in a rustle of silks and satins, leaving Maggie and Millie alone with their employer. Maggie's stomach quivered with nerves.

'Lord Anston has booked an appointment with you at ten,' she informed Millie briskly. 'Until then, take Maggie to the kitchen for something to eat, and afterwards you may show her around.'

'Yes, Mrs Wilkes,' Millie said meekly – but Maggie noted how her lips trembled and the colour had drained from her cheeks at the mention of her client's name.

'Who is this Lord Anston?' she asked as they made their way downstairs to the kitchen.

'You don't want to know,' Millie said bitterly. 'God 'elp yer if he takes a fancy to yer.' She forced a smile. 'Never mind, a bottle of brandy under me belt and I won't feel a thing. Thank God.'

And she was as good as her word. While Maggie ate the plateful of stringy meat and half-cooked potatoes Gladys plonked in front of her, Millie worked her way determinedly through glass after glass of rot-gut. By the time Maggie finished Millie's eyes had already taken on a glazed look and she was beginning to slur some of her words.

'Time for the grand tour,' she giggled tipsily. 'Show yer the ropes. Let yer shee what yer let yershelf in for.'

Finger to her lips, she tiptoed upstairs and along the corridors with the exaggerated care of the half-drunk. Swaying gently, she stopped in front of a panel in the deserted hall. Maggie looked at her in bewilderment. What on earth was she playing at?

'Sssshh!' she giggled, then, brow furrowed with concentration, she fumbled along the side of the panel until there was a quiet 'click' and it yawned silently open. Maggie gasped. It wasn't a panel at all. It was a small door, almost invisible because it had been carefully papered to match the wall. She stared apprehensively into the gaping darkness.

'Don' jush stand there gawping like a booby,' Millie muttered crossly. 'You want to give the game away?' She pushed Maggie inside, followed her and closed the door behind them. It was pitch black and there was barely enough room for both of them. They were crushed against each other and Maggie could feel the full length of the other girl's body against her own, smell the mingled odours of sweat and perfume and drink that came off her with every movement. She began to pant in terror as the darkness threatened to crush her. It was like being buried alive. But Millie's voice brought her back to reality. 'Gerroff!' she hissed, pinching Maggie to stop her squirming. 'He'll hear us.'

Maggie froze, even more frightened of the prospect of discovery. Who would hear them? And what would 'he' do if he did?

There was more drunken fumbling, the sound of something sliding back, and then twin rays of dim light split the darkness. Maggie blinked as her eyes adjusted, and her bewilderment increased. They appeared to be inside a small cupboard for some reason. What the hell was going on?

'Go on then,' urged Millie, pointing towards the two holes the light was coming through. 'Take a gander.'

Obediently Maggie stood on tiptoe, peered through – and then rocked back on her heels in shock. 'Th-that's disgusting,' she gasped under her breath.

Millie shrugged. 'Some of the gentlemen prefers to watch and toss themselves off,' she informed Maggie cheerfully, and then winked. 'Or have one of us girls give them a hand – if yer know what I mean?' She giggled. 'Bet yer the gentleman inside wouldn't be too 'appy if he knew he was performing for an audience. That'd soon put the kybosh on his capers. Mind you,' she went on knowledgeably, 'there's them as pays good money for that as well. Gives them an extra thrill to know somebody's watching.'

'But... but... how is it done?' gasped Maggie.

'Easy,' grinned Millie. 'Portrait on the wall with the eyes painted on a bit of board. Slide it back and Bob's yer uncle – it's a penny for the peepshow!' She snorted.

'Only old Ma Wilkes charges a damned sight more than a penny for a peep at this show.' Her explanation was suddenly cut short by a muffled shriek. Fascinated despite herself, Maggie stood on tiptoe and peeked through the holes again.

There was no way of knowing which girl it was, because she was bent over the ottoman with her skirts over her head. All that could be seen were the plump white curves of her bottom, offered up to the attentions of her master.

He was standing over her naked, holding a thin cane, and as Maggie watched in horror he raised it and brought it down viciously. It whistled as it cut through the air, then thwacked against the pale flesh, leaving a thin red line in its wake. There was another squeal from the helpless girl, and his excitement increased visibly, until his cock stood out from beneath his hairy belly like an iron bar.

Grinning avidly, he trailed the cane slowly the full length of the girl's shuddering body before raising his arm and applying it with fresh vigour. When the quivering bottom was a mass of red weals he flung himself on his victim, yanked her legs apart and thrust between them, his scrawny arse jerking as he humped her like a randy dog. Maggie closed her eyes in sympathy and horror.

'Seen enough?' asked Millie. Maggie nodded mutely and the other girl slid the board back across, hiding the scene of the other girl's humiliation. Millie clicked the door panel open and hurried her out into the hall again. 'Come on then,' she said, tugging her arm impatiently. 'I got the rest of them to show you yet.'

Maggie stared at her. 'Th-there are more?' she gasped.

'Course there's more,' Millie said scornfully. 'Most of the rooms has these little oobly-etts tucked on 'em. That's French for "hidey-holes",' she informed Maggie loftily. 'Not just French ticklers here, yer know. Told yer this was a classy house.'

Throughout this little lesson in language, she continued to haul Maggie along until they were standing in front of an identical panel. This time it didn't come as quite such a shock when it was swung open and Maggie was pushed inside.

But what did come as a shock was the scene that confronted her when she peered through the eyeholes this time.

For a start the room was like nothing she had ever seen in her life before. The walls were bare of ornament, painted to look like slabs of rock and draped here and there with drifts of black silk, that hung like dirty cobwebs – but what was most horrifying was the array of strange implements ranged against them. A rack of whips and paddles stood against one. Chains and manacles dangled from another, as if awaiting their next victim. Maggie gasped at the blasphemy; there was even a cross!

But strangest of all was the scene that was being played out before her eyes. The ingredients were the same: the same half-naked bodies; the same squeals of distress; the same pain and humiliation – but this time the roles were reversed.

In the centre of the room stood a tall girl, her fair hair pulled back tightly into a long plait, exaggerating her high cheekbones and the harsh planes of her face. She seemed to radiate power and cruelty like some pagan goddess or warrior queen – an impression heightened by her bizarre costume.

She wore nothing but gleaming black leather that hugged her body like a second skin. Her heavy breasts bulged from the complicated harness of straps that bound her chest. More straps twisted round her narrow waist and curled down between her thighs, revealing and concealing the lips of her sex as she moved. Her long muscular legs were cross-gartered to the knee, and her arms and hands were covered in long leather gloves that reached almost to the shoulder. From one hand drooped a wicked looking cat o' nine tails.

All her attention was focussed on her victim. His wrists were tied to a chain attached to the ceiling, pulling his arms above his head and forcing him to balance on his toes or have his shoulders dislocated. He was blindfolded, and a gag tied so tightly that it cut into his cheeks muffled his cries. His scrawny body was already covered in marks from the whip, and as Maggie watched, the girl lifted her arm and lazily flicked it at him again. He whimpered as each lash curled round his cringing form like a tongue of flame, leaving another weal behind.

But if the rest of his body was trying to cringe away, his John Thomas had a mind of its own. It was huge! Purple-red and grossly engorged, a tear of pleasure weeping from its bulbous tip, it seemed to grow bigger with every delicious bolt of pain.

As Maggie watched in fascinated disgust, the girl strode across to the rack of implements, laid down her whip and picked up something else. She frowned in bewilderment. What on earth was it? It looked like one of those children's puzzles, where you had to untangle the length of wood from the string. Then her jaw dropped as the girl shook it out and began to fasten it on. She could hardly believe her eyes; it… it was an enormous black artificial…

The dildo firmly strapped in place, the girl dipped her fingers in a jar of oil and greased it. Approaching her client from the rear, she pulled his buttocks apart, inserted the tip in his anus, slid it home and began to thrust. Maggie watched, spellbound, as it rammed in and out of his arse. Even oiled it must have been agonising.

As if in answer, every muscle in his body clenched. Arching his back like a bow he strained and shuddered, his cock jerking. A stream of milky-white spunk jetted across the room and he sagged against his bonds, his dribbling John Thomas shrinking rapidly.

Maggie pulled away from the peephole and gazed at Millie in bewilderment. 'I don't understand,' she complained. 'Why on earth would anybody want that done to them?'

'And pay for it too, remember,' Millie reminded her. 'There's one or two of our gentlemen what likes to get a bit of pain themselves instead of handing it out.' She sniffed. 'Comes from going to them posh schools if you ask me. All them masters with their canes. They gets a taste for it when they're nippers. That's why the Frenchies call it the "veece onglay".'

She chuckled. 'And when it comes to giving a good hiding, you can't beat our Ingrid. Her dad was a Swedish sailor – so her mum says – and she's like one of them bleedin' Vikings. Nothing she likes better than laying into some toff's fat arse. Lucky cow,' she added wistfully. 'Wouldn't mind being on that end of the business for a change.' She giggled, mood changing with the mercurial rapidity of the drunk. '"That end" … "arse"

... get it?' she asked, digging Maggie in the ribs with a sharp elbow as she ushered her out of the claustrophobic little cupboard. 'That's a good 'un, though I do say so meself.'

The 'tour' continued from room to room until Maggie was dizzy with what she'd seen. Each set of peepholes seemed to give another glimpse into the depravity of mankind. It was like gazing into the anterooms of hell. Finally – and mercifully – it was over and Millie led her back to the room where it had all begun.

'Time's getting on,' Millie said with a shiver. 'Better get meself ready for his lordship.' She tugged the bell-pull and after a few minutes Gladys shuffled in. 'Fetch us another bottle, love,' she said, and once it had arrived she helped herself to a brimming glass, seated herself in front of the mirror and began to repair her maquillage. Maggie watched fascinated as she applied more powder and rouge. 'There,' she said finally, 'that'll 'ave to do.' Her lips quivered. 'I'll need a damn sight more than that by the time that bastard's finished with me.'

The words were barely out of her mouth when Mrs Wilkes glided silently in and stood waiting.

'All right, all right, I'm coming,' Millie said, and drained her glass. 'Here's to a short life and a merry one.' Swaying slightly she exited, head in the air, leaving Maggie alone with Mrs Wilkes.

'Rose is almost finished with her gentleman,' the woman informed Maggie. 'She'll show you to your room. You may settle in before you begin to earn your keep.'

For the next few days Maggie was in a kind of limbo, slipping into the strange nocturnal rhythms of the house, but not yet a full-blown whore. Even her room reflected this. It wasn't as spartan as her old room in her previous existence as a maid, but nothing like the luxurious bedrooms frequented by the gentlemen on their visits.

There was no sign of Millie for two days after her appointment with Lord Anston, and when she did reappear she was bruised, limping and, despite Maggie's anxious questions, refused to say why. She too joined Maggie in limbo as she recovered from her ordeal.

If the threat of beginning to 'earn her keep' hadn't been hanging over Maggie, she might actually have enjoyed this strange period. Ironically, it was rather like being in an exclusive girls' boarding school. They were joined by other girls who were entertaining their 'monthly visitor', and spent the time laughing, chatting, reading or playing board games.

Maggie wasn't allowed out – in case she did a runner, Millie informed her – but she could listen to the girls who were and admire their purchases when they returned. If she tried hard enough, she could almost forget why she was there.

But one afternoon the pleasant idyll was shattered by the appearance of Mrs Wilkes. Silence fell as she bustled into the common room, holding a pile of cards. 'The invitations are back from the printer's,' she announced, passing one round for approval. When it reached Maggie, she stared at it in puzzlement, running her fingers over the embossing on the deckled gilt-edged card. It reminded her of the expensive invitations that used to sit on the mantelpiece at Lady Georgina's, announcing a ball or a wedding – but there the similarity ended. She gasped; Lady Georgina had never held an event like this!

Mrs Emmaline Wilkes cordially invites you to attend the auction of a prime young virgin on Saturday, September 6th, 1894.

Pity washed through her. What a dreadful fate – and Saturday was only two days away. 'That's shameful!' she exclaimed. 'Poor thing… who is she?'

For a moment Mrs Wilkes stared at her as if she was mad, then her hard face broke into a cruel smile. 'Why, my dear,' she laughed. 'How charmingly naïve. Don't you understand yet? It's you.'

Chapter Sixteen

Maggie stared at her in total disbelief. 'What?' she blurted. 'Me? That's impossible. I'm not a… a…'

'A virgin?' smiled Mrs Wilkes. 'Good heavens, child, what difference does that make?' She snorted derisively. 'For all their money and breeding, our gentlemen are as stupid as any other man. Most of them couldn't tell a virgin from the village doxy. Why, I could sell your maidenhead ten times over if the notion took me.'

'But I'm not some green girl,' protested Maggie. 'How do you expect them to believe I'm a virgin? They may be stupid, but they've got eyes in their heads, haven't they?'

Mrs Wilkes looked at her pityingly. 'You've still got a lot to learn, my dear. It's not what's in front of their face that counts – it's what goes on in their head. We don't just peddle flesh here; we sell dreams. Every man who walks through our doors, no matter how old or ugly, is an omnipotent sexual god with the power of life or death.' She raised her eyebrows. 'Why do you think they pay so much for the privilege? Besides,' she added, 'by the time we've finished with you, even your own mother would swear you were as pure as the driven snow.'

And she was as good as her word. For the next two days, Maggie was spoilt and pampered. Her skin was bleached even fairer with lemon juice, patted all over with rose water and smoothed with expensive creams until it was baby soft. Even her hands now looked as if she hadn't done a day's work in her life. One or another of the girls would spend hours brushing her hair and polishing it with a scrap of silk until it cascaded like a silky waterfall down her back, and all this unaccustomed attention would have been thoroughly enjoyable – if Maggie hadn't known why she was getting it. As it was, apprehension of what was to come lay like a heavy weight in her stomach, poisoning everything. She wished she could put Saturday off forever.

But regardless of her wishes it dawned bright and clear, and Maggie was woken by the sound of Gladys puffing and panting as she dragged a hipbath into the room.

'Piece of nonsense, if you ask me,' she grumbled, hauling it into place and giving it a kick for good luck. 'All this running up and down stairs with cans of 'ot water is enough to kill a body.' Her expression became pious. 'And if the good Lord wanted us wet all over, we'd 'ave been born in the sea.' Piety disappeared again as she gave Maggie a lewd wink. 'In my day a man liked a woman to smell like a woman, not a bleedin' chemist's shop.' Her smile became reminiscent. 'I remember one of my chaps as didn't want me to wash for a week afore his visit,' she said, with a gleeful cackle. 'Liked a bit o' fish, 'e did.' Maggie pulled a face at the vulgarity of Gladys' remark, but the old woman was off again.

'Well, this won't buy the baby a new pair of shoes,' she announced cheerfully. 'Can't stand around listening to you chatter all morning. Better start fetching the 'ot water to fill this bleedin' thing up, before 'er ladyship 'as conniptions.' She sniffed again. 'But I ain't breaking me back,' she warned. 'I'll get some of them bone idle young sluts to gimme an 'and. This time of day, they ain't got nothing better to do.'

The bath gradually filled up as the girls traipsed in and out with the water cans, chattering nineteen to the dozen as they did so. Maggie sat silently on the edge of the bed, watching them, her stomach an icy ball of fear. Finally the bath was full and they fluttered off like a flock of brightly plumaged birds leaving only Millie behind.

'Come on,' she coaxed, tugging Maggie's hands. 'Yer can't sit there all day.'

'Oh yes I can,' muttered Maggie, mutinously refusing to budge. 'You just watch me.'

'This ain't going to do any good,' sighed Millie. 'If you don't get into this bath yerself, old Ma Wilkes'll just fetch Jebediah and Arthur to give yer a hand. They'd enjoy every minute of it too, the bastards,' she added bitterly.

At the very thought Maggie leapt off the bed like a scalded cat. Slipping out of the petticoat she'd been sleeping in, she dipped a tentative toe in the hot water. She'd carried God knows how many cans of water for Lady Georgina's bath, but this was the first time she'd actually had one herself. She shivered with pleasure as she lowered herself into it, forgetting her fears for a moment as she revelled in the delicious sensation of the warm, perfumed water against her skin. It was lovely, and a far cry from the spartan experiences of her serving days. She smiled; what was it Emily used to say as they hastily took their sponge baths in the icy water from the ewer? 'Wash up as far as possible, wash down as far as possible – and let possible take care of itself!'

With a sigh of sheer contentment she slid beneath the surface and wiggled her toes. Her breasts peeped out like rosy islands from a sea of bubbles and her hair floated like tendrils of seaweed round her head. She sighed wistfully; if only she could turn into a mermaid and swim far, far away – out of reach of everyone…

'Don't just lie there,' ordered Millie, interrupting her pleasant daydream. 'Start scrubbin'. Ma Wilkes wants you as clean as a new pin, and the dirt ain't going to float away by itself. Here,' she added briskly, 'sit up and I'll do the bits yer can't reach.'

With a sigh Maggie hauled herself into a sitting position and allowed Millie to wash her back, then squawked in outrage as she pushed her forward and ducked her head under the water. 'What was that for?' she spluttered, surfacing again with water dripping down her face and into her eyes.

'Got ter get yer hair washed as well, ain'tcher?' chuckled Millie. 'Now stop being such a big baby and let me get on with it.' Maggie winced as the other girl scrubbed her head with cheerful vigour, poured clean water over her, then started the whole process all over again.

'Ouch!' she complained at a particularly painful point in the proceedings. 'You're supposed to be washing it – not pulling it out by the roots.'

'Nearly finished,' grinned Millie. 'Just got to wring yer out, wrap a towel round yer bonce and that's us done.' She suited her actions to her words and stepped back. 'Finished,' she announced with satisfaction. 'Now you just have a nice lie there and I'll be back in ten minutes.'

Relieved that her ordeal was over, Maggie did exactly as she was told. As the door closed behind Millie she leaned back and closed her eyes, trailing a hand idly through the bubbles.

The water was cooling now and she shivered, the soft peaks of her nipples rising and hardening in the damp air. A tremor of pleasure ran through her and she caressed them gently, her other hand slipping lower to find the secret place at the base of her belly. A tiny moan escaped her as she parted the lips of her vulva and found the hard little bud hidden in the folds of flesh and began to fondle it. Her thighs loosened and parted, and she slid two fingers inside, continuing to stroke her clitoris with her thumb as she began to move them in and out, slowly at first, then faster as the sensations mounted.

Then the door banged open and she snatched her hands guiltily away, her face scarlet. 'Here we go,' announced Millie, carrying a covered tray and laying it on the stand beside the bed. She picked up a towel, unfolded it and held it out. 'Up you get,' she ordered, and looked at Maggie critically. 'About time too, by the looks of it,' she said. 'The heat must be affecting you. You've gone quite red in the face.' Her comment only served to make Maggie blush the more.

Stepping out, she allowed Millie to wrap the towel around her, snuggling into the warm folds, and she was about to go and sit by the fire and comb her wet hair out when Millie's next words stopped her in her tracks.

'Where do you think you're going?' she demanded, and indicated the tray beside the bed. 'We ain't finished yet. Get yerself laid out there and get that towel opened.'

Maggie looked at her in bewilderment. 'What for?'

she asked.

Millie rolled her eyes. 'Use your head, girl. Yer gonna be an untouched maiden, ain't yer?' She fluttered her eyelashes in a grotesque parody. 'A sweet little innocent, trembling on the brink of womanhood. Don't want the sight of yer big hairy muff spoiling the gentlemen's, illusions now do we?'

For a few moments her words meant absolutely nothing, then their meaning filtered through to Maggie's brain. 'You... you mean you're going to shave me?' she squawked, her voice rising.

'As clean as a whistle,' Millie confirmed, grinning. 'By the time I've finished that sweet little fanny of yours will be as smooth as a baby's bum.'

'That's what you think,' Maggie said grimly. 'You're not coming anywhere near me.'

Millie sighed. 'I told you before,' she said patiently. 'There's no point kicking up a fuss. Do you really want Arthur holding you down while Jebediah comes at you with a razor in his hand?' She shuddered. 'It's not something I'd fancy – but you please yerself.' She sniffed. 'It's no skin off my nose.'

Maggie groaned; she was caught between the devil and the deep blue sea. She couldn't win; it was going to happen whatever she did or said, so she might as well give in gracefully. 'Oh, all right then,' she snarled, flouncing onto the bed and flinging off the towel. 'But you'.d better be damned careful with that razor. I want all me bits left intact, thank you very much.'

Millie stared down at her, admiring the plump breasts, the narrow waist and the long slender legs. She was a pretty one, and no mistake. The gentlemen would be falling over themselves to get their hands on her. She shook herself. Better get a move on before Ma Wilkes turned up and demanded what they thought they were playing at.

She pulled the cover off the tray to reveal a shaving brush, a bowl of shaving soap, a basin of hot water – and a glinting cutthroat razor. 'Put yer arms over yer 'ead,' she ordered. 'We'll do yer pits first. Break yer in gently.'

With a martyred sigh, Maggie did as she was told, squirming as Millie plastered the shaving soap beneath her arms. 'Stop wriggling,' snapped Millie. 'D'yer want me to 'ave yer arm off at the shoulder?' She giggled. 'Mind you, it wouldn't make much difference to the gents. There's them as likes a girl with a few bits missing.'

'I can't help it, it tickles,' protested Maggie. 'And what do you mean "a few bits missing"? What are you talking about.'

'We used ter 'ave a girl called "One-legged Doll",' grinned Millie. 'Very popular with some of the gentlemen, she was.' She shook her head philosophically as she deftly wielded the razor. 'Just goes to show, don't it. Yer could 'ave one eye, no teeth an' a face like an old boot – and there'd still be some bloke who'd pay good money ter shag yer. Warms the cockles of yer heart, don't it.'

'What happened to her then?' asked Maggie, interested despite her predicament and the absurdity of the tale.

'She hopped it,' Millie muttered absent-mindedly, then realised what she'd said and her hand flew to her mouth and they looked at each and began to giggle hysterically. 'One leg, 'opped it!' she guffawed. 'Blimey! That's a good 'un! And it just sorter slipped out, too!'

She recovered herself with difficulty and turned back to the task in hand. 'Right, that's yer arms done,' she said briskly. 'Now get them legs spread and let me at yer fanny.'

Reluctantly Maggie parted her thighs, closing her eyes so that she wouldn't have to look at Millie. She drew in her breath as the other girl applied the brush to her private parts and rivulets of warm soapy water trickled down the cleft of her vulva. She was still frustrated from being so rudely interrupted in her bath, and the tantalising brush strokes triggered off the sensations she'd tried so hard to suppress, so she bit her lip to keep back the soft moan that threatened to escape them.

'Don't you dare move now,' warned Millie, picking up the razor again, and Maggie felt the sharp blade gliding over her, icy cold against her feverish skin, and she bit her lip even harder as Millie continued and heat began to spread through her belly, so much so that it was both a relief and a disappointment when Millie stopped. 'There,' she said, her voice seeming to come from a great distance. 'All done. Just a spot of cream now and that's you.'

Maggie's eyes flew open as Millie's warm oily hand massaged the cream into the soft folds of her sex lips. 'What are you doing?' she gasped.

'Me?' asked Millie, in tones of innocence. 'Why, just finishing you off.' She smiled wickedly as she continued to knead the soft flesh. 'Feels nice, don't it?'

Maggie opened her mouth to protest, but emitted a low sigh instead as the busy hand continued to soothe and stroke. Her limbs felt warm and heavy and her eyelids drooped again as Millie parted the lips of her fanny and slipped two fingers inside. Her thumb found the hard nub of Maggie's clitoris and began to tease it gently.

'Like that, do yer?' Millie asked breathlessly, and Maggie's mouth opened in a soft sigh of agreement as Millie bent and replaced her fingers with her lips. She opened Maggie like a ripe fig and began to lap gently at the glistening pink flesh exposed to her attentions, flicking the swollen bud with her tongue. Maggie moaned and writhed as hot lust flooded her loins.

Smiling, Millie stood and slipped off her own shift. Her body was fuller than Maggie's. Her plump breasts sagged slightly under their own weight, the nipples large and dark compared to Maggie's. Her hips were lush and rounded and dark glossy hair gleamed at the juncture of her heavy thighs. She was like the painting of some fertile Roman goddess Maggie had seen once in a book.

With a sigh of pleasure she lay down beside Maggie and reached for her again, fondling her pert bosom, so different from her own, before leaning over, her own heavy breasts dangling, and taking each pink nipple between her lips in turn. Maggie tried to push her away, but her efforts were half-hearted; she had gone too far to stop now.

Millie took Maggie's hand and planted it between her own thighs, and Maggie gasped as she felt the other female's vulva beneath her fingers. Tentatively she slipped them into the hot wetness and began to move them as she would if she was frigging herself, and was rewarded by a moan of delight. Made bolder, she pushed Millie gently back on the pillow and bent her head to sample the other's breasts, sucking and nibbling at the dark swollen nipples, then trailing her mouth down the length of her body. The musky scent of Millie's excitement engulfed her as she plunged her tongue into her sex, lapping eagerly at the hot salty juices.

Her chin still wet, she retraced her path and their lips met, tongues entwining, breasts crushed together as their hands worked between each other's thighs, sensation mounting until they exploded in a mutual climax. Gasping for breath Maggie collapsed on the pillows, her body still alive with the after-effects of their pleasure – as horror at their unnatural passion washed through her like a crimson tide.

Millie looked at her shrewdly, noting the scarlet cheeks and the averted eyes. 'Feeling ashamed of yerself, are yer?' she asked, and Maggie nodded mutely. 'Don't waste yer time,' she advised, swinging her legs off the bed. 'All we did was give each other a little bit of comfort. Place like this, yer takes yer pleasure where yer can find it.' She snorted. 'And if yer worrying about what the Holy Joes would say, forget it. We got a few of them comes here, and they ain't half so holy once they gets their drawers off, I can tell yer.'

She slipped back into her clothes then leaned over and patted Maggie's hand. 'Now you just put it right out of yer mind, love.' Her lips set grimly. 'You got other things to worry about.'

Maggie stared at her blankly, and then comprehension and dismay rushed back. Of course, the auction! She groaned in despair. How could she possibly have forgotten about that?

Chapter Seventeen

The thought had barely formed in her mind before the door swung open and Mrs Wilkes bustled in. For once – no doubt inspired by the thought of the money to come – she was actually smiling. Over her arms she carried a linen clothes bag, which she laid at the foot of the bed.

The two girls sprang guiltily apart and Maggie got to her feet, hastily wrapping the towel round herself again, knotting it tightly above her breasts. Mrs Wilkes tutted, her good humour disappearing. 'For heaven's sake, girl,' she sighed in exasperation, 'why must you persist in this ridiculous false modesty? This is a brothel, not a nunnery. Get that off and let me look at you.' Maggie stepped backwards, clutching it even tighter, but in three short strides Mrs Wilkes crossed the room and wrenched it from her, leaving her standing naked and exposed. Arms folded, Mrs Wilkes inspected her from head to toe, nodding with satisfaction as she took in the soft breasts, the narrow waist and the sweet curve of hips and thighs. 'Part your legs,' she ordered.

Closing her eyes against the humiliation, Maggie did as she was told, shuddering with revulsion as Mrs Wilkes ran a hand over her newly shaven pudenda. For all the emotion she showed, she might have been checking over a horse she intended to purchase. 'Excellent,' she said, wiping her hand fastidiously on her apron. 'If any of our gentlemen callers can tell the difference between you and a proper virgin, I'll eat my Sunday hat – and give him his money back into the bargain.'

'Pretty safe bet then,' Millie muttered out of the corner of her mouth. 'The tight-fisted old bitch would rather have her teeth pulled than part with three farthings.'

Mrs Wilkes glared at her. 'Did you say something, Millicent?' she enquired icily.

'Er… no, ma'am,' Millie murmured, lowering her eyes. 'I didn't say nothing.'

'A good job too, young lady,' Mrs Wilkes said grimly. 'There's plenty of girls out on the streets as'd be only too pleased to take your place here. Just you keep that in mind next time you feel like being clever at my expense.'

'Yes, ma'am,' Millie said meekly.

'Right,' the harridan went on, turning back to Maggie. 'Time to get you dressed. The gentlemen will be arriving shortly, and we don't want to keep them waiting.'

Maggie shivered again. As far as she was concerned they could wait till hell froze over, but unfortunately she had no say in the matter, so she watched with apprehension as Mrs Wilkes picked up the clothes bag and opened it. What appalling costume would she be forced to put on for this charade? One of those gaudy skin-tight frocks the other girls wore, that exposed breasts and thighs to the lewd gaze of the clients?

She gasped as Mrs Wilkes drew out the contents.

'What did you expect, girl?' Mrs Wilkes asked shrewdly. 'You're a sweet virgin, remember, not some dockyard trull.' She held up the short white dress. 'This'll get their John Thomas' standing to attention,' she gloated. 'Dirty bastards; they'll be fighting to outbid each other once they see you in this. But first…' she produced a length of fine linen, rather like a broad bandage.

'What's that for?' Maggie asked nervously.

Mrs Wilkes raised her eyebrows. 'To bind your breasts, of course,' she said. 'Flatten you out a bit.'

'But... but won't the gentleman who...' she paused, barely able to say the words, '...who buys me, suspect something?'

'Mrs Wilkes laughed coarsely. 'Don't you worry, my girl. By the time he gets the clothes off your back he'll be too far gone to notice if you had tits like a sow.' She snapped her fingers. 'Come on, Millie, don't just stand there. Give me a hand.'

Between them they wrapped the bindings so tightly that Maggie's breasts were squashed flat and she could scarcely breathe. Once that was done, they slipped a lace-edged chemise over the top. White stockings and frilly pantaloons followed, then finally the short white dress, complete with wide blue sash around the waist – and a pair of black patent leather shoes with a strap that buttoned over the instep.

Next, Mrs Wilkes rummaged in the bottom of the bag and produced a pair of curling tongs. 'Stick those in the coals,' she told Millie, handing them over. 'We'll get her hair brushed while they're heating.' She then pushed Maggie into the chair in front of the mirror and began to brush her hair until it gleamed.

Satisfied, she clicked her fingers again and Millie gingerly handed over the tongs. Mrs Wilkes spat on them to check they were hot enough, then deftly transformed Maggie's hair into a mass of ringlets and topped it with a little straw boater with a ribbon that matched the sash.

Stepping back she admired her handiwork and smiled. 'There,' she chuckled. 'You look as if butter wouldn't melt in your mouth. Now stand up and look at yourself. Who could possibly resist such a charmingly innocent creature?'

Maggie stared at her reflection in disbelief and shuddered. What kind of inhuman scoundrel would pay to ravage such innocence – even if it was merely a façade?

She was soon to find out.

'Come along then,' ordered Mrs Wilkes. 'Your eager suitors await you.' Trembling, Maggie hung back, and the wicked old harridan gave her an evil grin. 'Or would you prefer Jebediah and Arthur to "escort" you? I am sure it would add a little frisson to the gentlemen's pleasure if you were to be dragged in kicking and screaming.' Maggie bit her lip and shook her head. There was no way she would give them the satisfaction of seeing her any more humiliated than she already was. 'Well then,' Mrs Wilkes continued, 'follow me and no more of this nonsense.' Turning on her heel she sailed from the room with Maggie stumbling reluctantly in her wake.

She could hear the so-called 'gentlemen' before they even reached the salon. The jeers and catcalls and coarse laughter made her cringe inside. They sounded like a pack of wild animals baying for blood. Her blood!

Mrs Wilkes pushed the door open. Silence fell for a moment as they entered – then the noise redoubled as they caught sight of Maggie. Ignoring it all, Mrs Wilkes led her to a chair on a dias at the front of the room and took her place at a lectern beside it. Surveying the room, she picked up a gavel and banged it on the lectern. Silence fell for the second time.

'Good evening, gentlemen,' she began. 'And welcome

to the auction. I trust you will enjoy yourselves.' A few hoots were instantly quelled by her cold smile. She waved her gavel at Maggie. 'Here we have tonight's prize – as sweet a young virgin as ever I saw in all my years as mistress of this house.' She gave a lewd smile. 'The gentleman who has the privilege of breaking in this little treasure will be a lucky man – the envy of his peers.' She smiled round. 'Now who will it be, I wonder?'

'Let's have a feel of the merchandise first,' bellowed a man at the front. Grinning, he made a lunge towards Maggie and she shrank back in terror.

'Naughty, naughty!' said Mrs Wilkes, sternly wagging a finger at him until he subsided. 'Untouched she is, and untouched she shall remain until her lucky purchaser deflowers her.' She looked round. 'Now, do I have any bids?'

'Ten guineas!' called a voice from the back, and Maggie stared in dismay at the man who had spoken. Grossly fat, his sweaty red face showed years of self-indulgence. He eyed her greedily and she groaned inwardly as she imagined that bloated body thrusting into her own. Dear God, please don't let him be the winner!

Thankfully Mrs Wilkes was not impressed. 'Ten guineas?' she smiled, raising her eyebrows. 'For a gem like this? Come now, Sir Oswald, you've wagered more than that on a hand of cards.'

'Twenty!' yelled another, and Maggie's eyes searched the room until she found the caller. It was difficult. A scrawny runt of a man, he could barely have come up to her shoulder. She drew in a shuddering breath as she recognised him as the one she'd watched through the peephole, beating that unfortunate girl. She closed her eyes. If he won, she would be the one spreadeagled as he took his vile pleasures on her helpless body.

As if the first two callers had released the floodgates, bids began to come fast and furious, from all corners of the room. Maggie's eyes darted frantically from face to face, trying to keep up, but it was impossible. They all blended into one nightmare entity. Wet, cawing mouths opened and closed as the bids were called and the price mounted.

Gradually they began to drop off as the cost soared beyond the pockets of most of those present. 'One hundred and fifty guineas,' said Mrs Wilkes with satisfaction. 'Do I hear two hundred?'

'Two hundred,' agreed a man in the second row.

'Do I hear two hundred and fifty?' asked Mrs Wilkes. She looked round enquiringly. 'Come, come gentlemen. A mere two hundred and fifty guineas for the pleasure of deflowering this lovely virgin? Cheap at twice the price.' She waited expectantly, but there were no further bids.

Maggie breathed a sigh of relief as she looked at the man who had purchased her. He might be the best of a bad bunch, but at least he was young and neither grossly fat or horrendously ugly. The ordeal of her 'defloration' might not be enjoyable, but at least it would be bearable.

Mrs Wilkes raised her gavel. 'One prime young virgin, sold to Lord Harris for two hundred guineas. Going once… Going twice… So—'

'Five hundred,' a voice called casually from the back.

There was a gasp from the room and all eyes turned towards the door. A tall bony figure stood there, leaning on a cane. Maggie stared in horror. He looked like a living skeleton that had just been dug up from a tomb! His raddled face was like a canvas on which some mad artist had depicted all that was depraved in humanity. But it was his eyes that were the worst; they glinted with cruel life as if denying the ravages of time.

Even Mrs Wilkes was flustered.

'F-five hundred guineas?' she repeated in disbelief, but then a satisfied smile crossed her face at the magnitude of the bid. She raised her gavel again. 'One prime young virgin,' she repeated triumphantly. 'Sold to Lord Anston for the sum of five hundred guineas. Going once... Going twice... Sold!'

Maggie stared at the man in horror as the words penetrated her befuddled brain. Lord Anston? Wasn't he the one Millie had refused to talk about? The one who'd been responsible for confining her to her bed for three days?

'No...' she said quietly, shaking her head in denial as she stumbled to her feet. 'Please... no!'

The room whirled round her for a moment – then everything went dark as she crumpled to the floor in a dead faint.

Chapter Eighteen

When she came to the first thing that met her eyes was a pale, helpless girl, floating upside down above her on a silk-covered bed. For a moment she thought she'd gone mad. Her mind whirled madly as it fought to make sense of what she was seeing – until it finally dawned on her that she was looking at her own reflection in a mirror on the ceiling. She became even more confused. Why would anyone want to put a mirror there?

Then the events of the last few hours rushed back and the question was pushed out of her mind by more important considerations. Sitting up with a start, she stared around wildly. Where was she – and even more to the point, where was Lord Anston?

The room appeared to be empty and she relaxed and began to take in her surroundings. She gasped. The predominant colour was scarlet. Scarlet silk hangings draped the windows. Scarlet turkey carpet covered the floors. Scarlet satin cushions covered the scarlet velvet sofa in the corner. It was like being inside some monstrous womb.

The reflection in the overhead mirror drew her eyes with dreadful fascination and she shuddered again; she lay upon the blood-coloured bedspread like a sacrifice on some pagan altar, her slender figure shockingly white against the scarlet silk.

Just then a figure loomed out of the darkness and she

cringed back – then sighed with relief as she realised it was only Millie.

'About time too,' she said, looking down at Maggie. 'I thought you were going to lie there like a dead 'un till kingdom come. Mind you,' she went on judiciously, 'that was a smart trick you pulled. I couldn't have done it better meself.'

'Trick?' Maggie echoed. 'What do you mean?'

'Conking out like that,' said Millie, and she winked. 'Nothing quite like a fit of the vapours to convince the punters of your maidenly modesty.' She pulled a wry face. 'Shame you hadn't thought of it before the bidding started. It'd have shoved the price up no end.'

At the mention of the bidding Maggie looked round and shuddered. 'Where's Lord Anston?' she gasped.

Millie shrugged. 'Knocking back the booze and bragging to his cronies about what a stud he is, no doubt. Why, you ain't panting for him to come and claim his rights, are you?'

'Oh no,' Maggie said fervently. 'I wouldn't care if he dropped dead right now.' She shivered. 'In fact, I wish he would.'

'Wouldn't we all,' Millie said bitterly. 'Vicious bastard.' She rubbed the fading bruises on her arms. 'God knows, most of them as comes through that front door are bad enough, but he's the worst. Half the girls in this house would pay a year's money to piss on the fucker's grave.'

She looked at Maggie's white face and softened. 'Sorry, love, didn't mean ter frighten yer. It's bad, but it don't last forever.' Her lips twisted. 'Remember what I told yer before; just close yer eyes and think of England.'

'But I don't understand,' wailed Maggie. 'Why is he so cruel? What pleasure does he get out of it?'

'The only pleasure he can,' said Millie with a coarse laugh. 'Ain't it a pisser? There he is, the lord of bleedin' creation; money, land, a title – and every street corner bullyboy without two ha'pennies to rub together is a better man than he is. Makes you think there's a God after all, don't it?'

Maggie stared at her in total incomprehension. 'What do you mean?' she quavered.

'You really are an innocent, ain'tcher?' scoffed Millie. 'What do you think I mean? The bastard can't get it up, that's what!' She held up her hand, quirked her little finger downwards and cackled gleefully. 'He's got a limp noodle. His John Thomas don't work!' She cackled again. 'Poor bugger. He's that desperate, if it ever stood he'd starch it!'

Her fit of laughter vanished as soon as it had come. 'Only trouble is,' she said grimly, 'he takes it out on us, don't he?' She snorted. 'Can't be his fault, can it? Gotta be ours then. And my gawd, he don't half make you pay for it.'

'What does he do?' asked Maggie, terrified of knowing but even more terrified of not knowing.

'Whatever he bleeding well likes,' said Millie cynically. 'He's paid for yer, ain't he? Got ter get his money's worth.'

Maggie buried her head in her hands. 'Oh,' she moaned, 'how will I ever bear it?'

Millie patted her shoulder. 'Same way as I do, love.' She grinned as she produced the bottle of brandy. 'Didn't think I'd let yer down, did yer? I brought a little something to help dull the pain.' She grimaced. 'Tastes like liquid shit, but drink enough of it and yer won't even notice what the bastard's doing to yer.'

Maggie reached for it gratefully, and the bottle was halfway to her lips when the door burst open and Mrs Wilkes flew in like a whirlwind. 'Give that to me this instant,' she snapped, grabbing it from Maggie's fingers. 'How dare you? Lord Anston paid for an innocent virgin, not some drunken trollop! I have a reputation to maintain.' She spun round to Millie. 'As for you, my lady,' she snarled, 'one more act of defiance and you'll be out on your ear so fast it'll make your head spin.' Her lip curled in a sneer. 'You won't be quite so headstrong when you're on your knees down the docks, sucking Lascar cocks for fourpence a throw! You can say goodbye to your little hat shop then!'

Cowed, Millie slunk from the room, leaving Maggie alone with Mrs Wilkes. 'That's better,' she said, straightening her black silk apron. 'You're a privileged girl, so let's have no more of this silly nonsense.' She looked Maggie over calculatingly. 'Come along now, sit up straight, brush your hair and tidy your frock. Lord Anston will be here any minute and we want you looking your best for him.'

With trembling fingers Maggie did as she was told. Deprived of even the small relief the brandy might have brought, the thought of what was to come terrified her almost beyond endurance – but endure it she must. She had no choice.

She had barely finished smoothing the tangles from her hair when the door opened again, and Lord Anston stood on the threshold, a look of casual arrogance on his face. A cigar hung from the corner of his mouth and the curling smoke from its tip wreathed lazily around his cruel features. To Maggie's frightened eyes he looked like a devil come from hell to torment her.

He dropped his cigar on the carpet and ground it out with his heel, and Mrs Wilkes didn't blink an eyelid.

'I do hope everything has been to your satisfaction, Lord Anston,' she gushed, bobbing a curtsey. 'The brandy? The cigars? The food?' It terrified Maggie even more to realise that the man made even a hard-faced old harridan like Mrs Wilkes nervous. The woman was practically gibbering. 'Is there anything else I can bring you?' she gabbled. 'Anything, anything at all, just say the word your lordship, and I'll have it fetched immediately.'

'Get out,' he growled.

'Yes, my lord,' she simpered, bobbing a last curtsey, 'certainly, my lord.' Holding her breath she sidled past, careful not to touch him, then fled with unseemly haste, closing the door behind her.

Maggie waited for him to pounce on her, but he seemed to be in no hurry. Instead he took out another cigar, lit it and stood in front of her, contemplating her for what seemed like an eternity. Finally he reached out, gripped her chin and forced her head up so that her eyes met his.

'So you're a virgin, are you girl?' he grated.

Mindful of her instructions, Maggie lowered her eyes modestly. 'Yes, sir,' she quavered.

The blow took her by surprise, stunning her with its force. She gasped with shock as much as pain, her hands flying to her face where the marks of his fingers were already beginning to form.

'Lying little trull,' he snarled. 'Do you think I'm one of those simpletons downstairs to be gulled by whatever fairytale you care to tell?' She shook her head dumbly. 'Good. Now we understand one another. You're a

202

whore, like any other in this house.' He smiled. 'The only difference is that you're a fresh whore and I haven't had you yet.' The smile widened. 'A situation I intend to remedy as soon as possible.' He waved an imperious hand. 'Now get those ridiculous clothes off and let me see what I've bought.' Fighting back the tears, Maggie stumbled to her feet while he seated himself on the end of the bed and watched as she began to fumble at her clothing. The sash went first, drifting to her feet, and then she tugged the frilly dress over her head and dropped it too. The petticoat and chemise followed, revealing the tight binding round her breasts.

She closed her eyes and waited for the explosion as he discovered the deception Mrs Wilkes had practised on him, but instead he let out a sharp bark of laughter. 'So,' he chuckled. 'More for my money than I bargained for, eh?'

Relieved, she began to unwind the binding, sighing with relief as her breasts sprang free from their confinement. They swung softly as she bent to roll down her white stockings, but he stopped her. 'No,' he ordered. 'Leave the stockings on. They add a little...' he raised an eyebrow, '...piquancy.'

Maggie straightened up again and stood before him, scarlet with shame and humiliation as he feasted his eyes on her body. His gaze lingered on the proud tilt of her breasts, then drifted lower to the narrow curve of waist and the soft swell of her hips and thighs. Her shaven sex was shocking in its nakedness, the sweet cleft exposed without the soft down of pubic hair to hide the pouting lips.

Then her humiliation turned to discomfort as he casually stubbed out his cigar, leaned forward and thrust his hand between her thighs. She gasped as he parted those lips and fondled her roughly, his bitten nails scratching her soft flesh as he forced a finger inside her – yet at the same time, a horrible excitement began to pulse through her lower belly. He laughed coarsely as he felt her moisten beneath his touch.

'Like that, do you, my little virgin whore?' he chuckled, never taking his eyes from her face as he forced another finger into her and began to move his hand.

She swayed, her legs beginning to weaken as the unwelcome feelings of pleasure began to mount, but it came to an abrupt end as he withdrew his hand and smacked her sharply on the hip, his hand leaving a scarlet print on her white skin. She opened her eyes and stared at him in shock as he slapped her hip again.

'We're not here for your pleasure, are we?' he gloated. 'We're here for mine.' He stood up and dragged the expensive clothes from his body, casting them to the floor as if they were rags. Naked, he stood in front of her, and she gasped with shock. If he'd looked thin when dressed, naked he was skeletal. She could see every rib standing out, stark beneath the paper-white skin. His belly was concave and his muscles stringy. He looked as if he was suffering from some dreadful wasting disease.

Her eyes dropped lower and her heart sank as Millie's words came back to her. His male member lay nestled in his coarse pubic hair, soft and asleep. He sat back down again, feet parted, and it dangled uselessly between his scrawny thighs.

'Well, whore,' he said. 'Don't just stand there. Be about your business.' She stared at him with incomprehension. What did he want her to do?

She soon found out. Reaching forward he jerked her legs so that she stumbled and fell to her knees. Then seizing her shoulders he dragged her close until she was kneeling between his parted thighs, gripped the back of her neck and pulled her face towards his flaccid cock. 'Suck it,' he ordered brusquely. 'Give me an erection.'

Gingerly Maggie leaned forward and took the wilted flesh between her lips, running her tongue around the soft gristle and sucking diligently, hoping to end the ordeal quickly. But it was hopeless; she might as well have tried to raise the dead. Desperately she tried harder, cradling his balls in her hand and fondling them as she sucked, but still there was no response at all.

Desperate to please him for her own sake, she remembered a tip Millie had given her, so she took her mouth from his prick, licked a finger, then once it was wet, slid it beneath him till she found the hairy pucker of his arse. Anxiously biting her lip, she forced herself to press her finger inside, then turned her attentions back to his cock with renewed vigour, her head bobbing in time with her thrusting finger. Nothing! Not even a flicker of life.

'Useless bitch,' he growled, pushing her away so that she sprawled on the floor in front of him. 'Call yourself a whore? You're as much use as the virgin you pretend to be.' He got up, bent over her, and grabbed the top of her arm. 'Well, there's more than one way to skin a cat, you little bitch. Just you wait and see.'

'No... please no,' she whimpered as he hauled her to her feet and flung her on the bed, but her pleas fell on deaf ears as he flung himself on her, his hands mauling her breasts, pinching the nipples until they rose hard and tight against his fingers. Taking them in his mouth he suckled them frantically, his teeth grazing the sensitive tips as his hand thrust between her thighs again. She moaned in a mixture of pain and pleasure as his fingers moved inside her.

'Want a cock, do you, you little bitch?' he gasped as he felt her unwilling response. 'Well, I'll give you one,' and holding her down with one hand he fumbled in the drawer beside the bed with the other, and her eyes widened in dismay as she saw what he was holding. It was a huge carved ivory dildo, at least ten inches long, the bulbous tip enormous. She gasped; surely he couldn't intend using that on her! She struggled to break free, but it was useless. Those wasted muscles were deceptively strong.

Grinning wolfishly he nudged her legs apart, parted her vulva and ran the tip of the dildo against the hot wet cleft of her sex until it gleamed with her juices. She whimpered as she felt its coldness against her, and then groaned in resignation as he began to push against her. Slowly, inch by awful inch he urged it deeper until Maggie felt she was being utterly filled.

The villainous man then paused for a moment, gloating over her helplessness, then pressed again and Maggie shuddered as it sank even further. He drew back, and then thrust it home again. Slippery now it slid more easily and she felt heat radiate through her belly. He began to move it faster and she whimpered again, this time with pleasure. Against her will her hips began to writhe as she raised them to meet each thrust. Above her in the mirror she could see each movement reflected; see him hunched over her; see the glistening dildo as it appeared and disappeared, each stroke bringing her closer to fulfilment.

'By, you're a hot one,' he grunted. 'You could raise the cock on a dead man.'

Maggie realised his words were true, and gasped as she saw his cock was no longer flaccid, but speared from his groin like a rod of iron, its swollen purple tip thrusting towards her. With a groan he pulled the dildo from her sex, cast it aside and threw himself on her, grunting with satisfaction as he plunged into her hot succulence. His hands gripped her buttocks, leaving red marks as he thrust and strained. Instinctively her legs wrapped around his hips to draw him closer and she squirmed beneath him, revelling in the roughness of their coupling, and at last she flung her head back and held her breath as she felt him swell and explode, his scalding seed erupting deep inside her – then she sank back exhausted as he collapsed onto her, panting against her smooth pale shoulder.

For a long moment they lay there, still entwined, his cock shrinking, then he rolled off her, sat up and calmly began to dress. She stared dumbly at the mirror in the ceiling. Reflected mercilessly was the proof of her depravity. She lay there, thighs lolling apart, the sticky residue of a strange man's seed glistening on her inner thighs. Bitter shame washed over her. There was no use pretending any longer. He'd been right; there was no difference between her and any other whore in the house.

Her bitter thoughts were interrupted by a discreet tap at the door and she hastily dragged the coverlet up to hide her nakedness as he barked, 'Come!'

Mrs Wilkes tiptoed in, glancing apprehensively at him as he stood there, pulling his embroidered waistcoat straight. 'I trust your purchase was satisfactory, Lord

Anston,' she enquired, with an oily smile.

'Excellent, I must say,' he admitted brusquely. 'Now see that her things are gathered and have her ready to leave in half an hour.'

Mrs Wilkes' jaw dropped. 'I beg your pardon, my lord?'

'You heard me, woman,' he snapped. 'Collect her things. I'm taking her with me.'

She stared at him, nonplussed for a moment, before collecting her wits again. 'I don't think you quite understand, my lord,' she said carefully. 'You merely paid for the taking of her maidenhead – not the girl herself.'

'Do you take me for a fool?' he demanded. 'Maidenhead, my arse! And for the five hundred guineas I paid you I could buy half the trollops in Piccadilly!' He paused. 'Still, I am not an unreasonable man. Name your price – within reason – and I shall pay it.'

A calculating expression crossed Mrs Wilkes' face as she weighed the advantages of pleasing Lord Anston against future profits, and her eyes glinted with greed. If the girl could please their most notorious client, what else could she not do? And no sensible woman gave up her capital when she could live on the profit. She made up her mind.

'I'm sorry, my lord,' she said. 'It's quite out of the question.' She drew herself up to her full height and the calculating expression was replaced by one of outraged morality. 'This is not a butcher shop to sell meat by the pound.'

'Isn't it?' he sneered, raising a cynical eyebrow. 'I'd have thought that's exactly what it was. And by the way, madam, I was not asking you, I was telling you.

Now get her ready.'

'Out of the question, Lord Anston,' Mrs Wilkes repeated stubbornly. 'The girl stays here.'

The smile that crossed his face was not a pretty sight, and Mrs Wilkes visibly faltered. 'You have the temerity to defy me, madam?' he asked with menacing softness. 'For all your airs and graces, you run nothing but a common bawdyhouse. A glorified knocking shop.' His evil smile widened. 'And how long do you think that would last if the magistrates no longer turned a blind eye?' He stroked his chin. 'Or even worse,' he went on conversationally, 'what if a gang of East End bullyboys were to break in, wreck the house and scar all your pretty young ladies?' He shook his head. 'It doesn't bear thinking about, does it? Now, would you care to reconsider my offer? What shall we say? Another five hundred guineas?'

Mrs Wilkes blenched as she envisioned her tiny empire crumbling to dust. 'Um, well, as you put it like that, of course, my lord,' she said, forcing herself to smile back. 'An extremely generous offer.' The smile became one of mock regret; he could have the girl, but she'd be damned if he'd have anything else. 'But you'll have to take her naked, I'm afraid,' she continued. 'She has no things of her own.'

With a curse he fumbled in his pocket and flung another twenty guineas at her feet. 'There, woman, will that cover the cost of the things she has now? I shall send round a banker's draft for the five hundred, first thing tomorrow morning.'

'Amply,' smirked Mrs Wilkes. 'Very generous, I'm sure.' She waved a hand towards Maggie. 'Help yourself, my lord. You may remove her whenever you please.'

Throughout this conversation Maggie had listened with growing outrage. How dare they haggle over her as if she was a cabbage on a costermonger's stall? And as for going with that bastard – she'd rather die!

'I'm going nowhere,' she said defiantly. 'You can't just buy and sell me like a pound of sausages. Lord Wilberforce abolished slavery, remember?'

The man and the woman stared at her with as much astonishment as if a piece of furniture had suddenly announced it no longer wished to be sat upon. It would have been comical had they not been casually playing with her life.

Mrs Wilkes recovered first. 'Ignore her,' she said. 'The silly little chit doesn't realise the honour you've done her, my lord. If you care to call your coachman, I shall deal with her.'

Ten minutes later, tied, bundled in a blanket and slung over Jebediah's shoulder, Maggie was deposited in the back of Lord Anston's carriage, to be carried off kicking and screaming into an unknown future.

Chapter Nineteen

The nightmare journey seemed to last forever. Half smothered beneath the evil smelling blanket, nausea threatened to overcome Maggie with ever jolt of the carriage. To avoid it, she concentrated on what little information she could garner from the sounds and sensations that penetrated the thick cloth.

At the start of the journey she could hear the clatter of hooves as the wheels of the carriage rumbled over the cobbled stones. As time passed, the hoof beats became muted and the familiar street cries died away, to be replaced by unexpected silence, broken only by the distant lowing of cattle or the occasional complaining bleat of a sheep. Where was he taking her? To some dark copse where he could ravish her again – or worse? She writhed against her bonds. If she could only break free she could jump from the carriage and flee to the nearest farmhouse. They would help her, surely?

Maggie sagged in despair as her struggles merely served to tighten the thin ropes until they bit painfully into her wrists. There was nothing to do but wait – and hope.

Eventually they drew to a halt. Strong hands hauled her out, dumped her unceremoniously on her feet and peeled the blanket away from her trembling form. For a moment she thought she had gone blind, then as her eyes adjusted to the half-light she realised it was almost dawn. Staggering, she sucked in a lungful of blessedly fresh air, opened her mouth – and screamed over and over again until the pain in her throat forced her to stop.

But it was useless. No one rushed to her rescue. No one knocked the villain to the ground and carried her off to freedom. Only the rooks, startled from sleep, wheeled above her head for a few moments before settling again.

And even more humiliating, her captor was lounging against the carriage laughing at her!

'Feel free to carry on, my dear,' he chuckled, waving an airy hand. 'My servants are well paid for their ability to turn a blind eye, and my nearest neighbour is five miles away, and stone deaf into the bargain.'

She closed her mouth abruptly, taking in her surroundings for the first time. The carriage sat on smoothly raked gravel at the foot of large stone steps that led up to the house. And what a house! It dwarfed the London mansions Maggie had been used to. The centre part alone could have accommodated three of them, and to each side was an additional even larger wing. Ivy grew up the grey stone walls almost covering the windows, and the pale dawn light reflected off them, giving them a look of ancient menace, like brooding, hooded eyes.

Maggie glanced around, frantically seeking an avenue of escape, but all she could see were acres of rolling parkland. There was no point in running; where could she run to?

'Well,' he taunted, 'you've gone very quiet. Cat got your tongue?'

'There's nowhere to go,' she said bitterly. 'You might as well untie me.'

'Certainly, my sweet,' he purred. 'Your wish is my command.' He produced a pocketknife and sliced through the rope at her wrists, and ignoring the pain as the blood rushed back into her fingers, she lifted her hand and slapped him as hard as she could.

'Bastard!' she hissed. 'You make me sick. You think your title and your money entitle you to treat girls like me as if we were dirt. I'll bet if I'd been Lady Muck you wouldn't have carted me off like a side of beef.'

'Actually, you're wrong,' he grinned, ruefully rubbing his jaw. 'That's exactly how I got my dear departed wife – and her fortune, of course. Abducting an heiress is very little different from abducting a whore. Only the stakes are higher.

'A few days in my bedroom and she was positively begging me to marry her,' he went on. 'After all, who else would want soiled goods?' He pulled a face. 'A rather vulgar girl, I'm afraid. Her family was in trade, you know. But sweet and biddable – after I'd trained her a little.' He smirked. 'And she did have the good taste to die in childbirth, leaving me with her money without the inconvenience of her presence.' He sighed. 'Pity she took the brat with her. I could have done with an heir.' He shrugged. 'But then, one can't have everything.'

Maggie stared at him, dismayed by his sheer callousness and the misery concealed in the brief story. Her heart sank. What hope had she if he could treat his own wife like that? Her thoughts were interrupted by the arrival of the housekeeper, carrying a small lantern.

'Welcome home, sir,' she beamed, holding it aloft. 'There's a good hot meal waiting in the oven and your favourite claret already decanted.' Her smile vanished, to be replaced by a look of hostility as she inspected Maggie in her torn white dress. 'Shall I put the young lady in the blue room?'

'The nursery, I think,' he said thoughtfully. 'If I remember correctly the bars are still on the windows. After all, we wouldn't want her to leave before she has fully experienced my hospitality.'

'Certainly, sir,' agreed the woman, with another simpering smile. She turned to Maggie. 'Follow me, girl,' she ordered, her lips twisting with distaste at having to deal with such dross.

Maggie stared back at her with equal distaste. The housekeeper wore the same uniform of respectability as Mrs Wilkes: a black silk apron over a black dress. The cold-hearted bitch must have known why she'd been brought here, but was prepared to accept Maggie's misery as the price of her own continued prosperity. How dare she look at her like that? The only difference between her and Mrs Wilkes was that she was pandering to one man, while Mrs Wilkes pandered to many – and at least she was honest about it.

Nose in the air Maggie pulled the blanket around her shoulders and swept past the woman as if she didn't exist, leaving her to bow and scrape to her precious master. In the entrance hall she hesitated, suddenly cut down to size by the vastness of her surroundings. The black and white marble floor seemed to stretch into infinity in front of her.

A surreptitious push in the back almost made her stumble. The housekeeper had come up behind her as she stood with her mouth open, gawping like a booby. 'This way, madam,' she sneered, stalking ahead of her, and reluctantly Maggie followed, her faltering footsteps echoing as she walked.

The nursery was in the west wing, up seemingly endless flights of stairs, and as Lord Anston had said, the windows were barred. Originally this might have been to protect its child occupant, but now it served equally well to imprison its present one. Maggie shivered. It was obvious the room hadn't been used for years – and that the servants had been neglecting their duties. She wrinkled her nose.

The room was icy cold and permeated with the smell of must and age. Dead ash filled the fireplace and layers of dust covered everything from the nursery table to the hideously snarling rocking horse in the corner. Off the playroom were two smaller rooms, one containing a cot and the other an old chest of drawers and a narrow iron bedstead with a mattress rolled up at the foot.

It was into this area that the housekeeper ushered her, in a parody of hospitality. 'You won't freeze,' she said. 'There're blankets in that chest under the window and coal and suchlike beside the fire in the playroom. I'll send one of the maids up with something to eat.' With a final haughty sniff she departed, her black skirt swishing with indignation at having to wait on one of the lower orders, and with a sinking heart Maggie heard the key turn in the lock behind her. She had heard that sound so often over the past few weeks that she'd learnt to dread it.

Left to her own devices, Maggie wrapped the blanket more tightly round her shivering body. She smiled ruefully. There had been no offer to start a fire for her, so she'd better get on with it.

Investigation proved that the woman had been almost right. There was coal in the scuttle, along with a few sticks of kindling, and a further search produced half a box of matches tucked behind a candle-stick on the mantelshelf – but there was no paper.

Undeterred, Maggie found the toy cupboard and several tattered board games pushed away at the back of the top shelf. They'd do, and she hoped they had sentimental value for that bastard. Smiling vindictively she tore them to pieces and used them as a base for her fire, carefully piling the kindling on top and adding the coal. Finally she crossed her fingers, struck a match, and coughed as a wave of smoke billowed out and for one dreadful moment she thought the chimney was blocked, but then the tiny flames flickered, caught and began to send out weak tendrils of warmth.

Satisfied, Maggie stood up, wiped her hands on the tattered remains of her white frock and began to look around. If she was going to stay here she might as well make herself as comfortable as possible, and doing something – anything – would help to pass the time. So she unrolled the mattress and made up the bed, wrinkling her nose again at the reek of dampness. Then, tearing a flounce from her skirt, she used it as a makeshift duster. What she really needed was a bucket of hot water and a scrubbing brush, but this would have to do.

By the time she'd finished the room was cleaner, but she was filthy and as hungry as a bear, so it was a relief when there was a faint tap on the door, then the sound of the key turning again and two young maids entered, one carrying a tray and the other a basin and a can of hot water. Casting frightened glances at Maggie – they'd obviously been warned not to speak to the scarlet woman – they put them down and hurried out as quickly as possible.

As soon as they'd gone Maggie lifted the cover on the tray and inspected the food beneath. Lord Anston might have been served his 'nice hot meal' but the same didn't apply to her. All she was getting was a hunk of hard cheese, the heel of the loaf and a jug of watered milk. She smiled ruefully; well at least she wouldn't have to worry about it getting cold while she washed.

Stripping down, she scrubbed herself, the firelight reflecting rosily off her pale, shivering body. Clean at last, she looked with distaste at the filthy white dress, unable to bear the thought of putting it back on. A rake through the chest of drawers produced an old moth-eaten uniform, which had obviously belonged to some long-ago nursery maid. Like everything else it stank of age and decay, but it would have to do, so she draped it over a chair in front of the fire and hungrily ate her bread and cheese as it steamed in the heat.

Once aired Maggie slipped it over her naked body, revelling in the warmth from the rough material. Fed and warm at last, the horrors of the last few days slipped from her mind and drowsiness overcame her, so she stumbled through to the other room, relieved herself in the chamber-pot from beneath the bed, then crawled between the unaired sheets, and within moments was sound asleep.

When she woke again it was still dark and confusion swept through her. Had she only dozed? Surely not? She felt completely refreshed. Rising, she went back through to the playroom and discovered that more food had been brought and the fire renewed, and she gasped as it dawned on her that she must have slept for a full twenty-four hours.

The food, beef stew with dumplings, was better this

time, even though it was cold. She ate gratefully, then sat gazing into the flames of the fire, dreaming wistfully and wishing she were anywhere but this cruel prison, until her thoughts were interrupted by the sound of the key turning in the lock and she sprang to her feet.

Lord Anston stood in the doorway, his smile evil in the red glow from the coals. 'So,' he grinned, taking in the shabby uniform she was wearing. 'Sitting doing nothing when you should be working.'

She stared at him blankly. What on earth was he talking about?

He stalked across the room and ran a finger along the mantelshelf, then held his dusty digit under her nose. 'Disgraceful,' he hissed. 'This room should be spotless. You have failed to do your duties, and maids who fail to do their duties must be punished.'

Slowly it dawned on Maggie that he was playing some twisted game, with her as the prize, so hastily gathering up her skirts she dodged past him and darted for the door – but it was too late. The brute seized her arm and pulled her to him, his breath hot on her face, stinking of brandy. She squirmed in his grasp but he held her easily, wrenching the dress from her shoulders with his free hand.

When she was naked he explored her body roughly, molesting the soft globes of her breasts and pinching her nipples into fullness. Panting, he pushed his hand between her thighs, fumbled with her sex and thrust his fingers inside. She whimpered with the mixture of pain and pleasure he was so skilled in producing in her, and shame flushed her cheeks as she felt the moisture begin to flow over his probing fingers.

He had no trouble with his John Thomas this time.

She could feel it pushing against her belly as he ground his hips against her. She moaned, her legs weakening as his mouth came down on hers and he thrust his tongue between her lips. Then pulling away he grinned savagely down at her.

'Enjoying it, are you, my little whore?' he sneered. 'Well, we'll see if you enjoy what's coming next.'

His words barely had time to sink in before he was dragging her towards the rocking horse in the corner. Brusquely twisting her round he pushed her so that she sprawled along its length, and she grasped at the horsehair mane to prevent herself falling.

He tugged her legs apart so that they fell each side of the horse's rump, offering her own to his greedy eyes, the soft pink flower of her anus exposed to his exploring fingers. She squealed and squirmed as he inserted his thumb into that most private of passages, while his index and middle fingers thrust into her vulva. The stumpy remains of the horse's tail tickled her clitoris with every movement, sending shivers of ecstasy through her belly and she whined in denial of the pleasure coursing through her.

His lips drew back from his teeth in a rictus of lust as he withdrew his hand and fumbled hastily with the buttons on his breeches. His cock sprang free and he pumped it in his fist until the swollen head looked as if it would burst, then with a savage grunt he thrust into her poor vulnerable bottom and Maggie wailed with discomfort and shame.

Smiling slyly, Lord Anston set the rocking horse in motion, moving it slowly at first, then faster and faster as his excitement mounted, his prick plunging in and out with each creaking movement. Helpless, with the stink of damp horse-hair in her nostrils, Maggie gave herself up to the wave of lust that pulsed in her loins and the feel of his rigid cock filling her, grinding her vulva against the horse's crupper with every roll and thrust.

Finally he juddered with release, his seed bursting deep within her, the pulsing column of gnarled flesh delivering her own shameful peak. Her eyelids fluttered, and a scream of pleasure escaped her as she reached her own climax.

He recovered first, and straightening his clothing he looked down on her, lip curled. 'Best ride I ever had on that thing,' he chuckled wickedly. 'It's good to be back in the saddle.' Aching in every muscle, Maggie got to her feet and pulled her frock back over her nakedness. Decent again, she stood with her head bowed, staring mutely at the floor. He looked at her thoughtfully.

'Who'd guess, to look at you, that you're such an accomplished little slut?' he mused hurtfully. 'It seems a shame not to put your undoubted abilities to wider use.' He grinned. 'In fact, I feel positively selfish not sharing your talents. A man should always share his good fortune with his friends.' Still chuckling, he strode out, locking the door behind him, his words chilling her to the core, and she stood on her own again, staring fearfully after the brute.

What did he mean by that?

Chapter Twenty

After he had gone she paced the room, his words echoing in her head. At each turn she caught sight of that damned rocking horse, its painted eyes and snarling grin seeming to mock the memory of her humiliation. Even if she closed her eyes she could still see herself spread naked across it, writhing in shameful bliss as her new owner took her savagely from behind, in her bottom.

On impulse she stalked through to the tiny bedroom, flung open the trunk beneath the window and hauled out a blanket, ignoring the foul waft of damp air that came with it. Then carrying it through she flung it over the rocking horse, hiding it – and her own wickedness.

Finally, wearied of her fruitless pacing, she slumped into the chair beside the fire and sat staring dully into the dying embers, until she fell into a troubled sleep.

She awoke, stiff and cold, to find a housemaid kneeling at the hearth re-laying the fire. For a moment it was like an innocent glimpse of her own past, before Jeremy and everything else that had happened.

'Good morning,' she said, yawning and stretching, and at the sound of her voice the girl leapt to her feet and backed away, her hands twisting nervously in her apron. Maggie wondered briefly what tales the housekeeper had told to cause such a reaction, and smiled wryly; you'd have thought she'd grown horns and a tail the way the girl was looking at her!

'Morning, m'm,' the maid whispered. 'Sorry, m'm, didn't mean to wake you. Mrs Grimes said you was to 'ave more coals.' She pointed placatingly towards the table. 'And I brung yer breakfast as well.'

'A good job too,' said Maggie, keeping her face straight. 'Or I might have eaten you instead!' But her weak attempt at humour fell flat as the girl's eyes widened and she backed even further away. Maggie sighed with exasperation; she must be simple or something. 'For heaven's sake, you silly ninny,' she snapped. 'Don't be ridiculous. I'm not some kind of monster. It was a joke.'

'Mrs Grimes said you was a minion of Satan,' the girl gabbled. 'She said I wasn't to talk to yer. She said "he who touches pitch will be defiled". She said—'

'She said a lot of things, didn't she?' Maggie interrupted crossly. 'If you ask me the old witch would be better off saying her prayers instead of frightening you by filling your head with nonsense.'

The girl stared at her for a moment, commonsense warring with her fear of the housekeeper – and finally commonsense won. 'She is an old witch, ain't she,' she agreed. 'Even ol' Meakes the butler is scared stiff of 'er. You should see 'is face when she—' the girl stopped abruptly as she realised she was talking to the 'minion of Satan', and then grinned sheepishly.

Maggie grinned back. 'You see?' she pointed out. 'You haven't been struck by lightening yet, have you?'

'I will be if Grimes catches me,' said the girl, pulling a face. 'She'll 'ave me on half rations for not doing me work fast enough. Not that full rations are much to write home about either,' she added wryly. 'Anything she saves on the housekeeping goes into 'er back pocket, so she'd 'ave us all on bread and water if she could get away with it.'

'I suppose that's what I'm getting for breakfast then,' Maggie said glumly.

'Oh no,' the girl assured her. 'The master said you was to be fed proper, and even she wouldn't dare disobey anything he said. ''E ain't 'ere 'alf the time,' she explained earnestly, 'so she's on a right cushy number. She wouldn't want to mess that up.' She shivered. 'And he's got a real nasty temper if he's crossed.'

Maggie smiled grimly; there was no need to tell her that. She'd found it out for herself. Still, 'what can't be cured must be endured', as her mother used to say, but at least if she had a morsel of food in her belly it might be endured a bit more comfortably, so getting up she walked across to the table and lifted the metal covers from the dishes to investigate.

The aroma of bacon wafted up to tantalise her. There was a mound of crisp rashers and half a dozen plump sausages, glistening with fat. Under the other cover was a huge plate of kedgeree, and beside it all sat a pile of thinly cut bread, thick with country butter. The whole lot was accompanied by a steaming pot of tea, and her mouth watered just looking at it.

But hers wasn't the only one. The maid was looking at the pile of food enviously and Maggie noticed for the first time how pale and thin she was. In fact, a puff of wind could blow her away. As she watched, the girl's tongue came out and unconsciously licked her lips.

'Lucky bugger,' she whispered, almost to herself. 'You got enough there to feed the five thousand,' then it evidently dawned on her what she'd said and her hand flew to her mouth in dismay. 'Oh, sorry m'm,' she

223

blurted, 'I didn't mean it.' She looked at Maggie pleadingly. 'You won't tell Mrs Grimes, will yer?'

'Don't be daft,' scoffed Maggie. 'She wouldn't listen even if I did. I'm a minion of Satan, remember?' She picked up two slices of bread, filled them with sausage and bacon, and began to eat hungrily. 'Fancy some?' she asked, waving her sandwich at the girl. 'There's plenty here for both of us.'

'Oh, I daren't,' she gasped. 'Mrs Grimes would kill me.'

'Well, I won't tell if you won't,' said Maggie, through her tasty mouthful. 'Go on, be a devil!'

Temptation and caution warred for a moment – then temptation won. Following Maggie's example she grabbed three slices of bacon and a couple of sausages, wrapped them in bread and began to chew ravenously, an expression of bliss lighting up her face.

'Cor,' she mumbled, grease glistening on her chin. 'I ain't had grub like this since I went into service. Me dad used ter keep a pig at the bottom of the garden. He used ter slaughter it afore the winter and we used ter feed fat for a month.' She grabbed some more and stuffed it greedily into her mouth, but had barely got it in when the door opened and Mrs Grimes stalked in. The maid sprang back from the table, swallowing frantically.

'And just what do you think you're doing, Harper?' Mrs Grimes demanded sharply. 'You should have been finished in here long ago. There's grates to be cleaned and fires to be laid in all the downstairs rooms yet.'

'Yes, m'm,' muttered the girl, eyes downcast. 'Sorry m'm.' Grabbing the coalscuttle she edged towards the door – but just before she disappeared she beamed at Maggie from behind the woman's back and gave her a saucy wink, making Maggie bite her lip to keep from smiling.

'As for you,' went on Mrs Grimes, looking at Maggie with unconcealed dislike. 'Lord Anston says you may be permitted to take a constitutional this morning.'

Maggie tried to hide her excitement; if she was allowed to take a walk, there might just be a chance of escape. Even though the estate was remote, she was young and strong. She could get a fair distance away before they even noticed she was missing, and surely not every cottager was beholden to him? There must be decent people somewhere who would take her in.

Mrs Grimes must have read her mind. 'You will be accompanied, of course,' she added with evident relish. 'At all times.'

Maggie's heart sank as her hopes of freedom shattered, and then a more alarming thought struck her. 'Accompanied?' she demanded. 'Who by?'

'By whom,' corrected the housekeeper.

'By whom, then?' Maggie impatiently corrected herself.

'The under-footmen,' said Mrs Grimes. 'My nephew, James. A good reliable boy, so you needn't bother trying your whorish wiles on him, because they won't work.'

'You may finish your breakfast,' she continued, 'and afterwards one of the maids will fetch you some more appropriate clothing.' She indicated the dusty bell-pull beside the fireplace. 'And you may ring when you're ready to be taken for a walk.' Without another word she turned and stalked out, leaving Maggie staring indignantly after her.

Taken for a walk? Hah! What was she, one of his majesty's horses or hounds to be exercised daily? Her appetite had gone now, and she looked at the food congealed on the plates with revulsion. Still, she needed to keep her strength up, so she forced herself to eat a little more, washing it down with hot sweet tea, and had barely finished when there was a timid knock on the door. 'Come in,' she called, smiling ruefully at the absurdity; the damned thing was locked from the outside, so why bother knocking? It wasn't as if she could open it.

'Mrs Grimes sent these up, miss,' said the girl, bobbing as she held out an armful of clothes. Maggie looked at them ruefully. The predominant colour was a muddy brown, and they'd been patched so many times they looked like a blooming quilt. But she shrugged, after all, who cared? She was only going for a supervised walk on the estate, not a hunt ball, and at least they'd be better than the mildewed attire she'd found to hide her nakedness.

'Thank you,' she smiled, and the little maid gave a sigh of relief and scurried off.

The clothes were just as ugly as she'd imagined. She looked like a dowdy governess, and a poor one at that with all the darns and patches. But they were warm and that was the main thing. Once dressed she tugged on the bell-pull, and despite the fact that she'd be forced to endure the company of the old hag's lumpen nephew, she was looking forward to escaping from the damp, claustrophobic room and getting a breath of fresh air. So she waited eagerly for his arrival.

It didn't take long. Five minutes later there was the familiar sound of the key turning in the lock and he was standing there, grinning at her.

Maggie stared at him coldly. The family resemblance

was clear; the same protuberant eyes, the same thin lips, the same pasty skin marred by pockmarks. Apparently none of the family had been blessed with good looks, though it was clear he didn't share her opinion. Running a hand through his greasy hair, he favoured her with what was obviously meant to be a winning smile, but was in fact a self-satisfied smirk, and when Maggie failed to return it his face twisted into a scowl.

'Well, get a move on then, girl,' he growled. 'I ain't got all day to stand around waiting for you.'

Maggie didn't deign to answer. Instead, she picked up the shabby shawl that had come with the rest of the clothes, threw it round her shoulders and walked past him as if he didn't exist, leaving him no option but to follow her. His scowl deepened. Snooty cow! Who the hell did she think she was?

A cunning smile curled the corner of his thin lips. Thought she could snub him, did she? Well, the bitch had another think coming.

Chapter Twenty-One

They were barely out of sight of the house before he pounced. Panting, he gripped her around the waist and pulled her towards him, his free hand groping at the heavy serge of her bodice, groaning as he felt the soft warmth within, his bony knee thrusting its way between her thighs as he pushed her against a convenient tree.

'Get your hands off me, you filthy brute,' she gasped, struggling against his vicelike grip. But in answer he wrenched the neck of her dress until it tore away, revealing the mouth-watering globes of her breasts. For a moment he feasted his eyes on them before burying his face in their softness. She gagged in disgust as his slobbering lips sought out her nipple and latched on like a leech. He had her skirts up round her waist now, his rough fingers parting the delicate lips of her sex, his freed cock hard and ready. She whimpered as she felt the swollen head push against her and braced herself for his unwelcome invasion.

But it never came.

There was a roar of outrage and he was plucked away and flung through the air like a straw in a gale. Blinking away tears, Maggie gazed hopefully up at her rescuer, then hope disappeared as she realised she was looking into the furious face of Lord Anston.

'Can't you go five minutes without causing mayhem, you little trollop?' he demanded, taking Maggie's breath away with the sheer unfairness of the accusation. 'As for you,' he snarled, turning his attention to the wretched creature on the ground. 'Pack your bags and get out of my house.' He punctuated each word with a blow from the dog-whip he carried, until the other man scuttled away like a whipped cur.

Ignoring him, Lord Anston seized Maggie's arm and dragged her back to the house, up the stairs and into the nursery where he flung her onto the narrow cot. 'Now stay there,' he growled. 'And keep out of trouble.'

He paused at the door and eyed her spitefully. 'You'll have quite enough to satisfy your greedy appetites this evening. More than enough!'

Even through the locked door Maggie could hear him laughing as he stalked off.

No one came near her for hours, leaving her plenty of time to brood over his words. When the door did open, it was only the young maid with a plateful of cold meats. 'Can't stop,' she panted, banging it on the table and turning to go. 'Mrs Grimes 'as got us scrubbing the reception rooms from top to bottom,' she announced excitedly. 'The master's having company. First time he's entertained in years.'

Maggie's blood ran cold at the thought, a dreadful suspicion materialising in her mind about what form the master's 'entertainment' might take.

And her fears were confirmed when he appeared several hours later. 'Put this on,' he ordered. Maggie held up the thing he had flung at her and looked at it in bewilderment. With its complicated straps and buckles, at first glance it appeared to be some kind of horse harness – then it dawned on her that it was some kind of bizarre corset.

'I can't wear this—!' she tried to protest, but the slap spun her halfway across the room and brought tears of shock to her eyes.

'I told you to put it on,' he grated, she struggled to obey, and when she'd succeeded she felt more naked than if she'd been completely unclothed. Broad leather bands – shockingly black against her white skin – crisscrossed between her breasts, forcing them into prominence. An even wider one encircled her waist, pinching it to an unnatural narrowness, and below that a thin thong disappeared between her buttocks and curved round in an inverted Y where her thighs met her torso, leaving her vulva fully exposed. It reminded her of the costume worn by Ingrid at Mrs Wilkes', but somehow she didn't think that she'd be the one in the dominant role.

She tried to cover herself with her hands, but he wrenched them away. 'Excellent,' he murmured. 'Just one more thing.' He reached out, and she winced as he pinched her nipples into hardness. 'There, perfect. Now come with me.' He turned and strode towards the door, expecting Maggie to follow obediently.

But she didn't.

'What on earth are you waiting for?' he demanded. 'I gave you an order.'

'And you can stick your orders where the sun don't shine,' Maggie countered defiantly. 'I ain't going nowhere.'

Anston was across the room in two strides, his grip biting into the soft skin of her arm. 'You'll do as you're told!' he growled, yanking her towards the door. She clawed at his face, but he avoided her easily. Frantic with terror she turned her head and sank her teeth into his wrist. He shook her free, bent, slung her over his shoulder and carried her kicking and screaming out of the room and along the corridors, past the occasional gawping servant.

The brief journey ended in the bowels of the house, where he banged her down so hard her head throbbed painfully. Giving her no time to regain her composure, he gripped her wrists, bound them, and then wrenched on the other end of the rope so that she was hauled onto her tiptoes, arms above her head. Wide-eyed with fear she hung there helplessly, swaying slightly. He gazed at her with satisfaction, rubbing his wrist where her teeth had sunk into his flesh. Stony-faced, he lifted the dog whip he had already used to such good effect on his impertinent footman.

'Behave like a bitch and you'll be treated like one,' he grated. 'If one of my dogs bites me, I beat it until it has learnt its lesson.' He smiled coldly. 'They seldom bite again.'

'No, please,' she begged. 'I won't do it again, I promise.'

Ignoring her pleas, he walked behind her, his eyes lingering on the smooth curves of her buttocks, where the black leather straps cut into the soft flesh. They made a very tempting target, so raising the whip, he brought it down across the shapely globes, grinning maliciously as they quivered beneath the stroke, the delicate skin turning first white, then red as the blood flowed back.

Maggie's mouth opened in a silent scream, the agony so monstrous it took her breath away – then as one blow followed the next she found her voice, and shriek after shriek pealed from her lips. Panting from the very enjoyable exertion, Anston stepped back to admire his handiwork. Her bottom was scarlet now, crisscrossed by a mass of thin weals where the whip had bruised the peach-like flesh. He ran a proprietary hand over it, feeling the heat radiate and savouring the way she flinched at his touch. A lustful smile touched his lips; the bitch would think twice before defying him again!

Maggie sagged against her bonds, her head drooping as tears of pain and humiliation coursed down her cheeks. Her backside throbbed abominably, but at least the worst was over... until the sound of a low titter brought her head up again, like that of a frightened deer. What was that? As she peered through the candlelit gloom she could just make out dim shadows and the glint of cruel eyes, and the full horror began to dawn on her. They were not alone. There had been an audience to witness her ordeal!

As Maggie shrank away the little her bonds would allow, the shadows began to move, closing in around her like a pack of rabid wolves. There were three of them and she could see their faces now, avaricious and pitiless. The tallest, his eyes sparkling greedily, reached to fondle her breasts, cruelly pinching her delicate nipples.

'Capital fun, Anston,' he lisped. 'And as pretty a filly as you'd find in a twelvemonth.' His next words chilled her to the marrow. 'So who's having first crack at her?'

Her eyes flew to Lord Anston's face, seeking some glimpse of humanity, but found none. Instead, he threw back his head and laughed. 'Impetuous as ever, Charles,' he said. 'I thought we'd cut cards. Highest wins the lady's favours – and the rest of you can wait while he enjoys them.'

Maggie watched in gathering terror as he produced a pack of cards and they each chose in turn. Oh, this couldn't be happening!

The tall one snorted in disgust as he showed the five of clubs. 'Last as usual, dammit!'

'I win,' chuckled the shortest one, producing an ace. With his flabby body and plump face, he looked like an evil cherub. He stepped forward to claim his prize and Maggie shuddered as his clammy hands began crawling over her. Grinning, he kneaded the soft mounds of her breasts, forced into vulnerable prominence by the thin leather straps that constrained her, and the fact that her arms were wrenched above her head. He tweaked her nipples viciously until they rose and hardened, then, satisfied, lowered his slobbering mouth to them, tonguing the hard buds while his hands roamed lower, wrenching her legs apart to find the dark secret gem between them. She winced as he forced his stubby fingers eagerly inside her quivering body while his friends looked on, jeering and offering lewd advice.

Closing her eyes, Maggie tried to will her mind away from her torment, to divorce herself from her helpless body and the disgusting buffoon mauling her. But it was useless. Despite his incompetence, her treacherous body was responding, the heat and pain from her beaten buttocks transforming into a more demanding heat that filled her lower belly. As she moistened, his fingers slid more smoothly in and out of her vulva, increasing the insidious tendrils of pleasure coiling their way through her.

There were more hands on her now. They fondled her buttocks, parting them to finger the puckered little mouth of her anus. They crawled over the soft flesh of her inner thighs. They joined the drooling tongue at her breasts. It felt as if every inch of her skin was being teased and tormented.

The fat one had his breeches open, his cock jutting from beneath the overhang his belly, thick and distended. Grunting, he parted the lips of her sex and gripped her hips as he pushed its swollen purple head between them. Maggie whimpered with reluctant pleasure as he eased himself home – then froze as she felt another persistent erection forcing itself between her buttocks and against her anus. She shrieked as it pressed, penetrated her tight muscle, and then the men thrust in unison, filling her completely. She hung helplessly between them, her breasts swaying as they heaved and grunted like beasts – and like an animal too, she gave herself up to the primitive lusts of the flesh, shrieking her pleasure as they both ejaculated inside her.

But that was not the end. As the first pair fell away the second took their place. Another cock thrust its way into her from behind, while a searching wet tongue lapped at the nub of her clitoris, sending her spiralling upwards yet again. She whimpered, fighting against the endless waves of foul excitement that washed through her, but her body had a mind of its own. She writhed in exquisite torment, her hips grinding against the source of her pleasure, forcing the anonymous penis deeper and deeper until she exploded once more.

How long it all lasted or how often they took her, she didn't know. When the ordeal was finally over Maggie hung from her bonds, perspiring and sated, her muscles trembling and aching, and she was barely conscious of Lord Anston removing her bonds, carrying her back to the nursery and flinging her on the bed.

Her last thought before exhaustion overtook her and she sank into oblivion was that she had died and gone to hell.

Chapter Twenty-Two

The only good thing to come from the nightmare night was that Maggie's treatment improved. Convinced he had broken her spirit and bent her to his will, she was released from her nursery prison, provided with decent clothes and ensconced in a bedroom on the main floor. She smiled bitterly; conveniently to hand should the master desire the use of her body.

Seated at the window of her new room, she stared moodily out at the empty landscape that stretched before her as bleakly as her life. She was trapped, like a bird in a gilded cage, and the last four months had been a study in insanity.

During the day she lived the life of a prim Victorian maiden; waited upon hand and foot, allowed nowhere without a chaperone and forced to pass the weary hours with pointless amusements such as pressing flowers or decorating endless boxes with sea shells.

But the resemblance ended with nightfall – or whenever else Lord Anston chose to slake his vile lusts. Then she was nothing but his whore; a human toy to be played with in whatever depraved way took his fancy. She shuddered; those fancies had taken her down many a twisted path. She had been forced to perform unnatural acts with other whores or play with herself while he and his friends looked on. Forced to endure the attentions of whomsoever he chose to offer her, almost every part of her body had been employed to provide pleasure.

And worst of all, she had grown to enjoy it all. Like an opium eater who craves the poison that will eventually destroy him, her body craved the evil mixture of pain and pleasure he had introduced her to. Each new episode left her filled with self-loathing and despair – yet hungry for the next.

Maggie's unhappy thoughts were interrupted by a peremptory knock on the door. Before she had time to answer, it swung open and Mrs Grimes appeared. 'The master will be with you directly,' she announced, stony faced. 'He wishes you to wear the red dress.' Duty done, she turned and walked out.

Maggie stuck out her tongue at the closed door. The woman made no secret of her contempt; she had never forgiven Maggie for the dismissal of her precious nephew and took her revenge by obeying Lord Anston's orders to the letter. Maggie's food and washing water were invariably cold, her fire was always on the verge of extinction, and her candles burnt down to the stump before they were replaced.

Still, that was the least of her worries, and a wave of anxious nausea washed over her. If she was to wear the obscene red dress it meant that once again he intended to indulge his depravities, but reluctantly she went to the wardrobe, pulled it out and slipped it over her naked body. It clung to her like a second skin, the bodice cut to reveal her breasts completely, the skirt split to the waist so that every movement uncovered her sex, but despite all this she felt the familiar wicked stirrings between her thighs at the thought of what was to come.

And she didn't have long to wait. She had barely seated

herself on the edge of the bed before the door swung open again and he strode in. The last few months had had their effect on him as well; his face held an almost unearthly pallor, the little flesh on his bones had melted away and his eyes glittered with a feverish brightness, like the last flare of a candle before it flickered out.

Maggie barely had time to register this before he was on her, his hands seeking her firm breasts, his mouth swooping down on hers as he forced his tongue between her lips, but suddenly he stiffened and pulled away and she stared at him with shameful disappointment. Had he spent his seed so soon?

But as she looked up at him his gaunt face contorted in anguish and a grunt of pain escaped his lips as he clutched his chest. As she watched in horror he swayed, staggered, then collapsed slowly to the carpet.

Maggie immediately knew what had happened, and for a brief moment she was tempted to watch and let him die – but she couldn't. Instead she tugged frantically on the bell-pull.

'Fetch a doctor!' she snapped at the first servant to appear, and then fell to her knees beside him. 'God damn you,' she said as she beat his chest. 'Don't you dare die!'

'I did warn him,' said the doctor, shaking his head as he closed his bag. He stared disapprovingly at Maggie and she pulled her shawl tighter over her naked breasts. 'With his weak heart it was only a matter of time if he didn't change his way of life.'

'How long?' she asked.

The doctor shrugged. 'A week... perhaps a fortnight. Who knows? There's nothing left to do but take care of him and hope for the best.'

For the next few nights Maggie barely rested, sitting beside his bed, frightened each laboured breath would be his last. What would she do without him? Return to Mrs Wilkes? Be passed on to someone even more depraved?

Finally exhaustion overtook her and she crept away to her own room and the blessed relief of sleep.

'Get up,' snapped Mrs Grimes, shaking Maggie roughly. 'The master wishes to see you immediately. There's no time to waste.' Panic-stricken, Maggie flung on her dressing gown and ran along the landing. At the door of his room she stopped. He was sitting up, propped up on pillows, and beside him stood a tall man she didn't recognise.

'Ah, come in, my dear,' Anston croaked feebly. 'This gentleman has come to do a little service for you.'

Maggie stared at him in dismay. Was there no end to his depravity? Did he intend to lie on his deathbed and watch her perform with another man?

Her feelings must have shown on her face, because he chuckled, but was quickly reduced to a bout of wheezy coughing. 'Come, come,' he eventually managed to chide once he'd recovered a little. 'A bride should look happy on her wedding day.'

For a moment she was speechless. 'What... what do you mean?' she asked warily.

'Exactly what I said,' he croaked. 'This gentleman is the Reverend Carstairs and he has come to join us in holy matrimony.'

Anger swamped her. How dare he torment her like this? 'Are you mad?' she said. 'This isn't some story from Peg's Paper. No gentleman marries his whore! What would people say?'

'They can say whatever they like,' he mused, his eyes glinting mischievously. 'I won't be around to hear them.'

'Oh, I see, atoning for your sins at the last minute, are you? Going to buy your way into heaven?'

'You underestimate me, my dear,' he grinned. 'Heaven sounds remarkably boring to me. I think I shall fit in much better in hell, don't you?' He coughed. 'I have only one heir, my nephew, who is a sanctimonious, disapproving prig.' He began to chuckle again. 'What better final joke can I play than to disinherit him by marrying a cheap slut from the gutter?'

He waved a bony hand at the reverend. 'Now get a move on man, I haven't much time left.'

When he died later that night, Maggie was left Lady Anston, heiress to one of the largest fortunes in England.

Chapter Twenty-Three

It took several days and a visit from Lord Anston's lawyers before it finally sank in. Not only was Maggie a titled woman, but the extent of her assets exceeded her wildest dreams. There was the country estate, a town house in London – and so much money she would have to live a hundred years to spend it all!

She laid the legal papers down on her bureau and a smile danced upon her lips. Money brought power and influence, and she intended to use both to the full.

There was a discreet tap and the door and Mrs Grimes entered, her face wreathed in smiles. 'Is there anything my lady wishes?' she simpered, bobbing a curtsey. 'Tea? Biscuits? A glass of Madeira?'

Maggie looked at her with dislike. The woman was a hypocrite, and a thief. She ran the house on a shoestring, leaving the lower servants to go hungry while she pocketed the proceeds, and while Maggie had been helpless she'd done her best to make her life a misery. Now here she was bowing and scraping as if her very life depended on it.

And it suddenly dawned on Maggie that this was indeed the case. 'Yes, there is something I would like,' she said slowly. 'I'd like you to pack your bags and be out of this house.'

Mrs Grimes stared at her in shock. 'But, my lady,' she blubbered, wringing her hands. 'What will I do?

Where will I go?'

'Do what you like,' said Maggie, raising an eyebrow. 'Perhaps you can join that precious nephew of yours beneath whatever rock he's crawled under. Now get out. I never want to see your wicked face again.'

Once the snivelling creature had gone, Maggie walked across the drawing room – her drawing room – and tugged the bell-pull. It was a few minutes before Sal, the young housemaid appeared, and one look at her fearful expression told Maggie that the news of her axe wielding had already spread through the servants' quarters.

'Please don't sack me as well, ma'am,' she begged, twisting her apron between nervous fingers. 'Mam's in the family way again and with dad out of work me family depends on me wages.'

'Sack you? Why should I sack you? But with Mrs Grimes gone, I shall need a new housekeeper. Do you think you could do the job?'

'Me?' squawked Sal, forgetting her awe of the new Lady Anston in her shock. 'But I'm just one of the housemaids!' She paused. 'Mind you,' she said thoughtfully, 'I'm young, but I ain't stupid. I was best in me school at 'rithmetic and I can write a fair hand. I could do the ordering and keep the household account books no bother at all.' She grinned. 'Yes, I reckon I could manage it. You're on, girl!' Her hand flew to her mouth as she bobbed a couple of curtsies. 'Erm... I mean thank you, your ladyship.'

'Excellent,' smiled Maggie. She reached into the bureau, took out a casket and counted out fifty guineas. 'There,' she said, 'that should cover the cost of your wages, with enough left over to keep your family in comfort into the bargain, and you may tell the rest of the staff that I intend to increase their wages too.'

Sal looked from Maggie's face to the money in her hand. She'd never seen so much in her entire life. The little 'uns would never need to go hungry again! She pinched herself to make sure it wasn't a dream, then, for the second time that morning one of Maggie's servants burst into tears. But this time tears of happiness. 'God bless yer, ma'am,' she blurted.

'He already has,' said Maggie. 'Now I'd like you to send word to my townhouse.' She paused to relish the words. 'And inform them that I shall be arriving tomorrow evening.' The smile became hard again. 'I have some business to attend to in London.'

'Yes ma'am, certainly ma'am,' beamed Sal, before disappearing to impart the good news to her fellow servants.

Maggie smiled after her retreating back, revelling in the pleasure of being able to reward as well as punish. Power was a heady drug!

The following morning found her on her way to London. Seated in her carriage, dressed in the black silk mourning dress Sal had found for her in the first Lady Anston's wardrobe, with a thick cloak and a hand warmer tucked in her fur muff, she gazed out at the passing countryside. She smiled ruefully. It was a far cry from her first journey, bound, gagged and bundled up like a pile of old rags. She passed the journey planning what she would do next.

At last the carriage drew up in front of the house, and Maggie gasped with shock. It was a huge Georgian mansion – and it was all hers! She felt like Queen

Victoria herself as the entire staff lined up to welcome her. It was strange to walk up the front steps when only a few months ago she would have been turned away at the back door.

The next week flew by as she invested in an entirely new wardrobe, partly through vanity, but mostly because if she were going to be Lady Anston, then she would have to look the part. Not that society ladies were going to beat a path to her doorway, she thought ruefully, but then she didn't expect them to. Once a whore, always a whore! Still, she was hardly going to lose sleep over the opinions of a flock of spoilt, empty-headed sheep whose husbands were no better than the whores they despised. She grinned – bugger the lot of them!

On Monday morning, wrapped in a dark cloak and with her veil pulled down over her face, she climbed down from her carriage, walked up the steps of Mrs Wilkes' and raised the heavy brass knocker. After five minutes banging the door finally swung open.

'Wot you want?' demanded a dishevelled, heavy-eyed Gladys. 'We ain't open. Come back tonight and Mrs Wilkes'll see yer then.'

'I think she'll see me now,' Maggie said crisply. 'Tell her Lady Anston wishes to speak to her… immediately.'

Grumbling under breath, Gladys shuffled off, leaving Maggie standing there. Five minutes later she returned, still muttering, and led Maggie upstairs to Mrs Wilkes' inner sanctum.

For a moment Maggie stood on the threshold, remembering the night she'd been brought there, quaking in her shoes, then she shook the memories away and seated herself at Mrs Wilkes' desk. The woman eyed her speculatively. It was virtually unheard of for a society lady to even acknowledge the existence of houses like hers, let alone patronise them.

'What can I do for you, my lady?' she asked politely.

'I wish to purchase one of your girls,' announced Maggie. 'Millicent Evans.'

Mrs Wilkes rose to her feet with dignity. 'I fear you have come to the wrong place, madam,' she said icily. 'I am no slave monger.' A little outraged dignity would help to raise the price nicely.

Maggie raised her veil. 'Then you've changed your tune since the day you auctioned me,' she said calmly.

Mrs Wilkes sat down abruptly, and then recovering herself she leaned back and smiled. 'Well, well, you've come up in the world,' she mused. 'Lady Anston, indeed. There's a turn-up for the books.' The smile became voracious. 'In that case, you can afford to pay well for Miss Evans.'

Maggie nodded. 'I can also afford to pay well to have Jebediah and Thomas treat you the way you treated me,' she said with dangerous softness. 'I am sure I can afford the price of their loyalty – and it would give me great pleasure to see you bound and ravished.' She smiled into the woman's horrified face. 'But I shall forgo that pleasure on three conditions.'

'An-and they are?' quavered Mrs Wilkes, wilting visibly.

Maggie's smile widened as she ticked them off on her fingers. 'One, you sell me Millie at the same price Lord Anston paid for me, and you can throw in young Eddie too. Two, you will loan me Jebediah and Thomas for an evening. I shall pay a reasonable fee for their services,' she added. 'And three, you will never take an unwilling girl into this house again.'

'And if I don't agree?' blustered Mrs Wilkes.

'In that case I shall have you bound, gagged and ravished fore and aft by your bullyboys,' said Maggie sweetly. 'Then I shall pay the magistrates to make sure this house is closed and you are flung out in the streets with nothing but the clothes on your back.' Her expression hardened. 'I think you'll find a return to whoring a little hard at your age. Now, do we have a deal, or not?'

The woman nodded dumbly and Maggie smiled again. 'Good.' She counted the money onto the desk. 'Now have Millie brought to me.'

Scraping the coins into her black silk apron, Mrs Wilkes scurried out, and when Millie opened the door Maggie was standing gazing out of the window.

'What you want with me, my lady?' the girl asked nervously.

Maggie turned round, smiling. 'Oh, I just thought you might like to come and live with me for a while.' She shrugged. 'Of course, if you prefer to stay here...'

'Maggie?' she gasped. 'Wot you doin' here? I was scared stiff. Old Ma Wilkes said some Lady Anston 'ad bought me.'

'She has,' said Maggie. 'That's me. I'll explain it all later. Now get your stuff together, you're coming with me. And fetch young Eddie – I'm taking him as well.'

Ten minutes later, after a few last instructions to Mrs Wilkes regarding Jebediah and Thomas, she ushered her two bewildered charges into the carriage and drove off home.

It was almost two in the morning before explanations were done and plans for the future made: Eddie to be properly educated; Millie to be set up in her longed for milliner's shop. 'I don't believe it,' she sighed happily. 'It's like one of them fairy stories for kids where everybody lives 'appily ever after.'

Maggie's lips set. Not everybody. There were a few scores to be settled yet.

First thing in the morning she called young Eddie in. 'You know the warrens in Whitechapel, don't you?' she asked.

'Course I do,' he boasted. 'Born there, weren't I? I could find me way round 'em wiv me eyes shut.' He grinned at her. 'What you want me to do, miss?'

'I want you to find the man who brought me to Mrs Wilkes,' she said. 'Do you remember what he looked like?'

'Who could ferget a face like that?' shivered Eddie. 'A real nasty piece of work.' He stuck out his scrawny chest. 'Want me ter sort 'im out for yer?'

Maggie suppressed a smile at the thought of Eddie, not the size of a decent scrubbing brush, tackling her brute of a stepfather. 'No thank you,' she said gravely. 'But I would like you to find out where he is and what he's doing. Do you think you could manage that without putting yourself in any danger?'

'Easy,' grinned Eddie. 'Consider it done, miss.'

Three nights later, Maggie was standing in the shadows outside a drinking den, flanked on either side by Thomas and Jebediah. The night was bitterly cold, but her cloak – and the rage inside her – kept her warm. When Bert finally staggered out, she was ready.

'Remember me?' she said, stepping out in front of him.

He stared at her blearily, and then recognition crossed his dull features. 'Well, if it ain't little Maggie,' he said, and then his eyes narrowed as he took in her fine clothes. 'Done well fer yerself, ain't yer,' he grinned. ''Ow's about a few bob for yer old dad?' He lurched towards her. 'An' a kiss fer old times sake?'

The first blow caught him full in the face, breaking his nose and his few remaining teeth, and as Maggie watched, Thomas and Jebediah systematically reduced him to a bleeding pulp, lying unconscious in the filthy gutter. She smiled with satisfaction. With any luck he'd spend his dying days broken and in the poorhouse, like her mother. She walked away without a backward glance.

'I wish it was as easy to pay back Lord Edward,' she said bitterly to Millie. 'He was just as bad, but people like him always get away with it.'

Millie put down her glass and stared at Maggie in astonishment. 'Ain't you heard?' she gasped. 'I thought everybody 'ad.'

'Heard what?' demanded Maggie.

'Hang on,' grinned Millie. 'I kept the papers. I'll fetch 'em and you can read fer yourself.' She was back in a matter of moments. 'Here you go, 'ave a butchers at that.'

So Maggie read the scandalous headlines. 'I don't believe it,' she gasped.

'Caught wiv 'is trousers down, rogering some bum-boy in Clarence Street!' Millie said with relish. 'Seems he fancied a bit of brown as well as a bit of the other.' She nodded philosophically. 'Course, 'e might 'ave got away wiv it, if he 'adn't gone bankrupt into the bargain;

invested every penny he 'ad in some bloomin' silver mine that went belly-up. Shot hisself, didn't he?' She grinned and raised her glass. 'And it couldn't 'ave 'appened ter a nicer feller!'

Warring emotions raged within Maggie. Pleasure at his scandalous end, and disappointment at being denied any hand in it. Then another thought struck her. 'What about Jeremy?' she gasped.

'Shame about him,' said Millie. ''E was the only decent one of the whole bloody lot of them. Dunno what's 'appened to 'im. 'E could still be at the 'ouse fer all I know. It's being sold to settle up some of his old man's debts.'

The following morning Maggie was standing outside the house, her stomach churning as she stared up at it. It already had a subtle air of neglect; the steps un-swept, the windows dull, weeds growing between the cracks in the basement paving. Feeling unsettled, she walked slowly up to the front door and raised the tarnished brass doorknocker.

The sound echoed through the house, but no smartly turned-out butler hurried to answer it. She was about to turn away when she heard a faint shuffling, and eventually the door opened.

'Jeremy?' she gasped.

'Maggie? I don't believe it. Come in.' Despite his welcoming smile, his face was carved in lines of suffering and he looked ten years older than the last time she'd seen him. Her eyes flew from the crutch to the empty space beneath his left knee, and pity and love almost overwhelmed her.

'Not very pretty, is it?' he said ruefully, following her

gaze. 'A little souvenir from India.' He shrugged. 'Anyway, come through to the drawing room; we might as well have a glass of wine before the vultures descend.' He stumped off and she followed him, noting the auctioneer's stickers on the furniture.

'What happened to you?' he demanded when they were seated. 'I wrote and wrote, but you never answered.'

'Never mind that,' said Maggie. 'What are you going to do when the house is sold? Where will you go?'

'God knows,' he shrugged. 'Join mother at her sister's, I suppose. I'm sure they'll enjoy demonstrating their Christian charity to the world by putting up with us, despite the scandal.' He smiled bitterly. 'Though I think my recouping the family fortunes by wedding some convenient heiress is rather out of the question. Who in their right mind would want to marry me now?'

Maggie's heart began to beat faster. 'I can think of someone,' she said softly. 'Me.' He opened his mouth to speak, but she held up her hand. 'Though whether you'd want to marry me, is a different story.' Blushing and stumbling she told him everything, then waited, heart in mouth, for the contempt that was bound to come.

But it didn't.

'Oh, you poor little bitch,' he said softly. 'What you must have gone through. I'd kill my father if the bastard hadn't already done the job himself.' He began to laugh. 'A disgraced cripple and a reformed whore; that should give them something to talk about! It'll be the wedding of the season.'

For Maggie relief was tempered with dismay. 'Is that the only reason you'd want to marry me?' she demanded, feeling hurt. 'To get your own back? To shock the world?'

'Of course not,' he said gently. 'The only thing that ever stood between us was convention, and we're beyond that now.' He grinned. 'Hell mend the whole damned lot of them. We can do whatever we like.'

For the first time since it had all begun, Maggie felt truly happy. He was right; damn them all, with their rules and their hypocrisy. The estate was there and waiting. They need never bother with so-called society again. She licked her lips; and there were so many new pleasures she could introduce him to...

'There's just one last thing,' she said demurely.

'And what's that?' he asked, raising a quizzical eyebrow.

'I've been a bad girl...' she said, smiling wickedly into his eyes as she began to undo the buttons of her bodice, '...and bad girls deserve to be spanked...'

More exciting titles available from Chimera

* * *

All **Chimera** titles are available from your local bookshop or newsagent, or direct from our mail order department. Please send your order with a cheque or postal order (made payable to *Chimera Publishing Ltd*) to: **Chimera Publishing Ltd., Readers' Services, PO Box 152, Waterlooville, Hants, PO8 9FS**. Or call our **24 hour telephone/fax credit card hotline: +44 (0)23 92 783037** (Visa, Mastercard, Switch, JCB and Solo only).

To order, send: Title, author, ISBN number and price for each book ordered, your full name and address, cheque or postal order for the total amount, and include the following for postage and packing:

UK and BFPO: £1.00 for the first book, and 50p for each additional book to a maximum of £3.50.

Overseas and Eire: £2.00 for the first book, £1.00 for the second and 50p for each additional book.

*Titles £5.99. All others £4.99

For a copy of our free catalogue please write to:

Chimera Publishing Ltd
Readers' Services
PO Box 152
Waterlooville
Hants
PO8 9FS

or email us at:
sales@chimerabooks.co.uk

or purchase from our range of superb titles at:
www.chimerabooks.co.uk

Sales and Distribution in the USA and Canada:

LPC Group
1436 West Randolph Street
Chicago
IL 60607
(800) 626-4330

***